Schrödinger's Ball

"*Schrödinger's Ball* is as funny as hell, charming and kind, and perceptive and moving. Adam Felber has an amazing feel for the interior lives of his characters, even while using the shifting points of view of a David Foster Wallace." —PETER SAGAL, NPR

"[A] crackling comic novel . . . [Felber] frolics in the fields of science. . . . His wit and linguistic acrobatics make this clever mind-bender worth the ride." —*Booklist*

"Few novels   e uncertainty princ   's debut is illogically   *rs Weekly*

"[A] raucous   e beautiful randomi   dern fiction's favor   comedy instead of a   *Reviews*

"If Einstein   his would be it. Felbe   d totally enchanted.   urprises, *Schrödinge   r original books."   0th Grade

Schrödinger's Ball

A Novel

Schrödinger's Ball

Adam Felber

Random House Trade Paperbacks

New York

A Random House Trade Paperback Original

Copyright © 2006 by Adam Felber

Published in the United States by Random House Trade Paperbacks, an imprint of The Random House Publishing Group, a division of Random House, Inc., New York.

RANDOM HOUSE TRADE PAPERBACKS and colophon are trademarks of Random House, Inc.

ISBN 0-8129-7442-5

Printed in the United States of America

www.atrandom.com

2 4 6 8 9 7 5 3 1

Book design by Simon M. Sullivan

for Jeanne
certainly

Cast *of* Characters

IN AND AROUND CAMBRIDGE, MASSACHUSETTS

The Gang of Four:

Johnny Felix Decaté, *a musician with severely limited gun-cleaning skills*

Deborah Johnstone, *an implausibly happy twenty-four-year-old temp*

Arlene, *whose cat, Furble, has recently died*

Grant, *a total geek*

Supporting Players:

Leonora Decaté, *Johnny's foxy grandmother*

Jack Kennedy, *Boston police officer and Leonora's considerably younger amour*

Dr. Erwin Schrödinger

Dori, *Dr. Schrödinger's young assistant*

Floyd, *a Harvard Square troubadour and former MIT researcher*

Brenda the Bag Lady, *a homeless counter-historian*

The Prophet Bernie, a.k.a. "Crazy Bernie," *chosen prophet of the Lord*

Colin, *a temporary sex partner to Deborah*

Lester the Rat, *a rat*

Melanie, *another rat*

Werner, *Dr. Schrödinger's cat*

An unnamed sparrow

An unnamed truck driver

Muldower, *geneticist and old school chum of Earl Anderson*

IN AND AROUND THE FREE STATE OF MONTANA

Earl Anderson, *the President of Montana*

Tammy Anderson, *the First Lady of Montana*

Dixon Reese, *Montana's Secretary of Defense*

Jimmy, *Montana's Secretary of Housing*

Boone Jeurgens, *a young Montana Free Militia soldier*

Murph, *a member of the President's Cabinet*

Deke, *the county sheriff, no longer recognized by the Free State of Montana*

Barbara, *the sheriff's wife*

An unnamed follower of Jebediah, prophet of the Jebedites

Schrödinger's Ball

Chapter 1

THERE'S A CAT IN A BOX in Cambridge, Massachusetts. It's about three-quarters of a mile from the firehouse in Central Square, which means that if someone launched a rescue operation now, the trucks could be there in half an hour. Or so.

Boston's roads started out in the colonial days as tracks and paths, routes for people and horses and cattle to travel from All Over to certain Important Places. In the fullness of time, the roads widened, lengthened, and were finally paved for the automobile, that newfangled machine whose basic operation still confounds most Boston natives.

So it's pointless to speak of Boston's "grid." Boston's roads were never meant to be urban thoroughfares—they intersect at odd, often precipitous angles, with frequently interesting results from an urban-design standpoint. Often, three or four roads will intersect in more or less the same place.

When this happened in an area unburdened with history, landmarks, or valuable real estate, the twentieth-century Bostonians created enormous disks of pavement where the roads collided, which they called "rotaries." The traffic laws governing how you enter and exit a rotary are poorly understood and rarely followed. Fortunately, the fact that a rotary *is* at the intersection of many roads ensures that there will be easy access for emergency vehicles, which spend a great deal of time cleaning up the messes that happen inside rotaries.

However, when many roads intersected in places that *were* historic, landmark-laden, or filled with valuable real estate (a set of conditions that can be best described as "almost everywhere"), the planners and pavers of Boston opted to create Squares. From a design standpoint, this roughly meant, "Do nothing and name the place after the principal reason why we can't have a rotary here."

In a Square you will find nothing that resembles an actual geometric square. In fact, the predominant shape is the triangle, as the intersection of many randomly generated roads would dictate. For drivers, Squares are nightmarish; because the roads rarely intersect at the *exact* same place, motorists can expect to encounter a confusing battery of traffic lights and signs every twenty yards or so. After running this gauntlet, Boston drivers can expect smooth sailing for roughly the next quarter of a mile, at which point they will come to another Square.

Harvard Square, Inman Square, and Central Square, the areas that we'll be primarily concerned with herein, all exist quite close to one another in Cambridge, Massachusetts. They are, naturally, made of triangles. Taken as a group, they form something of a triangle themselves (as is the wont of any three points). Not an isosceles triangle, mind you, but a stable and powerful shape nonetheless. Inman and Central are a bit closer to each other, linked by Prospect Street. Harvard is slightly farther off, to the west, linked to Inman and Central by Cambridge Street and Mass Ave, respectively.

On a map, if you look at the triangle formed by these three Squares, you might note that the shape they describe is a triangle with one dramatically acute angle, the one emanating from Harvard Square. The angle is sharp enough that the triangle looks very much like an arrowhead. If you owned a map of the entire United States big enough and detailed enough to depict the street-level configuration of this tiny section of Massachusetts—a map that would by necessity be approximately the size of your living room—you would be able to see exactly what this arrowhead is pointing at.

It's pointing, more or less, directly at Montana.

The President of Montana slumps low behind his desk and waits for the gunshots to stop. No doubt about it, the assassin's dead out there, but there's still a whole lot of risk from friendly fire. Dixon probably won't stop until he pumps thirty rounds into the pile of flesh that was a man thirty seconds ago.

There's a small corner of the President's mind that wonders if all the assassins who have come around here lately were actually assassins at all. By the time the President sees them, there's really not that much that can be done in the way of interrogation. They could be just ordinary visitors, couldn't they? Salesmen and milkmen and such. But why would Dixon shoot the milkman? the President wonders. No reason that he can see. Dixon *likes* milk.

Dixon comes in and sits in front of the President's desk. The President looks at his Secretary of Defense, watches him without moving. Dixon watches back. They spend a long while watching. The President is aware that Dixon is looking at a fiftyish "white" man whose lean, youthful pallor has given way to a fleshy, mottled, embarrassing red—the kind of red that lets everyone know that all efforts to lay off the salty fried food have been unsuccessful. The President also can't understand why Dix seems to look the same way he did when they were twenty-five.

6 · *Adam Felber*

It's not a good moment, from the Chief Executive's point of view. Finally, the President speaks.

"Assassin?"

"Yep."

More watching. They've been friends since they were small, but the President feels like these quiet staring times have been getting longer lately. Hell, friends don't need to talk. That's how you know it's a friend. But these silences have been getting . . . tense. Ever since he took the Oath of Office.

"Damn, I'm hungry! Could you ask Retta to fix me a big bowl of cornflakes with bananas? Could you do that for me, Dix? I got a lot of paperwork to do. . . ."

"Can't do that, Mr. President."

"Why not?"

"No milk."

"We're out of milk?"

"Yep."

Now, suddenly, the President of Montana is *scared*.

Johnny's first thought after the noise and the blood started was how incredibly cliché it was to have one's gun go off while one was cleaning it. Then he bled to death, realizing all the while that *that*, too, had been done before. *Done to death*, he thought. *Ha-ha.*

Fortunately, or unfortunately, no one came down to the basement for three days after that, so Johnny Felix Decaté didn't actually die until his grandmother opened the basement door three days later. Well, really, he was dead long before that. But not really. It's hard to explain.

———

Dr. Schrödinger was trying to explain quantum physics.

"Imagine if you will," he said, "a cat in a box with a vial of deadly gaseous poison which may or may not have been broken by a trip-hammer before you open the box." Everyone imagined this. "Now let me tell you that, in terms of particles, the cat is neither alive nor dead until you open that box, but it is in fact simultaneously alive *and* dead AND neither alive *nor* dead until a human observes it!" Everyone was thrilled. Captivated.

"Only in terms of particles and waves, of course," continued Dr. Schrödinger. "I'm not talking about a real cat, of course. And this is somewhat of a counterexample." No one was listening anymore, the idea was too grand. "Really," plied the doctor, aware that he was losing his audience, "we're talking about subatomic particles here, not cats. *Not cats*. Please, let's forget about the cat, okay?"

By this time, Dr. Schrödinger had pushed everyone a bit too far, and he was given his coat and shown to the door, still grumbling something about being misunderstood.

In a small one-bedroom apartment in Cambridge, Massachusetts, Deborah Johnstone is having an orgasm.

Johnny Felix Decaté was in a bar. This was several hours *after* he accidentally shot and killed himself. But he hadn't been found yet, so he wasn't actually dead—he was both alive and dead, and neither alive nor dead, and he was drinking a beer. Being dead wasn't a problem at the moment; it was just an *eigenstate*.

———

We called Dr. Schrödinger on the telephone to find out about these eigenstates. He was eager to oblige us. Frankly, he seemed a little lonely. He started to talk about subatomic particles, but we played dumb so that he would talk about the cat and the box. He then explained it like this:

"When I say that the 'cat' is both alive and dead before human observation intervenes, I *mean* it. It has the properties of both a dead thing and a living thing. At that point, it is said to exist simultaneously in two opposing eigenstates: alive and dead. At the moment of observation, it retains all the properties of one of the eigenstates and loses all of the other's. The cat becomes either truly alive or truly dead."

Then Dr. Schrödinger let us know that this only applies to subatomic physics, that we should substitute "particle" and "wave" for "alive" and "dead," that, tellingly, complex physical systems don't behave with the same indeterminacy.

"How would you know?" we ask, and he gets very quiet for a moment. Just enough time for us to hang up on the tiresome old codger.

Deborah Johnstone is still having an orgasm in Cambridge. The same orgasm. She is sitting upright, straddled across a man, her head is thrown back, and rivulets of sweat are running down her neck. Her eyes are closed, her jaw is clenched, and her body jerks and flails spasmodically.

Deborah has been having this orgasm for three minutes, and it's a *very* powerful orgasm, and it shows no sign of abating. In fact, it's intensifying, all of her soft but strong nether muscles convulsing in an uncontrollable spastic rhythm as a low, open-mouthed moan dances around the very back of her throat. Bear all this in mind.

Arlene ordered another cognac and tried to cry again. No dice. It's too soon, she thought. It's not real to me yet. I still expect to come home and find him waiting for me.

The Abbey was still in the frozen sobriety of pre–nine o'clock drinking. Within an hour or two, Arlene mused, alcohol will help us create a consensual reality in which all of us here believe we're entertaining, intelligent people who really like each other. Depressed though she was, Arlene couldn't quite swallow the thought. She knew there was at least one truly intelligent, entertaining person in the bar, who just so happened to be having a bad day because none of her real friends were here and *her fucking cat just fucking died for no fucking reason at all*. She suddenly noticed the tear running down her cheek and over her lips and she had to smile at it, and her toothy grin and moist eyes made her look like a newly crowned Miss America in the smoked glass behind the bar. She licked up the tear just in time to feel another one rolling down the other cheek, and her smile grew wider. "It's about time," she said softly. "I've been waiting for you fuckers."

Deborah Johnstone's orgasm is at six minutes and counting. She's leaning forward now, her moist palms pressed against the chest of her supine lover, a fine sheen of sweat highlighting her extended neck and swaying breasts. Her pale blue eyes are wide with wonder, and her smile is beatific. If you're a man, you've never felt anything quite like what Deborah is feeling right now. If you're a woman, you probably haven't, either. That's why it's so important. Take note; she is moving purposefully atop her lover, to milk every last drop of ecstasy from her exhausted body. Easily, though, as if she's done this before. In fact, she has done this before. Many times.

In the bar, Johnny Felix Decaté was feeling curiously *light*. Couldn't pin it on the beer; he wasn't even finished with mug number 1. Come to think of it, he'd felt pretty, uh, *light* ever since he'd finished cleaning his dad's old gun this afternoon. A funny feeling—like when he broke up with Stephanie, but without the pain. Like when he told Men's Nipples to find a new bass player, but without the second thoughts. He let his hair fall like a bronze curtain over his face as he stared directly down into his drink and instantly fell in love with the golden facets of the beer-filled mug. He thought: This is the beauty that the commercials want us to see. They film the pouring of the beer in slow motion to make you feel the *moment*, to help you forget who's pouring the beer and who's drinking and why, and just appreciate the simple beauty of beer in a mug.

Johnny slowly poured more beer from his bottle into the mug, even though it was mostly full already. Light danced in the little cylinder of falling beer, and Johnny realized that he could follow the stream as it plunged into the standing liquid in the glass. He could see the stream slow down as it sank and then divide and splay like an octopus and then curl like smoke, and then, for a tiny instant, Johnny understood that there was an extremely good reason why octopuses and smoke behaved like beer, and the understanding made him laugh, even though it was gone in an instant. He thought: I'm sitting here at the bar staring at a beer and laughing like a stoned moron, and I'm not *on* anything! What's up with that? What do I usually do when I drink alone at the Abbey? he asked himself.

Oh, I dunno, Johnny, you usually just think about stuff.

What stuff?

Oh, you know, John-man—your life and stuff.

Oh. Yeah. But I don't feel involved with that shit tonight. I'm watching a different channel, y'know? I feel . . .

. . . light?

Yeah, light.

We just received a letter from Dr. Schrödinger. He might be angry or he might be apologetic, as near as we can figure. We haven't opened the letter yet. Being sensitive, we call him on the telephone to ask him what the general tone of the letter is so we can be prepared to read it. "How should I know what the tone is?" he asks. "It won't be either apologetic or angry and it will be both until you open the letter, right?" He hangs up. If we didn't know him better, we might suspect that there was a note of sarcasm in his voice just then.

She's still coming! Nine minutes have passed, and Deborah Johnstone's monumental orgasm is still going strong. Now she's sprawled across her lover, her face buried in his neck, as she sobs and moans and laughs and writhes against him. It is necessary that you appreciate just how wonderful she is feeling right now. Deborah Johnstone has been on a plateau of ecstasy for a long, long time.

Deborah Johnstone has a life, of course, full of friends and ambitions and hobbies and concerns. But those don't matter right now. In the operating system of her brain, this climax is the only open application. There are no other open windows in the background consuming RAM and providing distractions.

This is full-screen, a singularity of consciousness that takes contemplative monks a lifetime to perfect.

It is a feature that comes standard with Deborah Johnstone.

That *is* Johnny at the end of the bar, Arlene thought. He looked . . . different, somehow. But in what way? Well, for one, he was looking straight down into his drink and giggling, which was admittedly a new thing for him, but that wasn't quite it. He looked—*dangerous*, like a hyperactive boy with a grenade in his belly. No, that wasn't it at all, Arlene realized, though she took a moment to congratulate herself on the imagery and hope briefly that she'd be able to recall it later, when she had a pen and paper and a less emotionally fraught moment. She shook her head to refocus her mind. Johnny looks different tonight, she thought slowly and carefully, because my cat is dead.

She was almost right about that.

A few facts about Deborah Johnstone:
1) She is twenty-four years old.
2) She is disease-free.
3) Everyone who meets her instantly likes her.
4) She genuinely cares about her friends and family.
5) She is capable of experiencing astounding amounts of ecstasy.
6) She's always at least as happy as you were on the happiest day of your life.

It was a dark and stormy night. A knock on the door awakened us. Unbelievably enough, it was Dr. Schrödinger. He was soaking wet and looked kind of desperate, water streaming down a face too frantic to be handsome, hopelessly unfashionable glasses fogged and partially obscuring those disconcertingly wobbly blue eyes. He was too pitiable to turn away, so we let him in. Just for a minute.

"The thing you must remember," he says as he huddles under a blanket and sips from his miserable little thermos of hot cider, "is that quantum theory is not the theory of relativity, though they are of course inextricably interrelated. Relativity talks about how you look at things. Quantum theory depends on *whether* you look at things."

"Meow . . ." we suggest hopefully.

"Oh, very well!" he snaps. "If no one opens the 'box,' the 'cat's' fate remains not just unobserved but really undetermined— it honestly behaves like a 'cat' that is both 'alive' and 'dead' until you look at it."

This is great stuff, as long as you ignore the sarcastic quotation marks that the doctor makes with his fingers when he says words like "cat" and "alive." Which we do. Pointedly. Then he lapses into his usual blather about particles and waves, and we leave him there to sleep on the couch.

Before Johnny Felix Decaté could get bored with his revelatory beer glass, he sensed something looming to his left. He didn't look up immediately, because the sensation of something *looming* was so delicious, and when you look right at a looming thing it ceases to really loom properly. Eventually he heard his name spoken, and in a sunburst of flashing connections he identified the loomer as a person, a woman, a friend. Arlene. This is the conversation that followed:

"What's so funny?"

"Looming."

"Was I looming? I'm sorry."

"Don't be. Nothing wrong with looming. If more people loomed, less people would be getting directly in your face."

"Am I in your face now?"

"Are you, like, oversensitive today?"

"Yes."

"Oh."

Pause.

"Do you wanna know why?"

"Can I help?"

"No."

"Then no."

"What!?"

"The past is a total burden. I have enough trouble forgetting my own without having other people's to forget."

"Fuck you!"

Pause.

"And stop that!"

"Stop what?"

"You don't smile lovingly at someone who just said 'fuck you' to you. It's rude."

"I like you."

"My cat died."

"So did Winston Churchill."

"What is *wrong* with you tonight?"

The most active part of Deborah Johnstone's orgasm is over. It is now eleven and one-half minutes since she sat bolt upright and, well, *squeaked* through her suddenly constricted throat.

Now, as she sprawls and stretches over her lover, she begins to feel that she is floating, and she thinks to herself: Now here comes the *really* good part.

The bathroom was actually much nicer than one would expect, especially for a place like the Abbey. The black tiles on the floor and halfway up the walls were as shiny as the white grout between them was white. A streamlined sink curved up from the floor like a black porcelain cobra poised to strike. The very large mirrors accurately reflected that there was no one in the room.

It was obvious that Schrödinger had nowhere to go. He spent the whole morning puttering around, drinking herbal tea, and trying to get us to talk about physics. He was none too subtle, either, trying to disguise his intent through "idle chit-chat."

"Bit of a drizzle falling this morning," he observed slowly, watching us out of the corner of his eye.

We agreed, warily, that there was.

"Do you see," he began, with bone-crunching nonchalance, "how the rain appears not as a series of plummeting drops but, rather, as a set of flickering points as some droplets happen to refract photons into your eyes?"

We tried to tell him that we really didn't want to get into this. . . .

"What I meant to say," he corrected himself hastily, "is: See how the rain sparkles?"

The rain did indeed sparkle, we allowed.

"Well, oddly enough, that effect can be replicated in a lab by directing a beam of—"

We rushed to the door and headed off to work, telling this one-hit wonder of popular science to please be gone when we returned, and that the door, independent of any observer, would lock itself.

"Let's do something."

"We *are* doing something, Johnny. We're drinking. This is what we do."

"Well, let's do something else. I'm going to—"

"No, wait. Hang. Everybody will be here by ten."

"And I would dearly love to see my friends, with whom I've shared so much. . . ."

"What are you—are you high?"

"I think that friendship is just a habit. A *good* habit, but don't be fooled into thinking that it has any other power on you besides force of habit."

"Well, that's a pretty strong force, isn't it? I mean, Furble died today, and I still *feel* him, scratching the couch with his little claws and begging for food and—"

"It's only strong because you say so, Arlene. You decide how strong things like that are."

"Yeah, but I don't *consciously* decide. It just happens."

"We'll come back in an hour and a half."

"What are we going to do?"

"Are you coming?"

"Why do you want me along?"

"You're here."

"Thanks."

"And I clearly remember that I've always liked you. . . ."

"Oh . . . thank you, Johnny, really. I'm sorry I'm crying. . . . I guess I just really needed to hear something like that, weirdly put or not. . . ."

"Bye."

"Wait, fucker!"

One half-hour after Deborah Johnstone first began to climax, she finally comes back to herself. First she becomes aware of her heartbeat and her limbs, slightly cramped. Soon the body underneath her begins to take form and gains an identity: Colin. She feels a surge of gratitude toward Colin, who has waited so patiently for her to return. But a quick look at his face tells her that thanks are not necessary; he is awestruck and proud, now *convinced* that he is truly the most remarkable lover the city has ever known. So everybody wins, Deborah thinks. She rises off him gently and watches him stifle a slight twinge of fear and loss. Deborah doesn't say anything about it—such comments are never well received, being taken for emasculating at best. Instead, she stands above him, stretches, looks at the clock. It's eight thirty. Perfect. "Just enough time for a bath or a shower," she thinks aloud. She's out of the room before there's any reply from Colin, who actually *was* waiting for a round of applause.

At 8:55 P.M.:

1) We are in the corner of the Abbey, watching Dr. Schrödinger bore an old barfly. We're hoping he doesn't see us.
2) There's this box going *meow*. And it's not going *meow*, too.
3) Deborah Johnstone is showering and thinking about tonight, slipping her life back on like a comfy sweater.

4) Arlene is screaming.
5) Montana, in most people's opinions, is still a state in the Union.
6) The bathroom of the Abbey is *really* quite nice. And empty.
7) Colin is wishing he'd gotten everything on videotape.
8) Johnny Felix Decaté is on fire.

Chapter 2

THE ABBEY HAD ALWAYS BEEN THERE. Tim always bragged that it had been the first bar to open when Prohibition was repealed. But if that was the case, it must have been mere coincidence; the architecture made it pretty clear that Prohibition had been *exactly* what the Abbey'd been built for. The two windows in front were tiny, round, and thick-paned, little more than portholes. Johnny Felix and Grant were known to argue drunkenly whether this was because the Abbey flew (J.F.'s opinion) or swam (Grant's view). The theories were both based on the idea of Pressure: Grant thought that the Abbey was a submarine, its stucco walls and thick-paned windows keeping the enormous pressures of the outside world from bursting in and flooding the cabin. Johnny Felix Decaté had always maintained that the Abbey was an airplane and that if the windows ever broke the feverish social energies that were generated by their intense clique would fly out and be loosed upon the world all at once, in a rush that would make Pandora's box look like a bargain-bin firecracker. One particularly drunken evening, the argument had grown so heated that they raced to the windows and began hammering away at them with black plastic ashtrays to settle the dispute once and for all. Tim had to come out from behind the bar to show them the door and, in a tough-but-considerate manner, shove them through it. The door, it had already been agreed, was a magical airlock that allowed people to pass in and out without too much discomfort (though Grant was fond of pointing out that one often experienced "the bends" when leaving the Abbey, further proving his theory; the others called this a premature hangover).

At 10:11 P.M., Deborah Johnstone and Colin enter the Abbey Lounge, walking like cowboys. Colin's walk is a swagger: "cocksure," thinks Deborah, grimacing to herself. Deb herself has other reasons for her gait, and those reasons are all that are keeping her from ditching Colin right there and then. Still, she thinks as he claps an arm around her and "leads" her to *her* corner and *her* friends, this guy's definitely got an early expiration date tattooed on his ass.

Arlene isn't moving, but she's thinking, sort of:
Johnny's dead, Furble's dead. Furble's dead, Johnny's having a beer. I saw Furble dead. I saw Johnny die. I didn't see Furble die. I didn't see Johnny dead. They both died. Johnny died but he isn't acting dead. Furble must have died, because he's dead and you need to die to get that way. But you also have to be dead after you die. That's a rule. You have to play that way. Should I tell Johnny that? He really seems to be enjoying his beer and the company, the last thing he'd want is some killjoy telling him that he has to put his drink down and be dead— that's rude. "Killjoy"—ha—I get it. I wonder if it's ever been used in that sense before. . . .

"She's laughing," said Deborah's voice. Johnny assumed that Deborah had said it, but he was too busy looking at the wood grains in the tabletop.

"Who?" asked Johnny Felix Decaté as he completed tracing one line all the way across the table.

"Arlene. She laughed—she's stopped now. It's like some kind of a coma. Johnny, what happened to her?"

"Lots of things. To hear her tell it, she's led a rich life. . . . But today I'd say two things of importance happened."

"Yeah? What?"

"Well, her cat died . . ."

"Furble? Oh no. Shit. And . . . ?"

". . . and I didn't."

"So she's upset about her cat dying?"

This voice was different. It had strange, soupy, adenoidal contours, not as familiar as Deb's or Arlene's, so Johnny looked up and reminded himself: Colin, Deb's lay du jour. Johnny looked at his face, loving all the unfamiliar details—the big Roman nose, the absurdly pronounced cheekbones, the light-brown stubble. None of this, he knew, mattered to Deborah. She had described her criteria for a Level 1 Lover (which Colin obviously was) very specifically to her friends: Agreeable Personality, At Least Six Inches Long, and Good Stamina. Higher levels had more stringent intelligence and charm requirements as well as more exacting physical specs. She truly had it down to a science.

"What?" Johnny asked.

"I said, she's like this because her cat's dead."

"No, I think it's more because I'm not. She's sort of in shock."

"What the fuck? Did you die sometime recently?"

"You see me here, don't you?"

"That's my point, fuckhead!"

That was *it* for him, Johnny realized right away. Not that Deb disliked profanity. But she had the very strong conviction that the word "fuck" should be reserved for phrases that actually had to do with fucking. If Deb had had any hopes for Colin, she'd be correcting him now. Johnny gave Deb two beats to speak up. Nothing.

"I'm really sorry, Deb," he said.

"Thanks. It's no big deal."

"What's no big deal? Come on, what the fuck are you talking about?"

Johnny looked at him with compassion. "I was telling Deb that I was sorry that you two weren't going to work out."

"Johnny! Shut up!"

"I wouldn't be so sure of that if I were you," said Colin, settling smugly into cliché. He draped one arm over Deb's chair back.

"If you were me you wouldn't be here right now."

"Oh yeah? I—*what?*"

"Johnny, what's with you tonight?"

"I'm just saying what I'm seeing."

"Yeah, well, I just wouldn't be so sure." Colin's eyebrows didn't move as a unit, Johnny suddenly realized. The right side was always the first to rise, but it followed the left brow downward. Amazing. Johnny wanted the eyebrows to move more. And he wanted Colin to know what an ass he was making of himself. And these two desires were in perfect harmony.

"Listen, Colin, man, you're working with incomplete info. Deb is an incredibly, uh, *gifted* woman. We all envy her. But if you think you're special, just keep this in mind—she once had a twenty-minute orgasm with two fingers and a stalk of asparagus! So, before you decide that you can be an asshole to everyone else, bear in mind that you probably only slightly out-performed a thin green vegetable."

"And it was probably better company, too," piped a small, dazed-sounding voice.

"Arlene!"

"Welcome back, sweetie."

"I'm outa here. You coming, Deb? Deb? Fuck!"

We are hunched up in the corner, facing the wall. Dr. Schrö-dinger is just one table away, patiently explaining fluid dy-namics to a homeless man who is too toasted even to request another drink. The good doctor has already bought the bum's attention three times.

". . . So here comes the really tricky part: What if you cool the fluid very quickly—so quickly, in fact, that the molecules don't have time to organize themselves as a solid?"

"Mmrrgg . . ." says the homeless man, slumping down on the table. With morbid fascination, we watch Dr. Schrödinger press on.

"Ah! Very good, Mr. Barnes, very good! You're right—the lowering of the temperature can't occur without molecular re-organization; it was in some ways a trick question. However, just suppose for the moment that we were literally able to suspend molecular motion—"

Mr. Barnes collapses to the floor, destroying the aging Ph.D.'s feeble illusion of having an audience. He's obviously used to this sort of thing, however, and he resolutely begins to scan the room for fresh blood. We cower and turn away; if he sees us here at all, he'll approach. Just when we think discovery is in-evitable, a plume of cigarette smoke carries the word "cat" across the air. Turning toward it, Dr. Schrödinger faces a table in the corner where two perfectly innocent young couples are talking and smoking. Poor kids. They've unwittingly offered Dr. Schrödinger an opening for his one and only socially acceptable conversation-starter. As he sidles toward the table, one of the young men gets up angrily, shouts something, and leaves, pushing Dr. Schrödinger aside as he does so. The doctor doesn't even notice; all his attention is focused on the three young people at the table and the one suddenly, miraculously empty chair.

A plume of smoke wafting next to his head looks briefly like a pouncing cat, back arched. Before it can say "meow," it rises and breaks into smaller strands, a litter of pouncing kittens.

We feel a little bit remorseful. There, across the room, Professor Schrödinger is introducing himself. Exuding the cool, diffident charm of a very, very desperate man. Still, the three youngsters look up at him and appear to be at least momentarily amused.

There is a President in Montana and a truck outside of Ames. There's a plastic bag buried deep in a stack of its fellows in a convenience store. There's a lot of carbon in the world. There's a bird, asleep, in a tree on the Cambridge Common. There's a girl serving frozen desserts, a homeless woman buying yet another notebook, an egg in a carton, and a rat skulking beneath a city's streets.

None of these things have any particular connection to one another, apart from whatever you believe might connect *all* things. But beyond that, nothing. Nothing.

But keep track of them all anyway.

———

Grant entered the Abbey depressed, looking forward to a drink. *What a healthy habit for later life,* he thought. Immediately he saw Johnny, Arlene, and Deb—the little knot of humanity to which he belonged in a way that seemed to go beyond friendship. Grant made it a point not to let this always welcome sight please him, though. Depression didn't come very naturally to Grant, or at least *sadness* didn't. It had to be nurtured. Fortunately, there was an opportunity for this—the table had an extra occupant, some older guy, and Grant was going to have to pull up a chair. He realized that this was an extremely small thing as far as annoyances go, but when you're cultivating a sulk, every little bit helps.

"Grant!"

"Siddown, buddy!"

"Hey, lover . . ."

"Grant, this is Dr. Schrödinger. He's a physicist."

Grant pulled up a chair and surveyed the table, smiling weakly. *Amazing thing about people,* he thought, *we're all outside of each other. All I have to do is sit down and smile, and not even one of them has a clue about my inner torment.*

"Grant, what's wrong, man?"

"Yeah, you look like you been hit by a semi."

Whatever.

"Kinda," Grant conceded. "I just found out that the chick I've been dating online was lying to me."

"She's married?" asked Arlene.

"She's got a dick?" asked Deb.

"Both."

"Harsh."

"My deepest apologies, young man. It is an inevitable fact of life that things are not always what they seem. Take photon beams, for example—"

"Yeah, yeah," said Grant, staring into his drink. "Particle and wave, all depends on how you measure it. Subatomic indeterminacy. Yadda yadda yadda. Cat in a box."

Everyone stared silently at Grant for a moment. Now that he was more comfortable, it would have surprised Grant how truly disparate his companions' thoughts really were at this moment:

Arlene: " 'Cat.' Poor Furble . . ."

Dr. S.: "He knows my work. Does he know he knows *my* work?"

Deb: "We *have* to get him laid. . . . Arlene, maybe?"

Johnny: "Amber light and beautiful smoke. Grant's mourning his own liberation. Lungs fill and deflate like trained balloons."

Deb broke the silence. "I know just how it is, Grant. My lover just walked out the door."

Arlene: "You kicked him out!"

"Yeah, so that means it doesn't hurt?"

"He had these totally amazing eyebrows. Independent eyebrows," said Johnny, a little wistfully.

Grant said, "I gotta side with Arlene on this one, Deb. You look like you're fine."

"So it was a quick healing process. . . ."

Laughter all around. The four of them laughing in their usual polyrhythmic harmony. Grant thought the sound was perfect, gorgeous. They'd spent over a year practicing it at this table, working the unique acoustics of the Abbey, ever since they first came together in the orbit around Men's Nipples. Only tonight there was an odd, overly robust timbre to Johnny's laugh, and there was a hacking, gasping noise in Grant's left ear.

He turned to the older man and realized that the hacking gasp was likely an awkward and self-conscious attempt at laughter. The sound cut off abruptly, so that the man was able to speak long before the others had caught their breath.

" 'Healing process' indeed, quite good, quite good . . ." began Dr. Schrödinger. "You know, the actual human healing process, a kind of guided mitosis, is remarkably similar to the self-replication of certain silicate crystal structures or clay. Now, while some might point to this as a possible starting point for carbon-based replicators, or 'life,' I've always rather thought that it . . ."

As Grant listened to the strange old man tell him things he already knew, his gaze slid around the table. He briefly touched eyes with Arlene, whose tiny smirk told him that their guest was beginning to get tedious. Happened all the time at the Abbey. He saw Deb smiling indulgently; Deb had some time; Deb didn't want to hurt the old man's feelings; Deb was willing to wait it out for his sake; Deb's spherical breasts were resting comfortably on the table, just enough to make them noticeably oblate. For the seventy-five-thousandth time in recent memory, Grant made himself look away from Deb . . .

. . . and looked right at Johnny, who was just *weird* tonight. Johnny was staring right at him, and his eyes were . . . naked, somehow. When their eyes met, Johnny Felix Decaté broke into a startlingly angelic smile, so bright, so joyful, so full of love and recognition that Grant felt himself falling toward feelings that he didn't remember how to feel. He felt a heartbeat that was bigger than his own, and he felt safe and accepted and thought that he must be having a stroke, he must be dying.

And then the feeling passed and Grant was fine and Johnny Felix Decaté was on his feet and headed toward the men's room.

Chapter 3

SCHRÖDINGER'S CAT IS IN HEAT. But it's not a sexual thing—
it's just the blind, overwhelming urge to reproduce. It paces
nervously around and around in Schrödinger's brain. It can
smell fertile minds nearby. All at once its powerful haunches
contract, it freezes for one tense moment, the end of its tail
twitching slightly, and then it springs, propelling itself cleanly
out of Dr. Schrödinger's mouth.

No ordinary cat, Schrödinger's Cat leaps on all three of its
targets at once, desperately, blindly trying to replicate itself.

In Deborah Johnstone the Cat finds fertile ground. The Cat
scampers around the inside of Deborah's head and manages to
construct a decent likeness of itself. A bit short on details perhaps, the fur looks a little cartoony rather than finely drawn, but
a decent job, all in all. Schrödinger's Cat gently recedes, leaving
its progeny behind.

In Grant, the Cat is surprised to come face to face with itself.
Obviously, it's been here before (though it doesn't, in fact
couldn't remember it; can't possibly remember anything, really).
It inspects its doppelgänger closely, ready to plug any gaps, heal
any wounds, but Grant's resident Cat is more or less perfect,
and Schrödinger's feline emissary withdraws.

In Arlene the Cat encounters a few problems. Familiar problems, as far as Dr. Schrödinger is concerned. The Cat moves in,

begins building a model of itself, and immediately gets tangled up inside all sorts of knotty strands in Arlene's mind. Strands of "Cat" and "Death" and "Love," and there's just not enough "Hard Science" around to help untangle the knots. Bruised, defeated, Schrödinger's Cat retreats, leaving behind a ridiculous stuffed-animal version of itself dangling from the sticky webwork.

Arlene leans forward, staring intently at Dr. Schrödinger's leathery face. "You mean," she asks, incredulous, "that if I hadn't gone home after work and opened my door, then Furble might still be alive?" Dr. Schrödinger stares at her, speechless, a familiar reddening feeling spreading across the back of his neck and creeping into his cheeks. Inside his head, Schrödinger's Cat slaps its forehead with one paw, shakes its head sadly, and curls up, sighing, in a well-lit corner.

The bathroom was a bonanza for Johnny Felix Decaté. All the beauty that he'd rushed by in the past had waited patiently for him, and he was grateful. The shiny angles, the brisk *zzip!* of his jeans, the feeling of unfolding, the glorious sparkling golden arc (much like the beer, it *was* the beer) which wavered and trickled and was heard no more. The King Cobra sink, the rush of water, the mirror.

Nothing in his life could have prepared him for the sight that waited for him in the mirror.

Slowly, carefully, his fingers traced the outlines of his image. Long, lank blond hair, the cheekbones and chin, the wide gray eyes and amazed mouth. It was all familiar, but it was very different. Something wrong. A strange sentimentality overtook him, as though he were gazing at a snapshot of himself taken long ago. The entire emotional history of Johnny Felix Decaté flooded his mind and commandeered his senses. His cheeks tingled with the Talking Heads' song "Heaven," which was not playing in the bar, but the way he'd heard it the first time, as a kid. He smelled his first girlfriend, Cathy's goodbye note, shocking and enormous in the hand of Suddenly Tiny Johnny. On the back of his tongue he tasted the last day of summer camp, and somewhere in the pit of his stomach rumbled and echoed the voice of his aunt as she lay dying slowly in a hospital bed.

Just as he'd made the decision to throw himself on the floor and writhe and scream, all the pain went away. The sensations and the memories remained, but they just hung there in plain view, for some reason no longer hard-wired to pain and shame and remorse.

Johnny's reflection laughed, and Johnny waved goodbye to it as he bounded for the door. The door opened and shut.

The bathroom remained empty.

By the time the last Cabinet members arrive, the President of Montana is still pointedly finishing his cornflakes. He's *sure* that one of those "assassins" last week was the milkman, and that's going to get them all in trouble, so he'd sent Dixon himself out to buy some milk. No questions, no accusations, just a request to go out there and get the President some milk. It was brave, the President of Montana tells himself, a brave thing. Leaderly. Much more leaderly than actually confronting Dix point-blank. Yeah, give him room to mend his ways. Tomorrow I'll send him out for a newspaper.

"All right, we're as here as we're ever gonna get," says the

President of Montana, pushing his bowl forcefully aside. Sorta toward Dix, too, who acts like he doesn't notice. "Let's do the roundup. Jimmy?"

"We got another wall up," says the Secretary of Housing brightly.

"Yeah, I saw," says the President. "Now we got five plots, with one wall apiece. We may not have any place to put our families, but we got five really nice handball courts." Most everyone laughs, and the President feels good. He bears down on the SoH. "What the hell are ya doin', Jimmy?"

Jimmy's looking all mumble-mouthed, but Dix cuts in.

"That was my call, sir," Dix says crisply. "I figured that, while the houses are still being built, five strategically placed walls could provide us cover in case we're attacked."

"In case we're attacked," repeats the President carefully.

The Secretary of Housing turns his little rat eyes on the President. "I told him, sir! I told him that buildin' the walls separate would mean that no one could move outa your house till February, but he made me do it anyhow."

"Security's a higher priority," says Dix.

The President knows he's gotta do something. He looks at Dix, still seeing the sandy-haired boy who used to ride that rusty old bicycle. Sorta. "You wanna run those little 'overrides' by me next time, Dix?"

" 'Course, sir. Oversight. Sorry."

The President of Montana is about to do the hard thing. The Confrontation. But then he has another thought.

I'll give Dix the last house that gets finished, thinks the President of Montana. *That'll send the message loud and clear.*

———

The good doctor's alone again, and he's obviously gathering his strength before seeking out fresh company. We watched him moments ago, as the long-haired young man returned to the table and muttered some quick words to his companions. Dr. Schrödinger gamely unleashed a flurry of concepts and scientific anecdotes, but his targets had become vaporous—the quartet of youngsters flowed easily around him and out the door, intent on some new mission.

Which leaves our insatiable doctor alone. We get up quietly from our table and sidle toward the door, embarrassed at our own cowardly furtiveness. Dr. Schrödinger is still facing the far wall, and our getaway is clean as we slip out of the bar.

But the key is hardly in the lock of our car door when a chillingly friendly voice behind us intones, "You know, the continued predominance of the internal-combustion engine is more an artifact of business than one of science or efficiency." We don't need to look to know who it is. We assure the aging Ph.D. that we are aware of this unfortunate fact, but no force on earth can stop Dr. Schrödinger from magically transforming this sorry excuse for a conversation into a ride home.

Of course, no sooner does he crowd into the car with us than Dr. Schrödinger falls deeply into a slightly drunken sleep. At first we're grateful, but we soon find that the doctor can't be roused at all, not even to give us his address. A grim terror grips us as even the most violent nudges and loudest throat-clearings only make Dr. Schrödinger snore louder.

We're pretty sure he's faking it, but we've got no choice but to drive home. *With* the good doctor. Who, naturally, wakes up as soon as we pull into our driveway.

He's far too good at this to take any note of our heavy sighs and disdainful grimaces as we offer him our couch once again. He trots gamely ahead of us to our door, for all the world like an overexcited puppy.

God preserve us from physicists. It's going to be a long night.

". . . and then he just burned up!"

Grant was having some processing problems. In his ear Arlene urgently whispered a mad tale about Johnny's demise. His eyes, forward, were fixed on the backs of Johnny and Deborah, who were leading them down a quiet semi-urban street toward Harvard Square. Well, to be honest, his eyes were mainly fixed on the lower part of Deb's back, where everything seemed to slope gracefully inward on its way down, compacting, gathering its energies, before it *exploded* into the most glorious hips and buttocks that Grant had ever known. Despite the dissonance between the inputs of his ears and his eyes, Grant's mind was even further afield. He was thinking about the silence that existed right in front of him between Deb and Johnny. It was the easy, casual silence that seemed to belong exclusively to the very, very cool, and seemed forever denied to Grant. He was half tempted to accelerate, catch up to Johnny and Deb, join their silence, and become part of it. But he knew he'd start talking right away, or even if he didn't Johnny or Deb would make some conversation, locking him out of their silence as they tried to make him comfortable. He couldn't get in there without altering it. Damn. *Damn.*

His ear demanded attention. Arlene had stopped talking, but this was the kind of silence that meant he was expected to say something. His mind dutifully replayed the last few seconds of what his ears had gathered up and advised his mouth on the best course of action.

"So, uh, it was close, huh?" he asked.

"No. It happened."

"What are you talking about?" Not a brilliant thing to say, but Grant was backpedaling. Arlene had turned really interesting, and his mind had to channel more power into the conversation.

"That's what I'm trying to tell you! We stopped at this café and he leaned into this tiki torch or whatever to get a better look at the flame and he just . . . *went up!*" Her "whisper" would have made any Shakespearean actor envious at this point, but Johnny and Deb had pulled pretty far ahead. "So he's burning, and I mean *really* burning, like hair on fire and skin crackling— and it actually looked kind of cool if you can believe that—and then somebody like tackled him and I poured my water bottle on him and it *smelled*, Grant. It smelled like hair and meat."

"He looks okay. . . ."

"I *know*. After we douse him, he gets up and he's *totally fine!* And— What? What? You don't believe me?"

"Well . . . it's like when two of your friends break up, isn't it?"

"Being on fire?"

"No, I mean like when two of your friends break up and they both tell you stories about the other one and you don't know who to believe between the two. . . ."

"Grant, Johnny's not *denying* what happened! He's just not talking about it much. It's not like you have to choose between Johnny and me."

"No," said Grant, "but I *do* have to choose between you and Reality, seeing as you've broken up and all. . . ."

"Thanks a lot."

Floyd slouches through Harvard Square toward the Coop, guitar case in hand. Everyone's out tonight. Shitloads of kids.

As he crosses Brattle, he sees a mini-army clustering around that creepy magician guy in the little Swiss hat who everybody loves being insulted by. Past him another newbie tie-dyed kid without a voice trying to tune up as two lethargic neo-hippie chicks paint each other's faces and sway as though the music has already started. If Floyd had a spare million, he'd bet it on the kid opening with either "Knockin' on Heaven's Door" or "Dark Side of the Moon." The universal call of that unrare bird, the Common Street-Busking Hack. Floyd smiles and waves as he passes, thinking, *Give it up, you little shit.*

Floyd's mood is ugly, and he knows that it will stay that way until he starts playing.

Most everyone is out; Floyd's free arm is getting tired just from waving. Fact: Even though Harvard Square sucks and everyone cool will be in Central Square by eleven, every major night all summer long begins in Harvard Square. And Floyd, and Floyd alone, knows why this is.

Central Square's got every bar and club worth shit, Harvard Square has diddly: tourists and undergrads and overpriced everything. But, still, those hip enough to know better start every summer night over here, for a reason they can't even admit to themselves. But Floyd can. Floyd sees: Nights start here because the ice cream is way better.

He gets to the big arch in front of the Coop, and Marylou is just finishing. A killer cover of "All Dead, All Dead." None of these tightasses recognize the song, but they love Marylou—sweet voice and cute little alterna-baby persona, can't miss. She smiles at Floyd, he signals her that it's cool, she can do one more. No rush—Floyd's gotta get his ax ready.

Floyd strums along idly with Marylou, trying not to look at the crowd, so he doesn't have to hate them right away. He's briefly impressed as he fingers the chords: This song was clearly written on a piano, and it feels strange on the guitar. Just getting the idea to cover it is pretty cool, let alone coming up with a decent way to do it. Not that the crowd appreciates it, thinks Floyd; they'd be just as happy with the standard-issue teen campfire crap that passes for a repertoire around here.

Marylou finishes, says good night, collects an unbelievable amount of bills in a dirty flowered hat, kisses Floyd, vanishes. Floyd's plugged in, he's playing, feeling slightly less dead inside, but only slightly, as the crowd sways and Floyd sings:

"So, So you think you can tell / Heaven from Hell / Blue skies from pain. . . ."

Bang! The President of Montana can't sleep, so he rereads his manifesto.

THE UNIVERSAL DECLARATION OF FREEDOM

We, the people of what has been known as the State of Montana, do hereby proclaim our complete independence from the Union of States known as the U.S.A. We have suffered enough, paid enough, seen enough to know that the International Governing Cartel behind the so-called democratic government of the U.S.A., . . .

Bang! The President's attention starts to drift. It doesn't have the same zing it used to. And that stuff about biodegradable GPS transmitters in fast-food burgers seems, well, kinda loony. *Bang!* It all suddenly seems kind of silly, even though the President knows he started most everything himself. It's just that tonight makes everything seem different, what with Dix questioning his authority in front of everybody and all. For a minute—*bang!*—the President thought that Dix was going to shoot him right there where he sat. Just because he said that he thought too much money was being spent on ammo. And that was true, damnit—they need more building materials, not to mention food, if they're really gonna make a go of it. But Dix wouldn't have any of that. So now the President can't sleep.

Bang!! But it's more than that, and the President of Montana knows it. He slowly lets his head take in what he's been avoiding noticing these last two hours. He looks out the window, and there's Dix, only twenty yards away or so, standing about fifty feet from a man-sized shadow drawn onto a freestanding wall, which is now hopelessly damaged. Dix has never been subtle. The President watches him reload and level the shotgun at the shadow once again.

The President of Montana looks away, pretends he didn't see it, pretends to read, pretends not to know that his wife is only pretending to sleep next to him. He feels cold and his mouth tastes like metal and his heart is racing and he hopes he's having a heart attack but he knows he isn't and he squeezes his eyes really tight now turned away from his wife trying to shut out everything and become a tight little ball that can't see or hear or take in anything. . . .

Bang!

Arlene said, "It's good to be with you guys, just sitting here, eating ice cream, y'know? It makes everything seem less fucked up right now—sorry, Deb—'messed up.' "

Grant was partly listening, partly savoring the taste of his Double Fudge Brownie Swirl. But mostly he was trying not to look like he was compulsively ogling Deborah.

She *had* to get a cone, he thought ruefully. He tried to casually eat a bit more ice cream, and nonchalantly plunged the cone into his eye.

"Are you all right, Grant?"

"Yeah, fine," Grant said, taking the napkin from Arlene, wildly looking for a distraction. He found a handy one nearby. "At least I'm getting more of it down than Johnny. . . ."

This was true. Johnny Felix had more or less plunged his entire face into a dietetically evil-looking sundae, seemingly trying to eat it from the inside, and now was sitting there staring into space with an unsettling smile on his lips.

"Everything feels a little strange tonight, doesn't it?" said Deb.

"It's the humidity, probably," said Grant idiotically, mainly to keep Arlene from going into her Burning Johnny thing again. Sometimes Grant's perception of Deb-as-unreachably-desirable-woman overwhelmed his perception of Deb-as-just-one-of-us. This was one of those moments. He was about to make things worse by justifying his statement with a mini-lecture on positive ions and Summer Seasonal Affective Disorder and related minutiae when his overactive mouth was bailed out by his overactive friend.

Johnny got up. His face was turned skyward, and he moved like a sleepwalker, charmed, transfixed.

Heading straight out into the sluggish traffic of Harvard Square. Grant and Arlene and Deb watched him for a long second, exchanged a few glances, and followed.

Pok! Pa-pok!

We're trying to sleep. Trying to ignore the sound coming from the living room, an absurd, occasional *pa-pok*-ing sound that we can't quite identify, though we know two things for sure about it:

1) The sound is being made by our guest for the second night running, Dr. Schrödinger.

2) He is making the sound precisely *because* he wants us to come and inquire as to its nature.

Resolutely, we resist the urge. The old scientist will not have his way with us tonight!

Pa-pok. Pok. Pokitty pokitty pok.

Sighing, we throw off the covers and go to investigate. Quietly. We're thinking that maybe we can take a quick peek and, curiosity satisfied, sneak back off to bed undetected.

He's sitting up on the couch wearing the spare pajamas we lent him. He's somehow located a few Ping-Pong balls. These he is tossing over his shoulder behind him. They bounce off our sliding glass door and hit the floor with the familiar, (now) unmistakable *pok*-ing noise. Aha. As we watch, Dr. Schrödinger gets up, retrieves the balls, counts them, chortles, and scampers back to the couch. He then repeats the procedure.

Pokkitty pok. Pa-pok. Pok. Pok pa-pok pokitty pokitty-pokpokpokpokpokpok . . .

It's no use. We were lost as soon as we left the bed. Beaten, we clear our throats and ask the old maniac what he's up to.

"See!?" he exclaims. "It's like I said—big objects don't behave like subatomic particles! I've just proved it."

"How?" we ask hopelessly.

"Why, I'm not observing the flight of these balls, am I? Therefore, they should remain as simultaneously particles and waves until observed, right? But *they don't*. Oh no. They're bouncing right off the glass door instead of passing through it! Proving?"

"That they're Ping-Pong balls?" we ask dully.

"Exactly. Not like subatomic particles. Oh no. More like cats. Real cats." As if it were cued by this, we suddenly hear a distinctly feline yowl emanating from somewhere with the house. *Our* house. Dr Schrödinger stares at us tentatively. He seems to be hoping that we won't say anything about it. But we do.

"Oh, that's just Werner," says the physicist, in what comes across as a music-hall parody of casualness. He doesn't seem inclined to explain where "Werner" is or how he managed to smuggle the cat into our house in the first place. Instead, he returns to the subject of Ping-Pong balls. "Now, if I were to toss Werner toward the glass, the result would be much like that of the Ping-Pong balls, which—"

"Good night," we say, withdrawing. Then a thought strikes us: "But you *hear* them."

"I beg your pardon?" asks Dr. Schrödinger.

"The balls—you hear the balls as they hit the glass."

"Yes . . ."

"Isn't hearing a form of observation?" we ask, perhaps a bit more sharply than we need to. But it's late. And it's *our* house.

"I suppose it is."

"Then of *course* they're bouncing off the glass. You're observing them."

Dr. Schrödinger is crestfallen. So much so that we begin to feel bad for having burst his bubble. But his face brightens almost immediately, and he chuckles and points to the little white ball in his hand. Then he tosses it behind his back and in one smooth motion covers both his ears.

Pok. Pokitta pok pok.

Grinning now, he scrambles to his feet and locates the ball behind the couch. Wordlessly, he holds the ball up in triumph.

We inform him that *we* were observing it that time.

We really wish we hadn't said that. Now we are compelled to sit next to the demented old coot, facing away from the sliding glass door, as he holds a ball aloft.

"Now, on the count of three, shut your eyes and plug your ears, all right? One, two, three!" He tosses the ball. We follow his instructions and count to ten. When we open our eyes, the doctor is already scrambling around, muttering, looking for the ball.

We can't find it. We look everywhere, even though we're really very tired now. Dr. Schrödinger is beside himself, rambling, insisting that the ball is Definitely in the room. He's probably right—we never saw the point of this anyway. We talk him down, assure him we'll find the ball in the morning, give him a glass of water, and stalk off to bed.

In the morning, on the patio, just outside the sliding glass door, we find a Ping-Pong ball.

Chapter 4

WHERE'S JOHNNY? Johnny is not here. Grant and Arlene and Deborah had him in their sights but he kind of slithered ahead in the crowd, so now they're heading in the direction Johnny was going. Grant allows Deborah and Arlene to lead the way.

They are walking in rhythm, Grant realizes. The rhythm of a guitar, playing just ahead. The music is familiar, fascinating, completely new. They walk toward it, not exactly forgetting Johnny but temporarily not thinking about anything except the music. . . .

The President of Montana has declared war, and all construction has ceased. This is exactly what the President didn't want to do, but Dix forced his hand. Well, Dix didn't actually *say* anything, but the President felt the need to act swiftly and shockingly. Just to let Dix and everybody else know who the *real* power around here was, who started it, who had the real vision.

He'd needed a pretense, of course. He'd taken the most foul-sounding Nonpayment of Taxes threat he'd been sent in the last few months (they all were pretty dire, and more or less identical), and read it aloud at the last meeting.

"Can you believe this?" he'd thundered. "They really think these threats are going to scare the Independent Nation we've worked so hard to build? No, friends. No!!" At this he pounded the table, and reached slowly underneath it. . . .

"As of this moment," he went on, "a state of war exists between the United States and the Free State of Montana." Then he raised up his shotgun. "And may God have mercy on their souls." Cheers, of course, followed.

So now they were taking a ten-minute break, after which they'd reconvene and decide exactly how they were going to break the news to the United States. And their own families. The President of Montana looked out at the compound. His wife wasn't going to like this. Most of the people weren't going to like this. The President hoped that actually declaring war wasn't going to attract much attention or get anybody in trouble. Why should it, after all? They hadn't really *done* anything (except for the "assassins" that Dix had . . . dealt with, who were doubtless being searched for, and whom the President tried not to think about). What is this country coming to, thought the President of Montana, when a God-fearing, formerly taxpaying citizen can't secede and declare war on his country without causing some kind of self-righteous PC ruckus?

"Mr. P-p-p-p-president?" This was Boone, Molly Jeurgens's boy, a member of one his new nation's most unstintingly loyal families. A model Montanan. "The C-c-c-c-council is b-b-back. . . ."

"Thank ya, Boone." He put his hand on the teenager's shoulder. "Let's go kick some ass, huh?" Boone giggled hysterically for reasons that the President couldn't quite fathom. Eventually the giggles turned into a choking fit, as they always did with Boone. The President of Montana clapped the boy hard on the back and waited until he regained his breath; then the two of them headed back into the chamber.

———

Floyd doesn't know how it happened. One minute he was playing "Knockin' on Heaven's Door" for a mildly appreciative crowd, and the next he was listening to someone else play it for a *wildly* appreciative crowd.

The thin kid with the blondish hair had just walked right up to him, smiled, and kinda *hugged* him from behind, his hands smoothly taking Floyd's place without missing a chord, without a break in the rhythm. It felt good, which made Floyd again think maybe he was queer, and then made him vow to *never* fucking go out without underwear again. Floyd had just kinda sunk to the sidewalk, overwhelmed by something, and now he was several feet away, watching the kid play *his* guitar.

Beautifully. The kid is standing there, strumming, bending, improvising music that goes beyond sound. The growing crowd is transfixed. Some are crying. Floyd realizes that he is one of the ones who are crying. Something about the sound, the sweet smile on the kid's face, the arching melodies, something about it washes Floyd with the unconditional, easy forgiveness that can only be granted to him by music. He listens without trying. It's still "Knockin' on Heaven's Door," but it's a lot more than that. It's as if someone has answered the Door and invited everyone in for a nice slice of pie.

Or maybe it's *this*, Floyd is thinking: I thought the song was about the struggle to reach heaven. Or the futility. Or the sense of expectation about what's behind the door. Maybe nothing's behind the door. We don't know. Something like that.

But not now. With the familiar chords of the refrain swirling around him, the kid isn't playing about the struggle or the expectation. He's playing the joke of it all. He's playing how fabulous and ridiculous and wonderful it is that a single man can stand before the gates of heaven and knock on the door. It doesn't matter how hard it was to get there or whether or not someone will open the door or whether people created heaven in the first place only to imagine challenging it. What's perfect is the moment of the song, the audacious act of knocking.

It should be tragic, but it isn't. And Floyd should want his frickin' guitar back already, but he doesn't. Floyd is listening, and Floyd is *thinking* about listening, for what seems like the first time in a while.

Still, no music, no matter how transcendent, can completely erase several decades of *Floyd*. He's also thinking, *My guitar, my tips.*

We're starting to think that we cannot escape Dr. Schrödinger. We had had a hard day, we were walking through the Square, pretending to ourselves that we were *not* angling toward the ice-cream store, when we suddenly saw what looked like the outline of the renowned physicist in the crowd ahead.

Fortunately, the ice-cream parlor was right there, so we ducked inside. It's fate, we reasoned, so we got in line.

"You know, the crystalline structure of frozen yogurt is remarkably dissimilar to that of ice cream."

That voice. Unbelievably enough, it was him. He was right up at the counter, talking to a very bored, slightly chunky Latina girl who was scooping the doctor's ice cream.

"I knew that," said the girl implausibly, as her voice managed to convey absolutely no interest. The doctor took this as a sign of interest.

"In fact, crystalline structures themselves are fascinating. Clay, for example, reproduces its own structure much like an organism. There are some who speculate that life might have originated from a self-replicating silicate that somehow managed to incorporate organic substances in its crystalline structure. To give you some idea of the complexity at work here, let me . . ."

We were slowly edging our way toward the door when Dr. Schrödinger saw us and called us over.

Two minutes later, we were holding a match to the bottom of a sundae glass, our eyes locked in helpless camaraderie with the scoop girl, while the doctor illustrated a particularly "interesting" property of fudge.

Arlene was the first to snap out of it. Like everyone else, she was taken on a personal, private trip by Johnny's song (hers was, of course, mainly a cathartic experience of grief and hope for a certain recently departed pet), but she rose out of her reverie pretty quickly.

Because Johnny was lying on the ground.

He'd hit that last keening note and then just *melted* to the ground. Arlene got to him seconds later to find him conscious but a little bewildered.

"Johnny, you all right?"

"Yah. I just . . . What's with everyone?"

Arlene looked around. "I think they really liked your playing."

"Looks like it." Johnny giggled.

The crowd surrounded them, motionless, stuck in the last notes of Johnny's song. For a moment, short and infinite, Arlene felt that she and Johnny were the only animate beings in a world of frozen time. It was the single most intimate moment of Arlene's life, even though she had no clue as to what was going on behind Johnny's now perpetually goofy grin.

And then Deborah and Grant were with them, and they were helping their wobbly friend get back on his feet, and they bought him a Gatorade at the Store 24, and Johnny took the plastic bag and released it into the wind so that it flew, full of air, high above the pointy church and across the Common and into a tree, where it hung, open, waiting.

As plastic bags in trees go, it didn't have to wait very long.

Dear Diary,

A good day, except for some cruelty from some of the younger skate rats, who don't know better until the older rats tell them that the crazy old bag lady is Brenda the Crazy Old Bag Lady, and they'll end up as friendly as the others, though they won't really know why. But I know. A name is all you need in this life, it's the magic key, the difference between a stranger and a person, thing and friend, salt and sugar. And I'm <u>sugar</u>—it's my birthday and I'm taking stock and things look pretty damn good. Being a sad old whore, one step before being a crazy old lady, sucked the big wazoo. But once you've been out of the whoring game for long enough (and it's been a looong time since I've <u>actually</u> sucked the big wazoo! at least for cash—ha-HA!), no one remembers you were ever a whore to begin with. Gives you dignity. Absolution. If those confessional booths really were freezing chambers that unfroze you say after forty years then they'd <u>really</u> work, Hail Marys or no. That is not a great idea because then you'd need so many more booths and people's families would miss them and going to church would be like dying in a way and people just wouldn't do it unless they'd done something really bad and the whole thing would just fall apart, so let's not add that idea to The List.

Here's a new one for The List. What about making one day out of every year car-free? Maybe ambulances only, I guess, but that's it. Imagine that! What the cities would look like, what they'd sound like! It would be like a beautiful dream, like a snow day with no snow, like when everybody in that story realizes that the elephant wasn't crazy after all and there ARE little people living on flowers. Maybe not like that last one, but you get it, right?

Here's another one: a soda pop that tastes like pussy. All the boys who really like the taste would buy it, and all the boys who don't would have to drink it anyway or their friends would think they were homos. And all the queer girls would buy it too. You could call it Cootchie or something cute like that. It would sell, maybe.

I don't know if that second one's on The List or not. Think about it more.

Spent my whole birthday on Mass Ave, getting presents. Didn't even have to tell anyone it was my birthday, since I've been telling them all for weeks that it was coming. That's how you do it. Makes the day more special. I got a radio from Carl, and a new wheelie basket from Bonnie, and Mohammed gave me more donuts than even I could finish and he even lit a candle in one for me, right there out in front of his store! Stevie the skate rat ran into the 24 and got me a rose, which just goes to show what I've been saying about Stevie all along—he's different. Not just friendly, but he could've been my friend if things had turned out completely differently, like in one of those fancy alternative universes that you always read about but never get invited to. Stevie just has this glow around him. It actually LOOKS like a glow to me—I see it. That's almost definitely because I'm crazy and I spend too much time in my own head, but maybe that's just part of being old, too—your own version of the world gets more real than the world everyone agrees on. But, then again, that sounds a lot like crazy, too, doesn't it? Who cares! It's my birthday!

Numbers from today: 16, 59, 4, 600, and 3 (again!). Colors: pink, pink, orange, gray, and pink. Robots: 7—one new one, working in the Woolworth's, but he didn't see me see him. Good night and Happy Birthday!

Grant is exhausted. He was ready to sleep right after Johnny played—he was lulled, completely at peace.

Grant would never have put Johnny's playing down before tonight. Never. But if a shadowy government agency had abducted Grant and put him in a dark interrogation chamber with one overhead lamp and slapped him around and burned him with cigarettes and absolutely *forced* him to give his honest assessment of Johnny's playing, Grant might have been compelled to confess that there was a little too much artifice and attitude in Johnny's approach, like he was trying to be a rock star first and a musician second.

But not tonight. Tonight Johnny had played like a blues lifer on a Tuesday night who had no reason not to just put *himself* into it, nothing more or less. And somewhere in that solo, Grant heard a little of Grant in there. Not like Grant could play a note, not that Johnny was playing a portrait of Grant—it was just a phrase or two with a conversational cadence and sense of humor that Grant recognized as part of the "Johnny-and-Grant thing."

Grant knows that his structurally unsound ego is always casting about for additional support, but he honestly thinks this is more touching than having a song written for him, because it's an unconscious tribute to their friendship and Grant's place in it. Besides, Grant thinks, any song that Johnny actually wrote for him would probably have a title like "Give the Dweeb a Chance" or "You've Really Got to *Relax*, Dude."

Fortunately, there's not a lot of time to think about that now.

They've only just gotten free—part of the crowd actually followed them, like they needed to be close to Johnny. So they had to circle the block and meander and tell people to piss off for a solid hour. But now they're in the clear, and they can head to Johnny's house, which is only a couple of blocks from the Square in the first place.

Johnny's new house is actually his grandmother's house, and he moved in with her only about a year ago. That sounds weird when Grant thinks it, but he's aware that it's only weird if you don't know Johnny's grandmother. Then it's weird, too, but in a different way.

By the time they get to the door, Johnny's walking fine, totally unassisted, and Grant realizes how many Deb-watching opportunities he's missed in the last hour. He's *seen*, but he hasn't been really watching, so the mental jpegs and mpegs are a little fuzzy. This is what he's got:

1) Still frame, Deborah laughing as Johnny kind of topples over on her. She's holding him up, but in danger of falling herself. A small sound file of her wonderfully wicked-sounding laugh accompanies this, but it's crappy quality and might just be a splice from an older file.

2) Five seconds of decent-quality mind-video. Deborah looks right at him and says, "You all right, Lieutenant?" They'd been playing some kind of imaginary army game, Operation Johnny, trying to get him home and away from the crowd. She's smiling, it's a definitely intimate smile, with a slight attempt to play-act the smile away. A treasure.

3) Still frame: the silhouettes of Deborah and Arlene behind them once Johnny started walking better. Grant doesn't know what they're talking about, but there's a

sentimental cast to the image—it's a quiet, easy shot of two people he loves.

4) Eight seconds of surprisingly good video. It's from a minute ago, when they realized it was safe to take Johnny home. Deborah is jumping up and down under a street light, crowing, "Free! Free, I tell you!" Amazing breast bounceage, plus tremendously adorable. Someone (probably Grant himself) goes "Sshhhhh!" and Deborah clutches her hands to her mouth, giggling, collapsing toward Arlene. All four of them are laughing with conspiratorial delight. It's a keeper. Grant makes sure his mind's got it firmly before he moves on.

They're in the house now, and Johnny's grandmother has apparently gone to sleep. Grant realizes that he is staring at the mantel, on which there is a wicker duck that he's never noticed before.

What draws Grant to the wicker duck is the amount of work it must have taken to fashion it. To weave all those strands together, into that undeniably ducklike shape. It's incredible, really. And kind of sad: Let's face it, Grant thinks, this might be the absolute best wicker duck in the entire world. And even the best wicker duck in the world is still, when all is said and done, nothing but a wicker duck. What's it like, Grant wonders, to devote your life to something that no one will ever really care about and that at best will be bought by some old lady who'll probably never notice it again once it's situated on the mantel? Worse, what if it's not even really a *choice*? What if the creator of this wicker duck is someone who just happens to have an extraordinary gift for weaving wicker? Whatever he makes, no matter how good he is, it's not exactly a medium that's *ever* going to get him any kind of acclaim. There's no Wicker Wing at the Museum of Fine Arts. The Rodin of the wicker world is destined to see his work pawned off at garage sales like all his brethren's.

Grant has now thought the word "wicker" one too many times, and the word no longer makes sense to him. Wicker wicker wicker wicker wicker. He turns toward the kitchen to join his friends and get a few more glimpses of Deborah, the watching of whom, he realizes, might just be his one, true, useless talent in this world.

The President of Montana stepped out into the night, away from the lights of his big and overoccupied farmhouse. The last of the sunset was hitting off the police car at his gate, and he waved to the familiar figure leaning against it.

"Thanks, Boone. I'll take it from here. Hiya, Deke."

"Earl. Or should I call you Mr. President?"

"Might be a good idea. Especially if you step over the property line."

"Don't you mean 'the border'?"

"Right you are. Thank you, Sheriff."

"Uh-huh."

"What can I do for you, Deke?"

"Well, I just wanted to come check things out. How are you all?"

"Fine, fine."

"Is that Dixon Reese back there?"

"Yep."

"He looks kinda different. Dixon! Whatcha doin' with that big ol' gun, boy? *'I shot the she-riifff.'* Is that it? Ha! . . . He's pretending not to hear me."

"That's Dix."

"I dunno. Something's just not right about him. You better keep your eye on that one."

"I kn—. . . I . . . Don't worry, Deke. We're just fine."

"Okay . . ."

". . ."

"So—what's this I hear about you declaring war on the United States?"

"Just that, I guess."

"Wasn't seceding enough for you boys?"

"Guess not."

"Well, listen, Earl, I'm an employee of the government. Now, if it were up to me, I'd just go on letting you all do your thing, just like I been doin'. "

"I appreciate that, Deke."

"But now you go and declare war, and it's kind of a problem, you understand?"

". . ."

"See, it's *news* now, and Jackson over at the County's breathin' down my neck and tellin' me to take care of it. So I'm here to ask you to stop it."

"Stop what? We're not attacking anyone or anything."

"Yeah, but you declared *war*, Earl."

"Yup . . ."

"Well, can't you just *undeclare* it? Declare peace or something? Just so we can go back to where we were at last week."

"I don't think I can do that, Deke. . . ."

"Why're you looking back at Dix when you say that, Earl? You scared of him?"

"No. Dix is my best military man. But he's *my* man. Look, Deke, I'm sorry we had to declare war on you and all, and I hope you know it's nothing personal against you . . ."

"Oh, I know that, Earl."

". . . but we did what we had to. For our country, the Free State of Montana. We're not gonna go looking for any trouble, but that's how it is."

"So you declared war, but you're not gonna do anything about it, huh?"

"Yeah. That okay?"

"Well, it's okay with me, Earl. But, honestly, it might not wash up at the County. I'm serious, Earl, I might have to come back here with a squad or something worse. You know, *beyond* the County . . ."

"You fixin' to pull a Waco, Deke?"

"Oh, for Christ's sake, Earl, I'm not kidding here! People could get hurt. Look, you don't really want to do this. I can tell."

"You do what you have to, Deke. I'm sorry."

"Oh Jesus, Earl, don't be like that. You really willing to do this?"

"Guess so."

"Goddamnit. Okay. We're in for it, then."

"Looks like it."

"All right. Well, I better head back, then. Sorry it went this way, Earl."

"Me, too, Deke."

"Love to Tammy."

"Right back at your Barbara, Deke."

"Uh-huh."

". . ."

". . ."

Dr. Schrödinger didn't even ask. After boring the entire popu- lation of Harvard Square, the man just jumped into our car and let us take him home, as though he's our new roommate. And the sound of his cat, Werner, continues to emerge from somewhere within our house. There is no doubt that the cat is not having a good time. When we ask Dr. Schrödinger what Werner's doing here, his ready reply is "Proving a point." He says this with the hint of a creepy smile. And now he's in our kitchen, prattling on about Chaos.

"—which is really a misnomer, you see. It's really about the surprisingly elegant equations that explain the exquisite order in *seeming* chaos. For instance, look at the pattern of frost on this glass that I put into your freezer while it was still wet. Ignore the fact that the glass has cracked a bit, and notice the distinctly *fernlike* frost patterns."

We stand there, only half listening, mainly aware that Dr. Schrödinger has frozen and cracked one of our best wineglasses, and that if he was conducting this experiment *today* he must have known he was going to be following us home tonight. And, slowly, one melodramatic yet half-serious thought begins to enter our minds:

Dr. Schrödinger must die.

Chapter 5

THE DECISION TO EMBARK on JohnnyWatch was made for two principal reasons, only one of which was spoken:

1) There was obviously something very wrong with Johnny, and

2) There seemed to be something very right with Johnny.

Those twin insights, far from canceling each other out, existed simultaneously and, for the moment, without any visible friction. Johnny needed help. Johnny could help. Either way, he bore watching.

Of course, for Grant, Arlene, and Deb, the only spoken reason was concern for Johnny's well-being; it seemed infinitely more morally defensible to tend to the unwell rather than to glom on to the godlike. Still, the unspoken reason loomed large, apparent to all, clinging to the air of the room with a third (also unspoken) reason: Everybody loves a slumber party.

For Grant, there was a lot of tension surrounding the decision. He could borrow stuff from Johnny, but Arlene and Deborah had to run home to get their "stuff," meaning that there was always the chance that they'd get home and decide that Grant could handle the situation on his own. Grant devoted a lot of energy to stressing out loud how much help Johnny might need in the dead of the night—*lots* and *lots* of help, making it all that much more important that they all sleep togeth—. . . um, near

Johnny. They promised they'd be back, and Grant spent the next forty-five minutes worrying that they wouldn't, while watching Johnny eat a full pint of Ben & Jerry's with whipped cream, chocolate syrup, peanuts (salted), and small cubes of cheese. Considering the amount of ice cream he'd consumed during their Square excursion, Grant was deeply impressed. Especially by the way Johnny would look up at him, messy-faced, after each bite, and say something like "Wow—this is totally *good*." As though it were his first bite. Every time. Grant would just stare back at him, smiling (which was apparently enough), gradually growing bored, and preparing himself for the dreadful disappointment he'd feel when the phone rang and he learned that Deb was not coming back. The phone, however, failed to ring. In less than an hour, the front door creaked open.

They returned, yes, thank you, Lord, they came back.

Dear Diary,

Just a couple hours later, and I'm up again! It's not my birthday anymore.

Why can't ol' Brenda sleep? For once, it's not the robots. Pretty quiet on that front. I'm not sure what's going on, but here I am. So we'll continue with the History. . . . Where were we? Somewhere around 1500. Just before Mr. Shakespeare . . .

1500—Bad year in China. The Emperor Ming had just replaced the entire Empirical Guard with ornamental vases, leaving him open to attacks from all sides. The people couldn't sleep at night, they were so worried. Somehow, all of the plots against the Emperor—mostly from his twelve sons, one of whom was a shemale—failed. Nobody remembers why, but probably because most of the plots were too damn tricky and subtle—real court-intrigue kind of stuff. Poisoned gloves and rickety ladders and whatnot. The Emperor ruled on, even though he was unguarded and usually naked. Finally, in 1506, the he-she gave up and just bashed the Emperor's head in with a vase and declared himself Empress.

Over in Europe, things were better. Everybody was all abuzz about America, and they were building ships and throwing parties like it was 1367 all over again. A man named Hans Glemperer bought six new hats on the same day just because he <u>could</u>! In France there was some kind of war going on, but nobody paid much attention—some of the battles had to be canceled due to poor attendance. It was a great time to be a European. Africa was still ruled by the ancient astronauts, so the people spent most of their time watching alien TV, which is just as bad for you as the human kind.

Right here in the New World, the Indians were enjoying their last few years of peace. But they were wise enough to know it wasn't going to last, so they spent most of their time writing their diaries and screwing. Who can blame them?

1510—More of the same in most of the world. China went through another couple of emperors and duchesses, until Wang took over. He was clever enough not to get himself killed, ruled for forty-five years, and then just vanished. Wang's real name was George Jameson, a time-traveler from twenty-second-century Minnesota. I met him near Inman Square last year, when he was just on his way forward to get some replacement body parts back home and then head back to become Elvis. A very nice man, even if he was going to kill the REAL Elvis in 1951 and take his place.

India was a hoot—they were writing the Kama Sutra and smoking opium. One weird thing, though—the <u>women</u> had balls until about 1540. Just hanging there, just like the men! So they had to change all the Kama Sutra books after all the women's balls suddenly went away. No, I'm kidding, they didn't have balls. That would be impossible.

Australia was nothing but Bushmen, as far as the eye could see. They had cities and steam-powered cars, and things were just fine until 1520, when they went to war with Africa and lost it all. You just can't fight the aliens. You can trick them, but you can't fight them, not even using songs as a weapon, like they did. The Australian Empire learned that the hard way.

Okay, that's all for tonight. Gotta stretch the legs—morning's coming.

When you can't sleep but you're not *supposed* to be sleeping, does it count as insomnia or not? The President of Montana was pretty sure it didn't, so he was kind of glad that there was something happening that kept him from not sleeping.

"What's the four-one-one, Murph?" asked the President, tying his Best Western bathrobe closed. The night air had a chill, but the gravel was warm under his bare feet. The President of Montana really liked asking what the four-one-one was.

"I'd say about ten cars in all, mostly from the County," said Murphy, who'd made an admirable transition from farmer to Secretary of Agriculture, the President thought. "They've sealed off the border."

"You mean the driveway?"

"Yeah." Murph was leaning on his shotgun, staring a hundred yards ahead at the assemblage of police cars down at the gate, lights awhirl. The President was alarmed to note that all the visible police had their guns out. Then he looked around and saw why.

"Murph, I don't want anything happening before we're ready for it. Tell the men to put the guns down for now."

Murph looked uncomfortable. "I . . . don't think I can do that, Ear— . . . Mr. President."

"Why the hell not, Murph?"

"Dix said we—"

"Well, Dix's not the President, is he? And the President of this free nation is ordering you to—WHAT?"

"War Powers Act, sir. We got copies of it today."

Murph handed the President of Montana a neatly folded piece of paper, obviously made on the President's own computer while the President wasn't in. The President read it, feeling a rush of cold blood around the sides of his head.

"What the hell? No one authorized this! The Council never voted on it!"

"It's not my place to argue about that, sir. . . ."

"You're *on* the Council, Murph."

"Yeah, I know . . . but Dix said—"

"Whatever Dix said, he's makin' it up! I said stand down, Murph!" The President was suddenly using his very best Voice of Command. Murph didn't even twitch.

Just like that, it was over. If the President of Montana (Deposed) had been a less perceptive man, he might have needed more evidence. But he saw the whole thing—he'd played right into Dix's hand by declaring war. And now the men were scared. And Dix owned their fear.

Dix, who had supported him all these years. Dix, who'd been there from the first meeting of the Montana Free Militia. Dix, who right now was staring at him across the lawn, with nothing on his face that the President even faintly recognized. Boone was approaching from there, looking uncomfortable even for Boone.

"M-M-Mr. P-p-p-president, D-d-d-dix says you gotta get your g-g-g-g-gun, sir. Th-th-then he wants to s-s-s-see you. . . ."

"Well, you tell Dix I'm not sure I *want* to get my gun, Boone."

Boone's face became what the P. of M. (D) was pretty sure was called a "rictus."

"N-n-n-not a good idea, sir . . . Th-th-th-that's what B-b-bobby tried to d-d-do b-b-before." Boone motioned with his head over toward the side of the house.

There, in the deeper shadows of the field, lay what might have been a sack of corn but probably, almost definitely, wasn't. The President maintained his outward composure but felt his insides turn into a warm, gooey liquid. Saying nothing, he turned slowly and walked as steadily as possible across the grass and toward the door. Though he'd been "ordered" to get his gun, he had a pretty good idea of what would happen if he approached Dix while carrying it. He was briefly impressed with Dix for thinking that one through. It was a perfect, if brutally simple, plan.

Perfect, that is, except that the plan involved taking over a three-hundred-acre Republic that was currently at war with and surrounded by a hostile superpower while deposing and executing the nation's only capable negotiator. The President began to think furiously as he walked, though for some reason he felt strangely lighter and easier than he had in years.

One shouldn't worry about appearing sexy when one is in mourning, thinks Arlene. But here she is worrying about it.

They're in Johnny's den, listening to a Stevie Wonder album from three decades ago. Johnny's completely wrapped up in the music, eyes closed, smiling mouth agape, like he's doing a bad Stevie impression. And Arlene doesn't really want any sexual attention from Grant, not really. So there's *no reason* why she should feel this way.

The reason, she realizes, is sitting right next to her, snuggled into an ancient beanbag chair, talking animatedly with Grant, and being toxically attractive. Willing herself not to compare, Arlene compares. She and Deb are basically wearing the same outfit: big T-shirts (hers reading "Tufts" and Deb's bearing a cuddly mascot of some sort—beer mascot, maybe), and soft cotton sweat-shorts. They have similar body types, at least on the face of it. But Arlene can't avoid noticing that Deb's outfit looks all slumber-party-esque, whereas her own looks like . . . like laundry day personified. Arlene's breasts kind of slump around in the T-shirt; Deb's *swell* against the fabric. When uncrossing a leg, Arlene's hated thighs are momentarily exposed; Deb's tanned limbs are *revealed.*

Arlene knows that this is partly or mostly a matter of perception and distorted body image (for which she astutely blames society, her parents, and her own damn self), but the knowledge doesn't help. She's angry at herself for being jealous of her friend, angry at herself for forgetting Furble so easily, and momentarily annoyed that the situation prevents her from rushing off and writing this all down for future use.

What's more, Deb's talking about some idiotic computer game, which Grant is also really into. So much so that he's forgotten to drool and stammer, which is his usual method of impressing Deb. *Oof, that's harsh*, thinks Arlene, and she's mad at herself for thinking it.

Stevie's masterpiece has ended, appropriately, with "Evil" ("Why do you infest our purest thoughts, with hatred?" *Double oof*), and Johnny is up on his feet, feeling the wall, leaving the room. He passes the basement door and begins to stagger a little, like he's going to fall over, but then he shakes his head and walks on out of the room. They all stare after him.

"I got it," says Arlene, barely acknowledging the grateful murmurs from Grant and Deb. She's aware of her breasts bobbling awkwardly as she clambers to her feet. *Next time,* she thinks at them as she pursues the vanishing Johnny, *you might try* swaying *or* bouncing, *for God's sakes. Would it kill you to* bounce *once in a while?*

At 3 A.M., our doorbell rings. Dr. Schrödinger, we're pretty sure, is already inside. Sensing an emergency, we go to investigate.

Before we're halfway down the hall, we hear Dr. Schrödinger's voice, pleasant and ingratiating. We hear phrases only: ". . . no trouble at all . . . just doing some reading . . . Like a drink? . . . Glad you came by, really . . ." With growing horror, we peer around the corner.

Impossibly enough, it's a woman. Well, a girl. The dull girl from the ice-cream shop! The one we'd thought was so bored by the good doctor, who, by the way, has now noticed us and is inviting us to join them.

"This is Dori, and she's come over to finish our talk about fluid dynamics and such," he says, a maddeningly proud smile frozen on his face. "Her shift ended late tonight, and cleanup was, in her words, 'brutal.' "

"Brutal," agrees the girl. We're convinced she has no idea what the doctor is talking about, and we can't fathom what would bring her here.

"We were turning our attention to more complex interactions," says Dr. Schrödinger.

"Like how Joukowski's circle inversion in the complex number plane to study airfoil shapes is rendered less useful in an environment of shifting fluids of varying densities," babbles the girl idiotically.

"Would you care to join us?" invites the doctor. Naturally, we demur: a busy day tomorrow, etc. No, we assure them, you won't keep us up. Good night, we bid them, good night, trying to ignore the agitated yowls and scrabblings of the mysterious Werner (where *is* he?).

As we retreat to our quarters, we hear that increasingly grating voice drone on: ". . . a sort of random turbulence of molecules rather than the orderly positioning found in solids. Note I say 'sort of' random, because there is now reason to doubt that assumption, or at least to better understand and imitate that particular kind of randomness. . . ."

She can't be genuinely interested in the doctor's prattlings, we tell ourselves. But the alternative's too horrible to contemplate. If Dr. Schrödinger is actually capable of getting *laid*, we think grimly, we may not get to kill him; we'll be far too busy killing ourselves.

Grant was beside himself. He felt like he was literally *beside himself*, cheering himself on, rooting hard for Team Grant as it struggled to gain, entertain, and sometimes just plain keep up with Deb.

She'd taken his recommendation, and she'd gotten *way* into "God Almighty," a world sim that had been occupying an embarrassingly large chunk of Grant's time. Not only was she into it, but for a novice she had some surprisingly good insights into the game. Grant's mind boggled: He'd thought that his fascination with these games was a pathetic sublimation of his sexual impulses disguised as a hobby. Having the object of his real-life desires involved in his sublimated-desire activity—it was great but seemed somehow *wrong*, like they should explode or something when they came in contact with each other, sort of a matter/antimatter thing. Or maybe his head was supposed to explode. He wasn't sure. He *was* sure that he had to stop wandering around in his own head and pay attention to his mouth, which was talking about "God Almighty" on autopilot.

". . . Good, well, it sounds like your planet's pretty much running right."

"After all those days of work, it oughta be," said Deb, idly pulling one strand of hair down over her forehead and staring at the ends. This should have looked ridiculous. It didn't.

"And your intelligent creatures—"

"Jehosaphats," corrected Deb. "They travel by jumping."

Grant grinned. "Naturally. Have they discovered space travel yet?"

"Oh yeah—they've colonized like their whole solar system. They are *stylin'.* "

"Well, then, you gotta go online."

"Why I gotta?"

"Well, that's the point. Once they can travel, you go online and start communicating with other people who have the game. Then you can have your Jehosaphats meet other races, trade with 'em—"

"Kill them? Mate with them?"

"Whatever."

"That is *too cool!*" Deb was ebullient, beaming, poking Grant's side with conspiratorial excitement. Grant was pretty sure he'd have tiny burns wherever her fingers touched.

She sat up again, thinking aloud. "I think I'd wanna start

slow. Could I somehow go online when you're on and start trading with you?"

"I was just going to suggest that," said Grant, who was *so* just going to suggest that. "The Jehosaphats will get along pretty damn well with the Labians."

"Labians?"

"They're like ninety percent lip."

Deb's laugh was music; Grant could have laughed along for an hour. When it stopped, there was a satisfied, smiling silence that was somehow even better. There was definitely a new level of intimacy here—nothing like a romance, he thought, but, still, something new, a little more. And Grant felt assured, even comfortable. Yes, *damn* comfortable, in fact.

Deb took a breath and said, "Okay, if the world was going to end tomorrow, and you could sleep with one person tonight, who would it be?"

ARRROOOOOOOOOOGAH! A thousand different neural pathways lit up at once in Grant's brain. The instinctual part of his brain told his body to go into full Panic Mode, which it promptly did. Another part of his brain was trying to stop the panic, another was sending an addendum to the face and body that said something like "And Try Not to Look Stupid While We Get This Under Control," while still another was desperately trying to process what Deb had said and formulate some kind of response. Anything. He couldn't lie to her—he was simply incapable of that. But he had to say something. Anything. He couldn't just *answer* the question; he was . . . unprepared. And time was ticking, the milliseconds stretching into milliminutes. He replayed her question, found a linguistic loophole, and dove for it:

"Uh, you mean like . . . a celebrity?"

"Yeah. Anyone."

"Oh. Hmmmm . . ." Whooooosh. His heart returned to normal operating parameters. It was going to be okay—this was just one of those games. Dealable.

"Okay, how's the world gonna end?"

"Grant, don't stall."

"No, I'm serious. It makes a difference."

"How?"

"For example, Christina Aguilera might be pretty high up on my list, right? Calm down—I said *might*, okay? Hypothetical. But if the world were going to end slowly, like with explosions, I don't want her there with me in the morning."

"She'd freak."

"Right, it'd be a nightmare—lots of screaming and crying and shit. It'd suck. Now, Macy Gray? Not so high on my list in the first-look category. But if it's gonna be a long thing, I'd want her there."

"She's so . . ."

"I just think she'd be a pretty cool chick to watch an apocalypse with, that's all."

Deb thinks about this, a smile creeping across her face. Strange kind of smile.

"What?" Grant asked.

"It's great. Even in a total no-strings-attached sexual fantasy, you find a way to make it into a relationship."

"Well, it's a short relationship. Just the morning after, really."

"No, don't be like that. Your answer's great. It's just . . . really, really sweet."

Wow. Grant actually blushed, so he pretended to pretend to blush: "Aw, stop it—"

"Who's a sweetie-weetie, *who* is?" Deb was pinching his face and making a baby voice. Grant was laughing and pretending to try to get away. Grant knew this was one of those moments that Regular Guys turn into Sexual Situations. It shouldn't be so hard, the Regular Guy in Grant's head argued, considering the lateness of the hour and the state of undress and the physical contact. . . . Grant began to plan how he might go about "making it happen." He'd narrowed it down to four or five possibilities by the time Deb stopped, sighed happily, and sank back down into her beanbag with a sound of finality and repose.

The Regular Guy in Grant's head slapped his forehead in disgust, turned out the light, and went to sleep.

It's ten minutes later, and the President of Montana (Deposed) is packing his bags in darkness as the First Lady of Montana (also Deposed, one would assume, albeit indirectly) sits cross-legged on their bed, an uncharacteristically girlish pose that some women (the PoM[D] thanks God for this frequently) never grow out of.

They're talking.

"You know, maybe if you just explain to Deke how—"

"It ain't up to Deke anymore, honey. You know that."

"Yeah, I guess that's true. You'd be in the clink till you're ninety. Federal prison too . . ."

"Mixing with the best and the brightest. Probably end up calling me 'Pops.' "

"Don't sell yourself short, Earl; you're still pretty cute. Some seven-foot-tall mass murderer would snap you up in no time. Would that count as infidelity, I wonder? Well, I forgive you in advance. Ya do what you have to. . . ."

"Funny. That doesn't help, you know."

"You're smiling. . . ."

"Reflex, darling, just reflex. I got any more socks?"

"Bottom drawer there. I can't believe it's come down to this. No way Dix can run all of it."

"I don't think he wants to. I think he wants . . . *this*. War. Can you believe that? All these people maybe dying over our over-due tax bill?" Big mistake there. The President freezes as he says it, hoping it'll pass unnoticed.

"A-*ha*!!"

"Aw, shit."

Now they're both smiling—the President guiltily, his wife tri-umphantly.

"I *knew* it!"

"No, wait, there's freedom and liberty, too. The new world order . . ."

"Too late, Buster Brown!"

She's laughing. The President can't help himself, grins, feel-ing lighter by the second.

"No, really—liberating the people!"

"Too late, you said it!" She's laughing.

". . . black helicopters, damnit!"

Now they're both convulsing with laughter, conspiratori-ally, like naughty children. Slightly hysterical, maybe, but it's worth it.

It lasts a long time, but not nearly long enough, and it ends suddenly as reality lumbers back into the room. They stare at each other for a while.

"Aw, Tammy, I'm sorry."

"I know, Earl. You let it all run away with you."

"Again."

"One of the reasons why I love you. You don't go halfway."

". . ."

"But I do wish you didn't have to escape *that* way. We might be a little peculiar *here*, but . . ."

"No way that Deke's gonna be watching the 'border' on Jebediah's side, so I'll make a start. And who knows? It mighta changed over there."

"If you believed that, you'd be taking me with you."

That's true enough to shut them both up. The President of Montana (Deposed) zips up his duffel, looks around the room a few times, makes to move one way or another, but doesn't go anywhere.

"I'll be okay. You just stay down, don't say much, wait till it all shakes down. Then . . . you know the places and times, right?"

"Yes. I'll be fine. Get goin', now, so I can spend my sunset years with you."

The President takes in his wife one more time, almost says something, doesn't.

Five minutes later, he's snaking his way across the damp grass in the darkness, moving away from the flashing red lights that line his country's southern border.

Arlene drifted off to sleep slowly, wondering why she'd never really thought about sleeping with Johnny before tonight, and if this was in some crazy way a fitting tribute to Furble. She hoped so. Next to her in the rumpled bed, Johnny Felix Decaté smiled in his sleep.

Grant can't sleep. He's thinking. First about tonight, of course, about Deborah Johnstone and Johnny's weirdness and the Square and Deborah Johnstone. And about Grant. He's thinking and maybe starting to sleep, but not really, and his thoughts become kind of unconnected, so that every once in a while he startles a little and reviews his last thought and thinks, "How did I get *there*?"

Here are some of Grant's last thoughts from tonight:

Somewhere, sometime back in human history, there had to be someone who actually spoke the first word. Had to be. Mathematical certainty. But here's the thing. . . . When that first word was spoken, everyone else who was there to hear it had absolutely no idea what it meant. How could they? They'd never heard a word before, they probably didn't even know that it was supposed to mean something. So the first word, whatever it was, was a total, 100 percent failure. So here's the thing. . . . What made the guy who said the first word and totally failed decide that he was going to say it again and again and again, until someone understood? If it were me, would I have said it again and again and again? No, probably not. It would have to be someone like Johnny. Or Deborah. What color are Deborah's nipples? Probably pink, light pink, but I bet they turn dark red when they get excited. I don't think I could have sex with her just once. If we had sex once and she made it really clear that it was just a one-time thing, then I would know for sure that my life was over, that the best possible thing that could ever happen to me had already happened. At some point, everybody has the absolute best time that they're ever going to have in their entire lives. How many people know it when it happens? Very few, I bet. Is it better to know or not to know? What *was* the first word? Or were there lots and lots of them, "first" words being invented over and over by different people, until someone had the gumption to just keep saying one until everyone got it? So what we're really talking about here is the first word that *stuck*.

The others don't count. I probably woulda been the guy who invented like seven words and never got anyone to listen, until some guy like Johnny came along and broke the ice with something like "food." Then, once words started to catch on, I'd have a whole bunch to teach people, and I'd have been really good at keeping track of what words we had and making up new ones, but Johnny would've been known as the guy who invented words, and that's not really untrue when you get right down to it. . . .

Okay, he's asleep.

Shhhhhh . . .

Chapter 6

ARLENE WOKE, yawned, looked to her right side . . .

. . . and moments later promised herself that she'd never again sneer at what she'd thought were overblown reactions and double-takes in sitcoms. In some situations—like this one, for instance—Jack Tripper's response would be subtle compared with her own:

She jumped out of the bed, taking with her a sheet that promptly got tangled in her legs. She wrestled it to the floor frantically, straightened up, realized she was naked, grabbed for the sheet, fell forward into the bed, and landed pretty much exactly where she'd been moments before, panting and staring wide-eyed at her still-sleeping bed partner.

She breathed, calming herself, and her mind lazily reminded her of the details, in no particular order:

- It was not clear whose idea it had been.
- They'd had safe sex, thank God.
- And then they'd had unsafe sex.
- And then safe again. Sort of.
- Johnny's pubic hair was blond.
- There was a lot of laughing involved.
- There was also what seemed like an unnatural amount of fluid.

- She'd had at least two orgasms, but the first one only sort of counted, because it was a physical response but she was totally uncomfortable, so it wasn't like it really counted.
- Even though she'd never been with Johnny before, she could tell that there was definitely something wrong with him.

This last item was hard for her to admit to herself, but pretty incontrovertible. For one, she thought *men* were supposed to be the goal-oriented ones, and previous experience had borne that out. But Johnny didn't even seem aware that there was a goal in the first place. Or even a guidepost, a few milestones, whatever. He kept getting distracted, taking side trips, suddenly becoming interested in an arm or a toe, whatever presented itself, regardless even of whether it was Arlene's or his own. His erections came and went easily, depending on what he was focused on.

Eventually, Arlene figured out some pretty surefire ways to *keep* him focused for a few minutes in a row. She was all for a sensitive, nonpressuring, non-goal-oriented lover (of course, what girl wasn't, at long last, chance of a lifetime, etc.), but after a while she began to see the merits of a more linear approach. Even the most sprawling novel *leads* to something, after all, builds up to a . . . thing. Or else it's a bad novel. Johnny had to be made to see that, which had taken a lot of pressuring on her part—in fact, what became borderline badgering. . . .

She stopped before she beat up on herself too much. After all, Johnny had really appreciated the results, like some infant who had to be shown how eating can make the stomachache go away.

It had been good, she decided. Weird, but good. And nothing to regret, of course . . .

. . . except for doing it on a night when her other friends were there, too. She realized this at the precise moment that she heard Deb's voice addressing her from the doorway.

"Good *morning*, stud!"

As dawn breaks, utterly gray and non-rosy-fingered, the Rightful President of Montana is hurrying through a damp field, swiveling his head, keeping low. His military training, what he remembers of it, actually would demand that he *crawl* the next couple of miles. But the RPoM's military training failed to take in contingencies like Arthritis, Assorted Pains, and Being Just Too Damn Old to Act Like a Goddamn Commando.

Besides, reasoned the President, there wasn't much to fear out here. From what he remembered of Jebediah's flock, back before they closed the gates, they weren't gonna be around at this hour. Jebediah used to invite everyone in the county to his "Sunrise Seminars" (a stupid name that the President of Montana [Retired] was sure he'd seen on TV before), and those were *endless*, according to Zack's father's niece-in-law, who'd attended one. So it was a pretty safe bet that all the Jebedites would be gathered in the now-hidden church, way over there behind that carefully planted stand of poplars.

So, if that's the case, thinks the PoM(R), is there any reason to be sneakin' around at all? His mood brightens with the sunrise, and he straightens up, relief washing over him, the long hike ahead of him suddenly surmountable. He whistles (yes, "Zip-A-Dee-Doo-Dah"), stretches, and strides out onto a rough path.

"It *is* a beautiful day, friend," says a sympathetic voice behind him, along with that really familiar sound of a shotgun being pumped. "I'll give you a couple of seconds to say goodbye to it an' all."

It is unthinkable. And it has happened. Within an infinitesimal margin of error, it's nearly certain that last night, in our house, Dr. Schrödinger had sexual intercourse. Got himself "some action." In a universe written by an infinite number of monkeys with an infinite number of typewriters, it would have to be one of the very last monkeys at the end of one of the very last rows that would ever construct a world wherein a man like Dr. Schrödinger managed to bed a young woman, but here we are. We make a quick mental note to hunt down that seedy little monkey at our earliest opportunity.

The good doctor and the girl (was it "Dori"?) are bustling about the kitchen, sharing a single set of pyjamas: he in the bottoms, she in the top. They're making breakfast.

Correction: She's making breakfast. He's lecturing on it.

". . . Of course, there's very little natural selection at work in chickens anyway. We've been breeding them for centuries. But if these were the eggs of wild birds—ostriches, let's say—you'll note that there'd be very little in the way of 'survival of the fittest': The eggs are taken at random, and selection starts when the survivors are hatched and the creatures are at large, as it were."

We pity her. She's actually fairly fetching, and her patient eyes are heavy-lidded with sleep. It's obvious that she hasn't heard a word that Dr. Schrödinger has said. (And we have no idea why a physicist is suddenly waxing on about Darwin. Must be the aftereffects of . . . We shudder to think.) She stretches, yawning, the spatula lifting skyward, and turns toward the doctor.

"But, like, what about the egg that looks more like a rock, you know? Or the one that's a little smaller and denser, so it ends up like closer to the bottom of the nest? You know, like, protected? That's selection, right? So the egg is part of the creature, right?" She persists, "I mean, because of these incontrovertible survival ramifications, we actually have to consider the egg part of the extended phenotype."

The doctor is flabbergasted, as are we. He because she's right. We because she was listening to the old man in the first place. She playfully lifts his lower jaw back up with the spatula, tweaks him somewhere in his midsection that we'd prefer not to think about, and turns back to flip the eggs.

Ten minutes later, we are all sitting at the table, eating our breakfast. Dr. Schrödinger is trying to be his merry self, but he's angry about something he can't quite speak about. For our part, we're delighted: If anyone besides *us* is going to get their drumstick battered in *our* home, it's a little more tolerable if they get intellectually emasculated in the process.

Dear Diary,

I am very unhappy about being in Inman Square instead of near my usual haunts (boo! ha-ha!), but last night's tug was a strong one. A real motherfucker. I had to go, though. At 4:35 A.M. exactly, I was behind a bar, storing my last jumbo farm-fresh egg in a crack between the Dumpster and the wall. It must have something to do with foiling the robots, but what doesn't, I ask you, what doesn't?

Another thing is I confronted another Man of Science! I was "looking for my purse" in the Dumpster behind the S&S deli when who walks out with a couple of grad students but Richard Lewontin! The neo-Darwinist, just like on his book jackets. I thought I'd actually have to hit the Harvard campus to get him.

As soon as I saw my opportunity, my mind began to focus, you know, overdrive, bullet-time, whatever.

I walked behind them for a few paces, cleared my throat real loud, and when they turned, I was ready. "Hey, Richie! Dick!" I shouted. "How'd you like to punctuate <u>this</u> equilibrium?" Then I hoisted my skirt and gave him a good look at ol' Lady Liberty. He headed off real quick, but I did manage to get one more shot in: "C'mon! <u>This</u> ain't just a spandrel!"

I'm pretty sure one of his students laughed at that one, but of course that's not the point. What's important here is that Lewontin is number eighteen in my Men of Science project. I think we'll be seeing some real results after twenty or so.

That's it until dinnertime. I'll be on patrol until then.

When "girl talk" happens, Grant is used to being discussed as though he's not there. This, however, is not the kind of thing that he's ever seen happen to Johnny. Johnny's always been their leader in some ways—that's only clear now that he's *not* anymore. He hasn't spoken a word all morning, so, though his presence is still commanding, it's more in an *objet-d'art* kind of way, like one of those anime giant robots that nobody sees until they're activated and start destroying the city. But for now, neither speaking nor playing music, he's a well-crafted curiosity, a wicker duck (Grant curses himself for having that damn duck still traipsing around in his brain).

So, as Arlene and Deb pad around the kitchen making an endless breakfast (Johnny's appetite remains prodigious—everyone else is getting only a bite or two in edgewise), there's little to indicate that they're aware of being listened to; Grant feels a bit like a large plush bunny at a girls' tea party.

Arlene flips an egg. "Wow, I can't believe that! I always figured you and Johnny had gotten together, you know, at least once." Grant had always thought so, too. But if he says so here, nobody hears it anyway, and history won't record it.

"No," says Deb, standing in the best patch of sunlight, stretching. "Never seemed . . . necessary. But it *is* necessary to hear all about it. I mean *everything*, girlfriend. Spill."

Well within the propriety-free zone that Deb generates, Arlene spills. Johnny chuckles occasionally, appreciating the recounting of his performance, flaws and all. Grant clears his throat repeatedly. The only reaction this gets is a sideways glance from Deb, who distractedly shovels more eggs onto the plush bunny's plate as she guides her friend's narrative. By the time Arlene gets to some of the more graphic details, Grant might as well *be* a stuffed animal from an appetite standpoint.

Grant's odd mixture of suffering and titillation (Deb's definitely not wearing a bra under that T-shirt, which is why Grant has requested scrambled eggs several times—oooh, that scrambling motion . . .) is interrupted when he feels Johnny's eyes on him. Grant turns to see that increasingly familiar new liquid and beatific stare. Johnny makes sure he's got Grant's attention, and then speaks for the first time in many, many hours.

"Grant?"

"Present."

"You're my best friend."

The President of Montana (Once and Future) cannot recall an odder conversation than this, standing in a field in the morning sunlight, a shotgun being leveled at his belly by a farm boy clad in a Cecil B. DeMille interpretation of Biblical robes. It would be more comfortable if the PoM(OaF) wasn't pretty sure he's about to die.

"You make some good points, but now I hafta kill you."

"Wait a minute. . . ."

"That's the rule, sir. We sent you guys a couple of notes about that."

"We stopped getting mail after we declared independence."

"There's a lot of signs posted at the property line."

"I crossed over before dawn."

"Shoulda brought a flashlight, I guess. Anyway, the warnings were a courtesy. Jebediah says that the uninitiated can never truly understand a warning, and their souls will pass on the same with or without it."

The President takes this in. He's already spent ten minutes debating with the Jebedite, and there seems to be no way to change his mind. Still, the fact that he's willing to talk gives the President hope.

"Don't think that there's any hope just 'cuz I'm willing to talk," says the Jebedite.

"I don't."

" 'The Truth shall be revealed even as the mind departs'— that's the way we see it, that's all."

"Oh. You're amazingly calm, I gotta say."

"I'm not the one about to be killed. Makes it easier."

"Good point . . . Say, maybe I could go back and get some better clothes—you know, go out with some dignity. I promise I'll be back."

"Oh, c'mon, I lost the rule book, but I haven't lost my mind." The kid levels his shotgun, sighting it at the President for the fifth time, but now clearly getting a little impatient. "You ready?"

"Wait—there was a rule book?"

" 'Course. Didn't think I was some kinda sicko who just *wants* to kill, didja? Is that what you thought?"

"No! But wait. You *lost* the rule book?"

"Misplaced it, yeah. But I can get another next week, when the new ones come in."

"So if there *was* some kind of loophole, some way for me to live through this . . ."

". . . I wouldn't know about it 'cuz I don't have the book. Kinda ironic, isn't it?" The kid's smiling.

"Yeah!" blurts the President. "It'd be, whaddyacallit, sacrilege to you, wouldn't it?"

"Calm down, mister, I was kiddin' you—there are no loopholes in there."

"Well, maybe *you* haven't found one, but . . ."

"Trust me."

"Well, I . . . what's your name, son?"

"Oh, I know this one—you get to know me, I start thinking of you as a person, I'll realize that you're just like me, and then I won't be able to pull the trigger, right?"

"Uh, right?" asks the President hopefully.

"Everyone tries that. Doesn't happen."

"Never?"

"Nope."

"Great." The President is starting to get tired, starting to think he'll tell the kid to just pull the trigger and get it over with, but he fights that thought off. He's already been told that not doing that and not moving from his spot are the only things that're keeping him alive.

He tries another tack. "This Jebediah—he eats and sleeps like other men, doesn't he?"

The kid's face takes on a look of revelation. "Oh, why, I never *thought* of that—he's not a god at all! You've freed me from my delusions! Now I *have* to let you live. . . ."

"You're being sarcastic."

"Don't you think I've heard that crap a few times before? Really, I'm tired of it. I know I'm not supposed to rush things here, but I've got a whole bunch of things to do this mornin'." The kid levels the gun again. It's the sixth time, but this time he means it.

"Wait! Hold on, damnit! You said you couldn't do this until you'd answered all my questions! You said the 'way of Jebediah' demands that you educate the condemned! You're gonna break your own holy rule?"

"That'll be our little secret, okay?" says the kid with a wink. His finger tightens on the trigger. The President's mind goes crazy, he's got a couple of other ideas, he's picturing his wife, he tries to wake up, his bladder lets go, he's got maybe a second left.

"Wait—" he starts.

Bang.

We've taken our lunch outside, shaking off the morning, enjoying the glittering Charles and the occasional Frisbees flying across our field of vision, a peaceful day, all too rare lately. We get up and stroll along the ribbon of grass, passing groups of students, sunbathers on blankets, and the occasional knot of audience members around some bank-busker or another.

One such group catches our attention, for there is no music emanating from the circle's center, and the group is particularly large and rapt. We push forward (politely, of course, but firmly), and get a better look.

We immediately wish we hadn't. We never should have had to see this.

At the center of the crowd's attention is a little card table laden with cheap-looking knickknacks. Nearby stands an easel on which rests an elegantly lettered placard.

It reads: "The Remarkable Dr. S."

Behind the table stands Dr. Schrödinger, wearing a tattered black cape and an absurdly large top hat over his usual fusty ensemble. At his side, jammed into a red satin showgirl's outfit with a matching headdress, and looking none too happy about it, is the girl from this morning, Dori. She's haphazardly gesturing at the little table as the Remarkable Dr. S. speaks.

"Yes, the humble carbon atom, ladies and gents, the essential building block, the life-giver. Able to bond in so many ways, so extensively that it can form molecules of astounding and unprecedented size and complexity. Today, right here on the banks of the mighty Charles, I bring you the newest, most exciting molecule the world has ever known. Larger than large, bigger than big, this molecule makes the 'buckyball' seem like a *quark* by comparison. The first molecule so large that it can be seen, seen quite easily, by the human eye. Ladies and gentlemen, I give you Schrödinger's Humdinger!"

The doctor's Lovely and Talented Assistant pulls aside a little curtain and the crowd gasps—actually, literally gasps. We're not even looking. How, we wonder, has this socially retarded physicist, this annoying and clingy man of science, so utterly transformed himself in a few days' time? Why now? And why can't we escape him? We ponder this as we walk away, the suddenly popular old prestidigitator's voice trailing off behind us: "Yes, for a limited time, you too can own Schrödinger's Humdinger, the world's first MegaMolecule! Step right up. . . ."

Over our shoulders we can see that the crowd, like our existence, is pressing in on him, spiraling slightly counterclockwise as they do so.

———

The others are still breakfasting as Grant wanders into Johnny's grandmother's library. He needs a couple of minutes to himself, some time to get centered, just like he always does after he spends a night away from home. He realizes that this makes him less cool.

Grant is thinking about the strange swirl of events in the past twenty-four hours, trying to compartmentalize a little bit, to separate Johnny's Condition from Arlene and Johnny from The Eternal Deborah Question from The Feelings Called Up by Johnny's Guitar. It's not easy, and the divisions between them all are artificial, but Grant, being Grant, needs some structure here.

He's idly browsing some of the books. Hundreds of them litter the library, as many off the shelf as on. After he has leafed through a few of them, an unfamiliar title catches his eye. A plain-looking but somehow evocatively titled little book. He opens it and reads:

> There's a cat in a box in Cambridge, Massachusetts. It's about three-quarters of a mile from the firehouse in Central Square, which means that if someone launched a rescue operation now, the trucks could be there in half an hour. Or so.

Odd, thinks Grant, and leafs forward. He's shocked to find his own name in there:

> Grant couldn't believe it—there, laid out beneath him, perfect, complete, was Deborah Johnstone, the Undiscovered Country. . . .

Despite his profound interest in this subject matter, Grant's a little freaked out by this. He riffles backward, seeing his friends' names, some pseudo-science, a lot of self-referential bullshit, etc. He comes across a frighteningly familiar passage and reads:

> Grant is thinking about the strange swirl of events in the past twenty-four hours, trying to compartmentalize a little bit, to separate Johnny's Condition from Arlene and Johnny from The Eternal Deborah Question from The Feelings Called Up by Johnny's Guitar. It's not easy, and the divisions between them all are artificial, but Grant, being Grant, needs some structure here.

He's idly browsing some of the books. Hundreds of them litter the library, as many off the shelf as on. After he has leafed through a few of them, an unfamiliar title catches his eye. A plain-looking but somehow evocatively titled little book. He opens it and reads:

> There's a cat in a box in Cambridge, Massachusetts. It's about three-quarters of a mile from the firehouse in Central Square, which means that if someone launched a rescue operation now, the trucks could be there in half an hour. Or so.

Odd, thinks Grant, and leafs forward. He's shacked to find his own name in there:

> Grant couldn't believe it—there, laid out beneath him, perfect, complete, was Deborah Johnstone, the Undiscovered Country. . . .

Despite his profound interest in this subject matter, Grant's a little freaked out by this. He riffles backward, seeing his friends' names, some pseudo-science, a lot of self-referential bullshit, etc. He comes across a frighteningly familiar passage and reads:

Grant is thinking about the strange swirl of events in the past twenty-four hours, trying to compartmentalize a little bit, to separate Johnny's Condition from Arlene and Johnny from The Eternal Deborah Question from The Feelings Called Up bye Johnny's Guitar. It's not easy, and the divisions between them all are artificial, but Grant, being Grant, needs some structure here.

He's idly browsing some of the books. Hundreds of them litter the library, as many off the shelf as on. After he has leafed through a few of them, an unfamiliar title catches his eye. A plain-looking but somehow evocatively titled little book. He opens it and reads:

> There's a cat in a box in Cambridge, Massachusetts. It's about three-quarters of a mile from the firehouse in Central Square, which means that if someone lunched a rescue operation now, the trucks could be there in half an hour. Or so.

Odd, thinks Grant, and leafs forward. He's shacked to find his own name in there:

> Grant ccouldn't believe it—there, laid out beneath him, perfect, complete, was Deborah Johnstone, the Undiscovered Country. . . .

Despite his profound interest in this subject matter, Grant's a little freaked out by this. He riffles backward, seeing hip friends' names, some pseudo-science, a lot of self-referential bullshit, etc. He comes across a fraughteningly familiar passage and reads:

AARRTTTIIIUUE090900000200030045764545 jrerhigerg 9ggfg32 Grant is thinkinggrant is thinking 000100010110 0101000010111 ARG OP SIT GLEW ffoej ffoef ffoet ffoeh. , ' : " ! CRRRRRRRRRRRRRRRRRR Six: Six: Six: Grant is Dr. Latina Johnny is is is is is not not not is not CORE ERROR 1679:

RESET Grant is thinking about the strange swirl of events in the past $$$$$$ SIGNAL 698959595 twenty-four hours, trying to compartmentalize a little bit, to separate Johnny's Condition about the strange swirl of events in the past twenty-four hours, trying to compartmentalize a little bit, to separate Johnny's Condition from Arlene and Johnny from The Eternal Deborah Question from The Feelings Called Up from Johnny's Guitar. It's not easy, and the divisions between them all are artificial, but Grant, being Grant, needs some structure here structure here structure here stricture here stricture hero strict are hero stric our hero STRUCTURE HEREEEEEEEEEEEEeoiitiyuty 93408503859483059485 573745837 435734 349834257205 748 v 9834539845 9834578934 Gran 4309850934769845 Is 4583578g67g348 thinking thin king 894508095830 OOOOO EEEEEEEEEE OOOOOOOOEEEEEEE 0-0-0-930930-309-30- 0-3 93094324 − 3 545904 - 2304- 04539 − 20349 - - 987598 98753498 89745 785787 7 STUS 8trte 03403094030404040 4040404040404040404040404040400000000000000000000000 0000000000000000000000000000000000000000000000000000 0000000000000000001000000000000000000110000000000000 1110000000000000000000000111000000000000000000000000 0000001111110000000000000000000000001111110000000001100 0111000011000010111111000010101011101010111010101010001 0010000111100011010010001011110110110110110000011010101010 0111010101000111001010010100010001010000000000001000 0000000000011110000000000000000000000000000000111111000 0000000000000000000011111100000000001100011100001100001 0111111000010101011101010111010101010001001000011110001 1010010001011110111011101100000110101010011101010100011 1001010010100010001010000000000000000000001111000000 0100000000100000000000011111100000000000000000000000011 1111000000000011000111000011000010111111000010101011101 0101110101010100010010000111100011010010001011110111011

1011000001101010100111010101000111001010010100010000101
0000000000000000000001111000000000000000000000000000000
0011111100000000000000000000011111100000000000110001110
00011000010111111000010101011101010111010101010001001 0
00011110001101001000101111011101110110000011010101001 11
0101010001100101001010001000101000000000000000000000
1111000000000001001000000000000000111110000000000000
00000000011111100000000001100011100001100001011111110000
10101011101010111010101010001001000011110001101001 0001
011110111011011000001101010100111010101000111001010010
1000100010100000000000000000000001110000000000000000
0000000000000111111000000000000000000000001111110000000
0011000111000011000010111111000010101011101010111010101
010001001000011110001101001000101111011011101 10110000011
01010100111010101000111001010010100010001010000000000
0000000000011110000000000000000000000000000000001111110000
00000000000000000011111100000000001100011100001100001
011111100001010101110101011010101010001001000011110001
101001000101111011101110110000011010101001101010100011
10010100101000100010100000000000000000000001111000000 0
0000000000000000000001111110000000000000000000000000011
111000000000011000111000011000010111111000010101011101
01011010101010001001000011110001101001000101111011101 1
1011000000110101010011101010100011100101001010001000101
00000000000000000000011110000000000000000000000000000000
0011111100000000000000000000011111100000000000110001110
0001100001011111100001010101110101011101010101000100 10
000111100011010010001011110111011011101100000110101010 0111
0101010001100101001010001000101000000000000000000000
111100000000000010100000000000000011111100000000000000
00000000111110000000000011000111000011000010111111 10000
10101011101010111010101010001001000011110001101001 0001
011110111011101100000110101010011101010100011100101 0010

100010001010000010100000000010011110000000000000000
000000000000111111000000000000000000000001111110000000
00110001110000110000101111110000101010111010101111010101
01000100100001111000110100100010111101110111011000011
01010100111010101000111001010010100010001010000000000
00000000000111100000000000000000000000000000111111000
00000000000000000001111110000000000110001110000110001
01111110000101010111010101111010101010001001000011110001
10100100010111101110111011000001101010100111010101000011
10010100101000100010100000000111111000000000000000000000
00000000000000000000000000011111111111gr-jo-de-ar 675 − 01 348
574857

098453333333333333333333333333333333333333333333333
333333333333333333333333333333333333333333333333333333
333333333333333333333333333333333333333333333333333333
333333333333333333333333333333333333333333333333333333
3333

This book has crashed. Please restart this book and try again.
FATAL ERROR: ch06/11

Chapter 6A

RESTART IND# 00007 RES. VER. 1.01

The others are still breakfasting as Grant wanders into Johnny's grandmother's library. He needs a couple of minutes to himself, some time to get centered, just like he always does after he spends a night away from home. He realizes that this makes him less cool.

Grant is thinking about the strange swirl of events in the past twenty-four hours, trying to compartmentalize a little bit, to separate Johnny's Condition from Arlene and Johnny from The Eternal Deborah Question from The Feelings Called Up by Johnny's Guitar. It's not easy, and the divisions between them all are artificial, but Grant, being Grant, needs some structure here.

He's idly browsing some of the books. Hundreds of them litter the library, as many off the shelf as on. After he has leafed through a few of them, an unfamiliar title catches his eye. A plain-looking but somehow evocatively titled little book. He DOES NOT TOUCH BOOK/LEAVES ROOM/DOES NOT RETURN/005003TXT.070167

ALT SEQ 73023-3434 FR: — walks back into the kitchen, where he hears a bustle of new activity. Over the general commotion he hears the strident, strong voice of Leonora Decaté, Johnny's grandmother and matron of the house, and he smiles.

The scene that greets him is not unexpected but somehow iconic, a neoclassical color-saturated tableau: Johnny, seated, staring up like a supplicant at the figure in the center of the room, a wide smile on his face; in a beam of sunlight, holding forth, Leonora, clad in a multilayered free-flowing dress of white and cream, impossibly young for a young man's grandmother; on either side of her, Arlene and Deb, their bare legs shining, offering coffee and toast, two nymphs attending an eccentric goddess; in the shadows, a uniformed figure, dark, confused, a busboy at the last supper.

At the entrance of Grant ("the Observer," he thinks wryly), the tableau breaks.

"Grant! Dear heart! My fiancé!" exclaims Leonora. Grant is her favorite, always has been, for reasons that Grant has forgotten and probably never knew. She wraps Grant up in her arms, her slight frame at once motherly and girlish. Grant savors the hug, then holds her out at arm's length.

"And where were you last night, young lady? You thought you could just sneak in anytime you want?"

"Sorry, Dad. Jack and I just lost track of the time, I guess. . . ."

"Uh-huh," says Grant, relishing the role, as always. He's vaguely aware of the girls smiling at him, Deb in particular smiling a smile he'd like to examine and think about and read into, but he presses on. "And who's this 'Jack'?"

"That's me," says an unfamiliar voice. The newcomer steps out of the shadows. He's a cop, and Grant notes without too much surprise that he's handsome and about twenty years younger than Mrs. D. "Jack Kennedy. No relation. And you're, uh, Leonora's father and fiancé, huh?"

"We're a very close family," Grant says, liking Jack, suffused with the glowing bubble of goodwill that tends to surround Leonora. Leonora, now swirling back toward the center of the kitchen, is chatting excitedly.

"Jack took me to that new restaurant downtown, and Aerosmith was there—at least the boy with the lips was—and then we rented *The Matrix*, and you were right about that one, Johnny, and then we—but we walked back from Arlington this morning, and—oh!—look at this. . . ."

She ecstatically reaches into her purse and withdraws a small round object, black and complex. "We got this," continues Johnny's grandmother, "from an adorably shabby old magician."

Grant can't identify the object in his hand, though it feels odd, multifaceted, dense. "It's a *molecule!*" exclaims Leonora breathlessly. "Carbon. Like a beckyball but bigger!"

" 'Buckyball,' " says Grant, idly. "But this can't be a single . . . A *magician* sold this to you? He's out there selling *molecules?*"

"Or a scientist. For all I know he teaches here." "Here," as ever for Leonora Decaté, is Harvard, which is in fact several blocks away.

"He should call them 'Satan's Golf Balls,' " Arlene says. Grant agrees—he's a little frightened by the feel of the object, and he puts it on the table. Leonora, characteristically, is already on to the next item on her ever-changing agenda.

"Johnny, dear one, you know you really could have invited the rest of your friends in last night. Jack and I had to step over them just to get in." She sees the look of puzzlement on all the faces. Arlene is the first at the front window.

"Oh God," she says. "Those aren't exactly our friends. . . ."

They all crowd around the window to see kids crowding

around the house. The lawn looks like a micro-Woodstock, a dozen or so ragged kids just arising, some with sleeping bags, some with nothing. Grant recognizes one or two faces from the night before. He attempts to explain to Leonora, but finds himself stuck on You Had to Be There. What does come across is that the visitors are uninvited. Jack, back in his element, volunteers to take care of it.

"We have an old shotgun in the basement," says Leonora. This is a mildly shocking statement—Leonora is perhaps the most welcoming and nonviolent person Grant has ever known. But the glint in her eye tells Grant that she'd just love to see her new man striding out heroically, weapon in hand. Grant can't help smiling as Jack jumps at the chance.

He follows Leonora's pointing finger, heads toward the basement door, grasps the handle. Johnny yelps and collapses. Arlene screams.

Dear Diary,

Bored out of my fucking skull. Time for more of the History . . .

1550—A Hawaiian woman named Weeio invents the hula dance. King Fahzik of Persia orders the digging of a tunnel to Rome, and fifteen thousand Musselmen start shoveling. Everybody's got the black plague except the Africans and the Chinese, who'd had it already.

Ivan the Terrible turns twenty and decides not to go to grad school. At this point, no one's calling him "the Terrible." His school nickname is "Ivan the Inky," thanks to his penmanship problems. Meanwhile, the Mayans and Incans were emigrating off the planet in droves to get away from the Spaniards. Three whole cities got airlifted in one afternoon, including El Dorado, buildings and all.

1560—Emperor Akbar's men, who've been tunneling to Japan,

run into King Fahzik's men underground, which means both of them were going the wrong way. It's one of those rare moments in history where everybody has a good laugh.

Leonardo da Vinci dies in hiding. His last invention is the video camera, which he gives to the Templars who've been keeping him alive all these years. They start shooting their secret Archive.

In China, Ming was the Thing and pottery was all the rage. The Empress commissioned the world's first vibrator, which was ceramic and required fourteen slaves to power it with cleverly designed pedals. It was installed at the Summer Palace, and by August you couldn't find a mah-jongg game within fifty miles of the place.

All right, ladies, I've got to go find some lunch elsewhere. Harvard Square is crawling with robots.

"Scientists should never philosophize," said Dr. Schrödinger, biting into his sandwich, unconcerned with the viscous mess spilling out the other end. "We should know better. But we can't help ourselves."

We were dining by ourselves, and then, suddenly, we were dining with the doctor, watching him fling his cape over a chair and overturn his top hat, now stuffed with currency. He seemed jaunty, almost robust, a marked contrast to the wraithlike and tedious blatherer of a few days before. We were, shockingly, faintly glad to see him, even though he had ordered without thereupon directing the waitress to us, and she promptly saved herself the trouble by ignoring us entirely, leaving us without any sort of meal for the moment.

"See, we scientists don't know anything more about the meaning of existence than anyone else. But we know people will listen. We're 'qualified.' But whenever a man of science steps out and makes sweeping pronouncements about life's mysteries, he inevitably says something extraordinarily dumb and accidentally brands himself a Nazi or a nihilist or worse. Because, of course, human ideas are scientifically inscrutable, despite what they're screaming about down at Yale or wherever they are these days."

We tried to summon up some fury, some of that "Dr. S. Must Die" fervor of the night before, but it somehow eluded us. Instead, we made a vaguely encouraging noise.

"So," said the formerly dorky doctor, "resolved: Scientists should never philosophize." He took another squelchy bite of his sandwich. "Now, let me tell you something about life. . . ."

INT DARKENED MOVIE THEATER--NIGHT

There's a large crowd, seated, watching the screen.

On the screen, we see the familiar five-second countdown, an invisible clock hand wiping each numeral away and revealing the next, Then ...

We see file footage (all black-and-white) of American flags being waved, parades, and U.S. soldiers marching in perfect unison.

MUSIC: Horn-laden up-tempo military march. Slightly distorted and tinny. Continues throughout.

TITLE: "Movietone Presents"

ANNOUNCER
(excited, authoritative)
Movietone presents ...

TITLE: "News on the March"

> ANNOUNCER (CONT'D)
> News on the March!

We see (in black-and-white) a farmhouse in the northern U.S., jeans-clad locals patrolling with guns.

> ANNOUNCER (CONT'D)
> Dateline, Montana. A small group of
> ranchers declare independence from
> the United States, proclaiming the
> Free State of Montana.

MEDIUM SHOT of a few freestanding walls, some with windows.

> ANNOUNCER (CONT'D)
> These would-be rebels don't see eye-
> to-eye with <u>anyone,</u> not even archi-
> tects, it would seem.

The audience giggles. Onscreen, we see a woman huddled against one of the walls.

> ANNOUNCER (CONT'D)
> (dripping with disdain,
> but still jaunty and positive)
> Here's a hint, madam—your "roof"
> might have a leak!

The audience laughs outright.

CUT TO a wide shot of soldiers performing exercises on an obstacle course in bright sunlight (in black-and-white, eternally, always in black-and-white).

> ANNOUNCER (CONT'D)
> But don't worry, our soldiers don't
> take any threat lightly...

CUT TO a shot of police and military personnel outside of the farmhouse.

> ANNOUNCER (CONT'D)
> ... and Montana's boys in blue take
> heart as literally dozens of our
> boys in green show up to lend a hand.

The audience applauds, chatters. CUT TO a wide shot of the rebels, sparsely placed but implacable.

> ANNOUNCER (CONT'D)
> Things seem bleak for the ninety-
> acre nation, as their "president" is
> already missing and time is running
> out....

TIGHT SHOT of two young boys playing behind one of the walls.

> ANNOUNCER (CONT'D)
> Today in class, Johnny's going to
> learn about Waco--the hard way!

The crowd guffaws, cheers, applauds.

CUT TO an overhead shot of the Charles River, sunlit (b&w--must we always remind you?).

> ANNOUNCER (CONT'D)
> (less serious)
> Meanwhile, in Boston, a new craze is
> sweeping the city...

MEDIUM SHOT of grassy bank, dozens of people holding little black balls.

> ANNOUNCER (CONT'D)
>
> . . . as everyone wants to get their hands on a "Dr. Schrödinger's Humdinger." Folks say they're useful. And fun. These handy little items are made of a single molecule!

We see a man holding a black ball aloft as a small cluster of people gaze in wonder. Followed by a shot of a small girl throwing her little black ball up a few inches and catching it. Followed by a shot of four young men proudly displaying their black balls for the camera.

> ANNOUNCER (CONT'D)
>
> These little wonders were just invented by the late physicist Dr. Erwin Schrödinger. . . .

File footage: Dr. Schrödinger with Albert Einstein.

> ANNOUNCER (CONT'D)
>
> This brilliant scientist is best known for the invention of your kitties' litter boxes, and with a second great advance to his credit, he's sure to make history.

A SHOT of a young Hispanic woman in a satin showgirl's costume and headdress. She is attempting to smile. She holds a small cigarette-girl's wooden box supported by a strap around her neck. In the box we see dozens of Humdingers.

> ANNOUNCER (CONT'D)
>
> And with a sales force as lovely as
> this one, no wonder these have rap-
> idly become the best-selling mole-
> cule of the century. Anything you
> say, miss--I'll take seven!

The audience chortles knowingly, particularly the men. Small children are heard pleading for their very own Humdingers and are quickly hushed.

CUT TO a wide shot of a suburban house. The lawn is covered with young people who are apparently camping out.

> ANNOUNCER (CONT'D)
>
> Meanwhile, just up the road, another
> craze has captivated the public
> imagination. Are these youngsters
> part of a cult? Are they stargazing?

We see a young blond man stepping out of the house with a guitar. He starts to play as the crowd extends their arms toward him.

> ANNOUNCER (CONT'D)
>
> No, they're just here to listen to
> musicland's latest phenomenon, Johnny
> Decaté.

FILE FOOTAGE of young women in a variety-show audience, scream-ing and crying. BACK ON Johnny, smiling and strumming.

> ANNOUNCER (CONT'D)
>
> This twentyish troubadour is caus-
> ing a stir with his growling guitar

    and his boyish good looks. It's like
    Beatlemania for the new century!

CLOSEUP of an ordinary-looking young woman at Johnny's side.

            ANNOUNCER (CONT'D)
    But sorry, ladies, he's already got
    a girlfriend. I guess love is blind.
    Plain Janes out there, take heart!

The audience chuckles.

            ANNOUNCER (CONT'D)
    Besides, this teen craze may not last.
    Rumor has it that Johnny may or may
    not have died just twenty-four hours
    before this film was taken!

WIDE SHOT of lawn, listeners enraptured.

            ANNOUNCER (CONT'D)
    But whether he's still with us or not,
    you'll hear about it right here, with
    News on the March!

Marching-band music swells, dopplers grotesquely.

BACK ON title screen, soldiers marching.

The screen goes white, then black, and the audience gossips excitedly until the feature begins.

  Bang.
  The President of Montana (On the Lam), having braced himself to remain standing with the shotgun blast's impact, fell

forward into the tall grass. He lay there, hearing groans that he didn't feel himself making, wondering whether this was because he'd already left his body behind. A voice called his name, full of compassion and concern, oddly familiar. . . .

Slowly, some ideas began to creep into his head. He'd fallen *forward*; he hadn't felt any impact; the groaning was coming from somewhere else; he could feel his body. . . .

"Earl? You all right?"

The PoM(OtL) looked up into a distinctly earthbound and friendly face. "Hiya, Deke."

"You're not hit, are ya?"

"Seems like I'm not," said the President, gradually sitting up.

"*I* am," came the voice of the Jebedite from several yards away. The Sheriff looked up, his gun still leveled in that direction.

"Serves ya right," said Deke curtly, then, turning his attention back to the President, "I figured you'd be coming this way."

"How'd you know I was gone?"

"When Dix started firing warning shots this morning, I knew it wasn't you in charge anymore. So I just added two and two. . . ."

"Dix *fired* at you?"

"Warning shots, but yeah. He's over the edge, Earl."

"Don't I know it."

"Some people are gonna get hurt."

"Some people are already hurt," whined a voice from nearby. The Sheriff looked up again.

"That's what you get," said the President, starting to feel better, "firing on a peaceful citizen like that."

"He didn't actually fire, Earl," said the Sheriff.

"Well, he was going to. . . ."

"True enough, and I don't let that kinda shit happen while I'm in charge."

"Well, you won't be for long," said the injured Jebedite, now breathing heavily.

"What?"

"You were trespassing! You're half a mile onto private property, without a warrant, and you fired on me. And I'm the only one with a right to be here!"

"You were gonna shoot me," said the President. "He was just keepin' the peace."

"Well, he's gonna have to tell that to the judge, because that's where I'm gonna take it. Plus, when Jebediah hears about this, he's gonna be wanted inside *and* outside the law! You *and* your family, Sheriff!"

The Sheriff considered this. Finally, he spoke, quietly. "Wow. That wouldn't'a been a really bright thing to say even if you weren't completely alone in a field at daybreak."

"What?" asked the Jebedite, the realization dawning way too slowly. "W-w-wait! Maybe I won't . . . You wouldn't—"

Bang.

"You're a hard man, Deke."

"Yeah, I guess. But Jebediah won't call this in. He never does."

"That's not what I—"

"I know. But those Jebedites rub me the wrong way, even if they haven't declared *war* on me yet."

"About that, Deke, I gotta say, I'm really sorry about—"

"Get out of here, Earl. Get to wherever you're going. Before I see you."

"Deke . . ."

"Now."

The President of Montana (in Exile) rose, brushed himself off, and looked at the Sheriff, who was now staring off at the rising sun. The President began to walk off, turned one last time. . . .

"Love to Barbara, Deke."

"Yeah."

Arlene doesn't want to go home—Furble's absence would be too much.

Deborah, as always, is fine right where she is.

Grant, as always, is fine right where Deborah is.

Johnny—well, there's no way to tell. He's talking less and less.

Besides, they're kind of trapped here anyway.

After Johnny fainted, and everyone came running, and they woke him up, and his grandmother sent Jack home, and Johnny looked out the window, and he smiled, and he got his guitar, and he went outside, and they followed him, and he played for everyone in the bright sunlight for an hour, and everyone listened . . . well, now that *that's* happened, they're pretty much under siege. The front lawn and the street are littered with people, mostly young, mostly peaceful, but there are just too many of them. They're out there with guitars and video cameras and picnics thrown together at the nearby Store 24, and they want one thing only: more Johnny.

Arlene looks at Johnny there across the living room, sitting cross-legged and smiling at them all, unhurried, and she thinks there *is* more Johnny than there ever was. And somehow that means there's *less* Johnny. Is he really there at all? The fact that she can see him, and the people outside, and the vague soreness between her legs are pretty overwhelming, evidence-wise. But she hasn't forgotten him aflame last night. And the changes: Johnny was always a positive guy, but not *this* positive; he was always talented, but not *this* talented; he was always sweet, but not *this* sweet. His signal's been . . . *amplified*, somehow—not beyond recognition, but almost, almost.

And it's still growing.

Arlene looks around at her little group, realizing how much she's loved this foursome, how much it's been thrown out of balance. It feels like they've always been there, roaming Boston, drinking, laughing, being alternately bored and excited, gathering and splitting and gathering together again, always connected, always knowing exactly who they meant when they used words like "us" and "we." She always knew it wouldn't last forever—time, love, sex, and the rest of the world were eventually going to break them apart the way a storm system, no matter how strong, eventually breaks up, scatters, dissolves into newborn breezes. Intellectually she knows this, that all is process, that product is an illusion. She knows that snapshots lie, because they seem to stop the unstoppable. Hell, half of her meticulously crafted but never-shared poems are *about* that, not to mention the short stories. But now she thinks that she's been writing to prepare herself and protect herself, that deep inside her she is, was, and always will be a creature that wants to hold things together, to prevent change, especially when things are good. And now Furble and Johnny have changed everything, and there's nothing she can do but ride it out until things settle down a little and she can once again, despite everything she knows, live in the illusion of an unchanging world.

Arlene rolls across the floor, puts her head in Johnny's lap, feeling his hand come down to play with her hair. Soon Grant and Deb have joined them, and they become a human knot, all sprawled and touching in some way, right there on the carpet, barely moving in the afternoon sunlight. They're reaffirming the Four of Them as a unit, but Arlene knows that this is something they'd never do if the Four of Them really existed anymore.

Chapter 7

"Your life," said Dr. Schrödinger as he ordered another diet soda and the waitress once again slipped by *us* without taking any notice, "is the story that you tell yourself about what happened to bring you to this point. But if you were to tell it accurately, you'd see that it couldn't have happened. That, from a statistical standpoint, it's all so unlikely as to be nearly impossible."

We don't know how it happened, but we had come around to liking Dr. Schrödinger. Somehow, this was the Dr. Schrödinger we always wanted, the man who told us stories about cats in boxes, the man who could regale us with mysteries and wonders rather than cold scientific pedantries. His company was now almost desirable, if one ignored the fact that nights in our house were still punctuated with the plaintive meowing of Werner. We didn't think about that. We listened.

"Any story, really, is impossible if you tell it right," he went on. "To survive, the human brain is programmed to see clear, smooth causes and effects. How else could we survive? We need to see the patterns, learn to identify the footprints of predator and prey, see where they lead, and react accordingly. We need to predict the predictable so that we can handle the unpredictable. We'd like to believe that history unfolds in a nearly inevitable way, that if Hitler had died young his role would've been fulfilled by someone else. But it's the *un*predictable that really runs the world. Not only did Hitler have to be Hitler, but he had to have eaten a certain rancid bit of cheese and gotten angry about it in 1926 or he never would have risen to power. Now, that's just allegorical, of course, an invention. I don't know anything about Hitler's cheese. The point is that *no* event of any significance has ever happened that didn't result from some nearly impossible web of happenstance, coincidence, and odd twists of fate. Mathematically speaking, these things shouldn't happen. Almost paradoxically, inevitably, events *do* happen."

We were following the doctor, but also thinking about ordering a dessert. Or something. Unfortunately, we were at one of those perennially overcrowded sidewalk cafés, where the lone overworked waitress had little motivation to squeeze through the dauntingly tight and circuitous maze of chairs and tables that led to our location. We couldn't help noticing that the doctor had, for the first time in our memory, left over some of his sandwich. We stared hopefully at it.

Dr. S. didn't notice. "Do you remember the cartoons of Rube Goldberg? An inventor of the most ludicrous contraptions. You know: A lever is pulled, causing a boot to kick a dog, whose bark motivates a hamster to run on a wheel which winds a pulley that raises a gate that releases a bowling ball and so on? Until, at the end, finally, the machine does something incredibly mundane, like making a piece of toast. Yes? Well, as it turns out, *that's* the world. All these incredibly complex, inscrutably intertwined Rube Goldberg machines that can only be seen in retrospect when something *happens*."

This was fascinating, yes. But we made some small sounds anyway, in the hope that Dr. Schrödinger might offer us the rest of the sandwich. Messy though it was, there was still a fairly sizable piece of meat in there. . . .

"Opportunities found or missed by a matter of seconds, random environmental factors, someone's full bladder or empty stomach—these are often all things that make an event happen the way it does, when you look back on it. Let me give you . . ." said the doctor, reaching for his plate. Our eyes lit up, salivary glands pumping double-time.

". . . an example," finished the doctor. And he plucked the largest slice of pastrami from the sandwich, lifted it delicately, and with a flick of his wrist tossed it away.

We watched it as it flew, a red and tasty deli morsel, glistening in the afternoon sun. It described a high and slightly wobbly parabola because of questionable aerodynamics, its long, flat sides meeting minuscule bits of air resistance before flopping and folding back and flopping anew. It sailed over the railing of the little sidewalk café, still rising, reached its zenith somewhere over the sidewalk, and then descended precipitously, completing the arc, until it came to rest with a moist, audible *thwack* in the street just beyond the curb.

Part of us was sitting in breathless anticipation, rapt, wondering how the old sage was going to use this sudden missile of meat as an illustration of life's vagaries.

And another part of us, the hungry part, was thinking: Fuck Dr. Schrödinger.

Night is falling again, they've been trapped like animals inside, but Grant thinks that things could certainly be worse. It's Saturday, so nobody's too concerned about work. Not that anybody is actually concerned about work anyway, thinks Grant.

They all are doing very temporary things (Johnny and Arlene are actually temps, in fact), and their lives have nothing to do with their work. Except Grant, of course, who truly enjoys his job in web design and programming, can see how he might be embarking on an exciting and increasingly lucrative career, and feels unaccountably guilty about the whole thing, as though his peers might bust him at any moment for being Insufficiently Disaffected.

Several times now, Johnny has gone outside. Sometimes, as the pilgrims keep requesting, he plays his guitar, sings, and casts an otherworldly, emotionally cathartic spell upon his friends and the assembled crowd. And sometimes he just goes out there and bullshits with people, seeming not to distinguish between people he knows and strangers. His conversation is elliptical and weird (or, to Grant, who knows him, *more* elliptical and weird*er*) and often unintentionally insulting, and this seems to hold the number of campers down to a reasonable throng.

The sun is setting now, and Grant is hanging with Johnny. The ladies have gone upstairs with Johnny's grandmother: It's going to be their second night at Casa Decaté, and they've decided to shower and then accept the older woman's invitation to raid her staggeringly large and diverse wardrobe. Girlish laughter tumbles down the stairs occasionally, making Johnny smile and Grant's head fill maddeningly with rounded, pink shapes.

"Grant," says Johnny suddenly, "what scares you?"

Johnny's been asking Grant these vintage *Breakfast Club* questions all evening. At first Grant was answering glibly, but Johnny's sense of humor isn't what it was a few days ago, and Grant started to get the feeling he was only entertaining himself. So now he tries to answer as honestly as possible, reasoning that this is what Johnny wants and there's nothing like free therapy anyway.

"Oh, I dunno, Johnny. Everything, I guess. I mean, I'm scared of more things than you are, that's for sure. But you know that."

"Tell me specifically. Pleeeeeaase . . ."

"Okay. Hmm. Anything that's not logical, I guess. Relationships, loneliness, sex, attraction, gambling . . . I'm not being specific enough, am I?"

"Nuh-uh."

"Sorry, John-man. Well, I'm scared of dying, of course. And even more, I'm scared of something bad happening to my brain and *living*, you know, without being able to think straight. So head injuries are a biggie with me. And I'm afraid of insects of all kinds except possibly bees, because for some reason I think they're kinda cute. Um, let's see. . . . Knives, subway platforms, terrorists, killer viruses, losing my teeth. Lots more. But . . ." Grant pauses, figuring, Why not? It'll feel brave at least. ". . . mostly, lately, I'm afraid of Deb. You know . . . finally making the, um, *move*. I'm afraid she'll sleep with me but that'll be it, I'm afraid she won't but that'll make things weird between us, I'm afraid she'll fall in love with me and I'll be disappointed or insanely, psychotically jealous or something. I'm afraid of losing the same desperate, obsessive longing that's making me miserable, if that makes any sense."

"No, that doesn't make any sense," says Johnny benignly.

"The fuck it doesn't!" yells Grant. "It makes perfect sense, ya dink!"

"Nope."

"It does! That's the way love works when you're spineless

and unsuccessful. You exist in a perpetual state of exquisite torture over the hell of your 'just friends' status, you complain to your buddies about it, you try to psych yourself up to make some kind of move and cut through the terror that paralyzes you, you look for something, anything, some event that will break the perfect equilibrium between the attraction of your love and the repulsion of your fear that holds you in stasis, and then . . ."

There's a pause. Grant breathes deeply, consciously, and finally hears Johnny echo, "And then?"

"And I don't know what comes after that," says Grant, finally. "Hence the fear."

Johnny's opinion of this doesn't need to be spoken; even before the current weirdness, he was always the kind of guy who *did* things, got the cards on the table, moved the ball downfield, etc. Grant sits there contemplatively, thinking that perhaps the events of the last day have changed the equilibrium a bit, put him on a footing where he'll be able to see Deb and the situation a bit more objectively and finally move things ahead, a New Grant now in effect.

"Hello? Anyone for Scrabble?" says Johnny's grandmother. Grant looks up and sees the three women on the stairway, catches sight of what Deborah has chosen to wear, and realizes that the "New Grant" exists in precisely the same way as "Grant the Home Run King" and "Grant the Galactic Hero."

It's late at night, and the President of Montana (Back When That Actually Meant Something) sits in the passenger seat of yet another big rig, sharing another companionable silence with yet another scraggly-looking trucker in a baseball cap, heading east, always east, on I-90 (sometimes I-80).

The PoM(BWTAMS) is feeling increasingly secure, too. He's

still a fugitive, of course, but as he gets farther and farther away from Montana, there's less and less in the news about him and the continuing standoff. More important, there are fewer and fewer images of him on the news. Which is good for two reasons: He's less likely to be arrested, yes, but he also doesn't have to look at that picture anymore, which is not his best photograph and makes him look a little, well, goofy.

So things are good. In fact—they're *great*. Ever since that gun went off, the sound that the President thought was meant for him, he's been feeling terrific, as though he's really escaped the web of angry paranoia he'd created around himself and his wife (whose presence here would make things *perfect*).

So the journey's been one of discovery rather than heedless flight. He hasn't behaved like a fugitive at all; he's been taking in the sights, some official and some serendipitous, and they've all been worthwhile and seemed somehow connected:

- In a truckstop diner in the Black Hills, he saw an old man nursing a baby while the child's mother cried into a cellphone.
- Fifty miles down the road from there, he visited a front-yard museum: dinosaurs sculpted from old automobile parts. One of the plaques read, "Ankylosaurus: Early Cretaceous Period. Its spiny plates and clublike tail kept this gentle herbivore safe from all comers. '75 Honda Civic, '82 Chevy, various ACDelco accessories."
- Near St. Paul, a couple offered to sell him a videotape of the two of them having sex. "We're Amateurs!" exclaimed the wife proudly. The President liked that so much he bought the tape, even though he had no intention of watching it. He then promised to visit their website.

- In Wisconsin, he attended a funeral for an old woman. He never actually claimed to be a relative, but he held several people while they cried, holding them in his big, fleshy arms, saying things like "She loved you, too," and "I can't believe she's gone, either."
- Chicago was the first major city he'd been in for quite a while. He spent most of his time inside a radio station's offices on the touristy Navy Pier. The view of Lake Michigan was spectacular, and as long as he toted around a vacuum he'd found, he was welcomed by all. Friday morning was particularly great—"Bagels are here!" one of his new friends told him, heading toward the communal kitchen. There were indeed free bagels.
- The trucker who took him through Indiana and Ohio and was in no hurry had an expanded back cab with a home theater, "complete with satellite speakers, Dolby 5.1 up to spec, and everything." Nights, they watched *Enter the Dragon*, *The Empire Strikes Back*, *Casablanca*, *The Matrix*, *Beverly Hills Cop*, and, oddly enough, *Sense and Sensibility*, which made the trucker cry. The President loved them all, especially *The Matrix*, which seemed to validate both his paranoia *and* his newfound optimism.
- Outside of Akron, there were signs advertising "The World's Largest Sweater," and he convinced the trucker to visit the site, which they did. It was.

Now, crossing Pennsylvania, the President of Montana looks ahead to the end of the road. Literally the *end* of this particular road. He misses his wife, can't call her for security reasons, and hopes she remembers their plan.

———

You should realize that Deborah Johnstone did not choose her outfit to drive Grant insane, though she does enjoy the effect it has.

Deborah, who likes to dress up and adores Johnny's grandmother, felt especially honored to be let, along with Arlene, into the old woman's trove. Together, the three women spent a hilarious half-hour selecting their "looks," Johnny's grandmother insisting on full vintage evening wear. They devoted the most time to choosing and fitting Arlene's outfit.

As they descend the stairs, despite the perfect fit of the strapless, spangly black gown, her not-bad-when-you-really-think-about-it figure, and good makeup, Arlene looks oppressed by her outfit. It's not that Arlene's unpretty, it's just that she's never been comfortable with the whole Woman thing; she's pretty sure that, whatever Feminine Wiles are, she doesn't have them. She doesn't know how to Slink. Her eyes don't Bat. She finds figure-conscious clothes and exotic lingerie attractive, but it would never occur to her that her own body might be a good place to put that stuff. Watching Arlene making her way down the stairs, Deborah smiles at her and thinks that her friend really *is* pretty—a photograph of Arlene taken now would look great, as long as you blurred the slightly pained and embarrassed expression on her face.

Leonora Decaté is a different story entirely. She comes down the stairs with a lifetime of exuberant confidence in tow. Her outfit, though riotously colored and more fit for grand opera than Scrabble, couldn't possibly outshine her and doesn't seem to be trying. Her ridiculously plumed headdress brushes the ceiling, and she uses the stairway expertly, as though it were a set from an MGM musical, her hips turned sideways so that one leg crosses over the other, showgirl-style, as she descends. If age has had any effect on Leonora, it's made her more playful, which is why, thinks Deborah, she can date uniformed men twenty years her junior.

Deborah brings up the rear in a silky burgundy gown, seemingly ripped right from the pages of a 1940s crime novella—that part where the PI's door flies open, a woman enters, and a host of tortured purple metaphors are loosed upon the world. Deb loves costume, and the costume seems to feel the same way about her. The low neck swoops in from the right shoulder, crosses over the swoop from the left, and gathers proprietarily at her right hip, clinging for dear life as Deborah's body flings itself in various directions with each step.

Deborah Johnstone is just naturally *good* at wearing things, Grant knows. She doesn't *try* to make her every move a symphony of elegant seduction, she doesn't *mean* to dangle her torso luxuriously over the board as she selects her first tile, she doesn't *intend* to stretch back languidly in a way that sets every nerve in Grant's body on edge.

But she is aware that this is precisely what's happening, she's conscious of the effect she's having (which is, Arlene suspects, what these elusive Wiles are all about). And for the first time, as Deb looks toward the end of the Scrabble game and the night beyond it and the awkward and beloved friend whom she'll doubtless be rooming with for the second straight night, she thinks, offhandedly, *Why not?*

To her surprise, her mind actually has a couple of pretty good, if not completely coherent, answers to that question.

The sun had already set when we gave up and paid the bill, even though we hadn't eaten anything. It was pretty clear that Dr. Schrödinger wasn't going to do it, probably didn't have any cash, and generally couldn't be bothered. He was still talking, in fact, and he showed no sign of letting up.

"I've made some mistakes," he said, "but none so large, I now realize, as my recent anger at people's fascination with 'my' cat. What I hadn't realized at the time is that there *is* a cat, and there *is* a box."

We were flabbergasted. Why, after his endless and angry denials, was the doctor suddenly changing his tune?

"Well, not really," said the doctor, not realizing how close this statement brought him to being punched in the mush. We controlled ourselves and waited. "But in some ways, yes. People *name* things. They name things constantly. They can't help themselves—anything that lasts more than a few minutes, any phenomenon, real or imagined, even parts of pieces of sections of things, get names. Recurring things. Wind patterns. Things that sometimes aren't even things unto themselves suddenly get promoted to proper nouns.

"And the act of naming really *does* change a thing. It's impossible to say whether the things really change, in a Heisenbergian sense, or whether it's our perception of things that changes. In fact, that distinction turns out not to matter all that much. Consider my sandwich," he said, gesturing to his plate. We didn't have to consider it—we knew the last piece of meat was currently residing in the street, about fifteen feet from its former, more desirable address.

"My sandwich," continued the doctor, "was easy to order. I simply asked for a 'Reuben.' Note I did not ask for a 'pastrami-and-sauerkraut sandwich on pumpernickel.' I wouldn't think to order such a thing. I couldn't imagine that it would taste good. But when I ask for a 'Reuben,' I am ordering something with a name, something that implies New York delicatessens with tubs of pickles and clever Jewish television writers gathered around linoleum-topped tables. The name, you see, identifies the thing much more than its constituent ingredients. I am ordering a certain kind of historical experience, not a mere plate of sustenance."

Dr. S.'s point seemed particularly obvious to us, for we'd been label-conscious for quite a few years and already knew that things like "blind taste tests" were utterly beside the point as far as being a professional consumer was concerned. But he seemed to be enjoying himself so much that we let him continue.

"So what I didn't realize is that when I came up with the 'cat' metaphor for quantum theory, I didn't just create a wonderful objection to Heisenberg's uncertainty principle. I also, in a sense, created a cat. 'Schrödinger's Cat,' to be precise. And if I'm willing to accept the indisputable importance of an observer when it comes to determining whether a subatomic particle has mass or wavelength, I suppose I need to accept the importance and effect of other human observations—even if they're based on confusion or misunderstanding."

As we got up, followed by the still-chattering scientist, we wondered, Is Dr. Schrödinger saying that reality itself is a matter of consent, that we create the world through naming, like the gods of the Australian Aborigines?

"I'm saying," said Dr. Schrödinger, "that reality itself is a matter of consent, that we create the world through naming, like the gods of the Australian Aborigines."

So where's the cat? we thought as we strolled away from the café. Is that "Werner"?

"The actual act of naming is only the beginning, though. Or, to be fair, the *middle* . . ."

Behind us, now glistening in the streetlamp's light, lay a fairly robust-sized piece of pastrami. It was, we couldn't help observing, no longer part of a Reuben. And it didn't seem to be part of any larger Machine, either.

Dear Diary,

Back in Central Square, where I should be. A good day—food was plentiful and robots were scarce, for the most part. I found one of those new "Humdingers" on a table near Au Bon Pain™, and I'll be selling it tomorrow. Why would I want it—what's a homeless old lady going to do with "the biggest molecule on earth"? Why would <u>anyone</u> want it? I'm pretty sure that slogan isn't true anyway—aren't crystals and other silicates technically huge molecules? I forget, they may just be strongly bonded . . . substances. Whatever, as the skate rats say.

Crazy Bernie's been hovering around, drinking up the courage to come over here. Not that yrs truly's necessarily going to open up the Gates of Heaven for him tonight. Ten years ago we might have—well, truth to tell, ten years ago we <u>did.</u> But that wasn't anything for either of us to write home about, especially since we don't <u>have</u> homes.

A warm body could do me some good, though, and Bernie's pretty harmless as schizophrenics go. The fact that a loon like me calls him "Crazy Bernie" ought to tell you something. Has anyone else noticed that schizos always have crooked johnsons? That's got to mean something—I'd look into it, but homeless ex-whores just don't get the big research grants these days.

Whoops—Bernie's just stopped muttering to himself, which means he's getting ready to be sociable. It's the psycho's equivalent of putting on a sport jacket and slicking down the hair. If he behaves, there may just be a big molecule in it for him. Time to sign off. Good night, ladies.

———

Deb: SEX

Grant: EXCITE

Johnny and Arlene: TERMINAL

Leonora: CEREAL

Deb: GAVE

Grant: YEN, SEXY, IN

Johnny and Arlene: FIN, FAT, AT

Leonora: GAVEL, SLOG

Deb: REAM, FINE

Grant: DUET, TO, US

Johnny and Arlene: S(H)ADOWS

Leonora: (A)T(H)EISM

Deb: MOVE

Grant: INURED, FATE, EXCITED

Johnny and Arlene: MOVED, DECAY

Leonora: EF, FINER, FEWER

"Schrödinger's Humdingers: harmless fad or deadly distraction? What *you* need to know about the popular new molecule . . . on *Eyewitness News*, tonight, after the game."

"Are your children safe with Schrödinger's Humdinger? After the movie."

"Molecules that kill and molecules that don't. Which are which? We have a 'humdinger' of an answer . . . tonight at eleven."

Chapter 8

IT HAD BEEN A CLOSE ONE, but Grant won at Scrabble, narrowly edging out Deb, Leonora Decaté, and the inconstant team of Johnny and Arlene. The game wasn't made much easier by the fact that Johnny's grandmother had broken out another bottle of Lagavulin midway through, and by the game's end everyone was warmed and giddy. A bottle of Talisker accompanied the arrival of the Monopoly board, and by the time Grant had his first house (a green single-family dwelling on Illinois Avenue, very convenient to the railroad), the room was a cacophony of laughter, screams, and silly accents. Grant and Deb reverted to the pseudo-Scottish brogue they'd evolved over the past year (which seemed to go nicely with the scotch), while Arlene tried to mimic Leonora's surprisingly accurate French dialect. Johnny mostly laughed. *Roared,* in fact, to the point of oxygen deprivation.

Though Johnny hadn't been outside for hours, the party continued out there, the assembled folk entertaining one another with acoustic guitars, domestic beer, and any number of illicit substances. The strumming and warbling provided a pleasant backdrop, further enclosing the five of them from the rest of the world.

Leonora, who'd made indecorous references to how little sleep she'd had the night before, was the first to go, uselessly trying to straighten her headdress while wobbling up the stairs and exhorting the others to keep going. Before leaving, she generously willed all her property to her surviving grandson. Nobody really minded this, because Johnny had made a complete hash of his initial assets and would need any help he could get just to stay in the game.

They drank, snacked, and played for another hour before Johnny was eliminated. Arlene went soon after that. Her rapid decline was more than a little suspicious, considering that she had well-developed holdings with good St. Charles and his purple fraternity. Still, Grant and Deb were clearly ahead, and were in the process of marshaling their forces against each other when Arlene drunkenly grabbed Johnny and more or less dragged him bodily back to his room.

The good times continued to roll out in the living room, until Grant's mind suddenly notified him that the fact that he was alone with Deb meant that he was in fact Alone. With Deb. The drunken, giddy momentum of the evening suddenly came to an abrupt, teetering halt.

This is what Grant took in at the instant that time stopped: They were on the living-room carpet, on opposite sides of the game board, both leaning on one arm toward Jail and Free Parking, their legs sprawled off toward Go and Go to Jail. Deb had just declared, "Ach, ye've taken the food from the mouths of me wee bairn babes!" and she was about to roll the dice. Her hair was a glorious mess, her dress had more or less abandoned its attempts to conceal certain things, torso-wise, and for Grant the all-important game of Monopoly had suddenly vanished into the thick air, leaving just some cardboard, paper, and plastic on the floor between them. . . .

Deb sensed it, too (or perhaps merely noticed that Grant had frozen, his mouth literally hanging open), and she stopped rattling the dice. Her smile grew wicked, and the room shrank, pushing the two of them closer together.

"Maybe," said Deb slowly, leaving no room for misinterpretation, "we should switch to a different game." Laughing lightly, she pushed the board aside and crept toward him, back arched, a knowing and extreme parody of a sexual predator.

The force of the come-on hit Grant like a sharp blow to the forehead—he was pretty sure his pupils were now different sizes. Here it was, here was Deb, laying it out for him like the gift he'd always wanted, and there was nothing even he could do to fuck it up now.

Sure there was.

Her breath was on his throat, and he tried desperately to think. He was so, so drunk. She read his face. "What's the matter, laddie?" she purred, Scottish again. "Aren't ya wantin' to toss yer caber a bit?"

"I . . . can't believe I'm saying this, but I don't think so, lassie. I don't think you'd be happy with the results. . . ."

"What?" As in most extremely drunken conversations, they were too loud, too animated, Grant realized. His thoughts were unclear, but he hoped Deb was getting it.

"Grant, if you're worried about my 'requirements,' that's kind of a joke. I don't care, really, and I make exceptions for people I really like. . . ."

She wasn't getting it.

"No! It's not the size thing."

"Thank God!" exclaimed Deb with exaggerated relief, and the tension disappeared, popped like a balloon as they laughed. Grant sighed gratefully.

"No, I knew that wasn't it. Unless you're trying to steal Leonora's antique pepper mill . . ." said Deb, staring down at Grant's lap and bobbling her eyebrows comically.

"Hey! Cut that out! Leave a guy a little mystery, can't ya?" Grant strategically placed a few Community Chest cards in his lap as they laughed. She "helped" him place a few, he restrained her, they tumbled over and destroyed a fortune in houses and hotels. Somehow they ended up on their backs, next to each other, and a deep silence took over the room.

"Why not?" asked Deb quietly and a bit petulantly, staring at the ceiling.

"You really don't know?"

"No."

". . ."

". . ."

"That's probably for the best," said Grant finally, taking her hand gently.

Within five minutes, they were curled up amid the game pieces, deeply asleep.

. . . 17. And it came to pass that, as the Time of the Crossing drew nigh, the Prophet Bernie did awaken from his slumber and thanked the Lord for His many Gifts. 18. And Bernie gazed down and saw the face of the woman he had lain with upon the hard ground, and his heart was filled with gladness. And lo! For in Bernie's pocket there now lay a talisman of many sides and of unknown purpose! 19. And the Lord said to Bernie, "Lo! For I have created a chill upon the air in the midst of summer, and though it shall pass, thine raiment protects thee not at present. Thine dungarees are thin, and thy flannel shirt hast been made threadbare." 20. "Therefore, Bernie," spake the Lord, "thou must go now to My servants in the Army of Salvation, which I have in My wisdom located conveniently on Mass Ave, not far from My Dunkin' Donuts. There Mine servants will adorn thee with a light Coat of Green, which shall protect thee from the chill." 21. "And the price shall be Reasonable, for I have ordained that they shall vest ye without Duress." 22. "For the Time of the Crossing draws nigh, and thou must keep thyself in readiness for it. Go now, and do as I have commanded." 23. And Bernie said unto the Lord, "Lord, thanks. This will I do. You're the best." 24. And Bernie did set out from his place of rest, and looked not back upon the Lot of Parking or the woman with whom he had lain, and he did as the Lord commanded. 25. And the Prophet Bernie did arrive at the camp of the Army of Salvation, and lo! It was as the Lord had promised, and the Army did clothe him in a Coat of Green. And though Bernie had lived as a beggar in accordance with the Lord's command, still was he able to pay for the Coat, for the Lord had seen to this. 26. And Bernie was pleased, for the Lord had provided many other Bargains for His servant there, and Bernie did spend much time enrapt by these good gifts. 27. And the Lord said unto Bernie, "Move ye! Thou who accepts My gifts; waste not thine time in idle Shopping, for the Time of the Crossing draws nigh, and there is much to do." 28. And Bernie was ashamed, and begged the Lord's forgiveness. 29. And the Lord said unto Bernie, "No Problem. For thou art My good servant, and it would please Me if thou wouldst go forth to My nearest House of Worship, and there thou wilt find that it is Sunday, and I have provided thee with a free Cup of Coffee." 30. And Bernie did thank the Lord anew, and did as He commanded. . . .

The President of Montana (As If He Still Gave a Fuck) stood in a parking lot in Springfield, Massachusetts, and wondered why he felt so much younger. He had three theories:

1) Because I just ran away from all the responsibilities that were making me feel old.

2) Because I'm going back to Boston.
3) Because the natural direction in the United States is east-to-west—westward ho!—and when you reverse that, you get younger. Like $E = MC^2$ or something.

The PoM(AIHSGAF) had to admit that that last one was a long shot—he didn't really know all that much about science. He guessed that number 3 was probably also a symptom of number 2—he was returning to the place where he'd gone to college, where speculation was a way of life, where he'd arrived as a Montana farmboy and had a million experiences, tried curry, had his mind opened up. . . .

When exactly, mused the President, had it closed up again? Well, no, not *closed*, really, but definitely *narrowed. Stream-lined*, he'd thought, but now it looked like he'd been being too generous with himself. Why hadn't Tammy told him about that? Why the hell had she kept that to herself?

The President's mind flashed back to the last couple of years and Tammy looking straight at him and saying things like "You're getting kinda close-minded there, Earl," and "Maybe you oughta try thinking more than one way for a change," and "Stop and smell the roses, Earl," and "Are you sure that all this antigovernment stuff isn't just a way of narrowing your life down to one far-from-personal goal so you don't have to think about the more complicated issues of aging and childlessness and our terrifying financial situation?"

Yes, the President had to admit, she may have *hinted* at it a bit.

He smiled, and looked back toward the sunset. The past few days had been easy, fun, even revelatory. North Dakota, Minnesota, Wisconsin, Illinois, Indiana, Michigan, Ohio, Pennsylvania, New York . . . What a *spread.* He'd been only mildly surprised to find no traces of the New World Order. Well, there'd been a lot more surveillance cameras than before, a lot of talk about being "on alert," a few more signs with warnings printed on them, and you basically couldn't smoke anywhere anymore. But it didn't really feel like a shadowy, controlling authority. More like a confused mess, like always, with no one really in charge of it all. Just like Tammy always said, and he once again wondered why that lady even bothered with him.

His key said "17," so he went to that door, opened it, and was greeted by a sad and musty little room with bolted-down furniture and a carpet stained with at least a decade's worth of the Unexpected. Tomorrow he'd board the 7:43 A.M. Peter Pan bus and ride I-90 upstream all the way to the source. This tiny, dank space was to be his shelter until then.

He instantly loved it, and he walked into the motel room with his arms open wide.

Arlene dreams of showering, of swimming, of wetting her bed at summer camp. She wakes up slowly, and dimly realizes that she's draped around Johnny, and that her hands and chest are wet. Johnny's wet.

Weird, she thinks, slowly bringing her hand toward her and opening her eyes. She sees an unexpected color, and first thinks that the sun is in her eyes. No, not the sun. But her hands, her arm, her chest are all wet and warm and shiny. And bright red.

Her heart pounds, and her veins fill with sudden adrenaline. "Johnny?" she asks, tentatively. She touches his shoulder and rolls him toward her.

He's covered in blood. There's no doubt where it's coming from, because the right side of his face is . . . *missing*. He's been bleeding for a long while—it's not even trickling anymore, and some of the blood is starting to dry. He's dead, Arlene realizes. Very, very dead. She screams, hard and ragged.

Arlene wakes up, or something. She's in the same position as before, sitting up staring at her hand, an inert Johnny turned toward her, her scream trailing off. . . .

But there's no blood. No wound. Nothing.

That, thinks Arlene, is one fucked-up dream. It didn't even feel like a dream, and just now didn't really feel like waking up. It felt like . . . *blinking* really hard. It's too weird, and her heart is racing and her throat feels raw, as if, for instance, she'd just screamed.

Johnny opens his eyes, and Arlene thinks she can see the pillow beneath through them. He smiles and she grabs his face, kisses it madly, throws her thigh over him. It's not enough. She flings the sheet, rolls onto him, finds him stiff as the proverbial board (*morning wood*, thinks a little voice inside her hopefully, *and not rigor mortis*), still holding his face, enveloping him desperately, slamming up and down, kissing him. It's not fun. It's not recreational. It's just *necessary*, if she's going to stay sane. . . . She looks in Johnny's eyes, and though he couldn't possibly have seen what she saw, it's clear that he understands on some level. She's sure he understands.

Whoa, thinks Johnny, *I am getting SO laid right now.*

Dear Diary,

Crazy Bernie was off and running at around eight, so I had to spend a half-hour pretending to still be asleep. No matter how old they get, they still wanna pull on their pants and hoof it before you're awake. And when you're waking up behind a Dumpster, every little bit of dignity counts.

Me, I don't need dignity.

Say this for Bernie—as far as nutzoid psychos with messiah complexes go, he's a pretty good lay. And completely nondangerous. I give him the thumbs-up. Though not the "thumbs-up" he asked for last night—Bernie's not exactly Mr. Hygiene, and a girl's gotta keep a little mystery about her.

Back to the History, boys and girls.

1570—The Iroquois League is coming together. They originally start off as a sports league, but they turn political real quick when they figure out they're never going to be allowed to play in any of the big stadiums. Mongols are overrunning China, which drives down property values, which makes the Europeans start smacking their lips and hunting for bargains. In Australia they're getting wind of the Europeans, so they start packing up their technology and sending most of the really cool stuff off-world. They draw straws to figure out who's going to remain behind to play the "Aborigines."

1590—The Ottoman Empire's as big as it's ever going to get. Suleiman the Magnificent is dead, but his son Suleiman the Adequate is holdin' down the fort. The new craze among the Turks is macramé, and they start hand-weaving things that shouldn't be woven. Like flatware and armor. Over in Europe they've managed to kill most of the Huguenots, which means Mercy and Understanding are just around the corner. The Huguenots don't mind because they're robots.

1600—Dawn of the new century. Everybody's happy, except the Russians, who've just entered the Time of Troubles and wish they'd named it something cheerier. Queen Elizabeth's just about had it, and it's Shakespeare's fault: He and his sister have been running her ragged in the bedroom. Meanwhile, the Shakespeares' musicals are doing great, but all of Vivian Shakespeare's songs are about to get edited out, because the public is getting tired of all that singing and dancing.

In Africa, a man named Sool marries his 12,952nd wife. He is so charismatic that each of his wives considers herself his "favorite."

In Morocco, they build the Tower of Foreskins, which stands anywhere between 150 and 400 feet, depending.

The clatter of dishes and the smell of coffee wake Grant. He's got that could-be-worse kind of hangover that comes from really good scotch. . . .

His surroundings slowly come into focus, and his memory struggles back online at the same time. He's still on the floor, curled up around Deborah Johnstone. Before he can even get worked up about this, he remembers: He turned her down.

What the fuck? thinks Grant. *Was there any logic to that? Or did I just feel like I had to obey the "logic" of badly written romantic comedies? Well, I'm not Tom Hanks. I'm not gonna get another shot. The most I'm gonna get is this right now, spooning with Deb, still dressed, with my hand on her breast—*

Oh God.

It's a natural position, what with his arm over her like this it's hard to imagine where else his hand *could* be right now. But the fact is that Grant's left hand is more or less completely covering Deb's right breast. And if her dress was covering it before they fell asleep, it isn't right now. That's *flesh* under his palm.

Panic sets in. On the one hand (Grant dimly finds this turn of phrase amusing), this is tremendously interesting. But mostly he's worried about Deb waking up and branding him a rapist, or at least a pathetic perv. A somnophiliac (is that the word?) who turns down girls when they're awake so he can feel them up while they sleep. Any second now, the sounds in the kitchen are going to wake her, and it'll all hit the fan. So Grant knows he's gotta fix this situation ASAP.

He gently begins to lift his hand straight off, but finds that perspiration (either from his hand or her breast or both) has made the area slightly sticky—her flesh rises with his as he tries to withdraw it, and either the stretching or the eventual elastic bounceback is *sure* to wake her. So he aborts that approach, slowly allowing his hand to sink back into its initial position, trying not to enjoy what his hand is feeling.

Attempt number 2 is a more gradual approach. He tries to use the sweat as a subtle lubricant, allowing him to slide his hand off of her as slowly and gently as possible. This seems to be working at first, but in only a few moments the unforeseen stops him in his tracks: The action of sliding his hand like that has caused Deb's nipple (hitherto undetected) to swell and stiffen. The terrain is no longer level, in other words, which makes the Sliding Ploy a complete nonoption.

Grant's desperate now, and he's searching for a way out. He begins and aborts several other Removals, various combinations of Lifting and Sliding, but nothing seems safe, every move brings a little too much friction.

If he were a little less panicky, Grant would realize that the cumulative effect of all his various Removal attempts is that he is now more or less *kneading* Deb's breast while pressed up against her in an ever-growing state of arousal. Which is pretty much how Deb perceives it as she slowly wakes up . . .

"Can I play, too, or is this some kind of narcophilia thing?" asks Deb. Grant screams, lifts his hand completely, notices he's leaving her exposed, puts it back, realizes what he's doing, removes it again, rolls over, gets up, sees he's in no condition to be standing, sits down, and begins to stammer an explanation.

Deb's laughing by now, an open, throaty morning chuckle. Soon Grant's laughing, too, and everything's okay again.

A tiny part of Grant's brain is once more reconstructing the web of fantasy and hopeless optimism surrounding Deb. A tiny part of Deb's brain is figuring out why she and Grant didn't get together last night and beginning to process it.

There *is*, it seems, the possibility of something here. But it's too weak, too embryonic. The friends are fragmenting as a group, and there's not enough time. Grant is too tentative, Deb too content. It's not going to happen.

Chapter 9

We'd been talking all night with Dr. Schrödinger. Or, rather, Dr. Schrödinger had been addressing us all night. Sitting there at the kitchen table, drinking White Russians nonstop, holding forth, his wispy white hair standing and flopping and seemingly gesturing the whole time.

There was some physics. And a lot of philosophizing. And a smattering of biology, sports metaphors, Darwinism, mathematics, futurist speculation, and molecular chemistry. It was mostly fascinating, occasionally pedantic, always delivered with a frightening intensity. And we had nothing better to do.

Here are some quotations from Chairman Schrödinger:

"One must not confuse scientific fact with scientific misconception. They're more or less opposites, of course. But a scientific misconception, if widely believed, creates a kind of truth of its own. This doesn't seem to make sense, but it's true."

"To talk about a 'thought pattern' is redundant. Thoughts themselves *are* patterns—huge, multilayered patterns built on custom-tweaked operating systems, no two alike. The idea of a single, expressible 'thought' is a lie. But believing that lie is the only thing that makes communication possible."

"Kahlúa is really, really good. It'd be more popular if it was a 'serious' drink, probably. 'Stoo unsubtle for the connoisseurs, I guess. Morons. Fools!"

"Me, Heisenberg, all of us, we always talked about the 'observer.' Never hit us that if that observer was allowed to stay around long enough, he'd start developing a personality. Nothing hangs around without developing a personality. Nothing."

"Physical evolution's over, that's for sure. At least for humans. There's never going to be a problem that we won't solve in a few years, never mind a few thousand generations, which is how long it'd take to adapt the old-fashioned way. Kind of sad, really: Because we built airplanes, we'll never have wings."

"Doesn't matter if we're down to cheap vodka, 'slong as we got Kahlúa, we won't taste the difference."

"What're these? 'Ranch flavor'? This is a great example. Packaging colors. I mean—what? All right, nacho cheese is orange, barbecue's red, that kind of makes sense. I'll even give you sour-cream-and-onion, though green for onion's a stretch, you gotta admit. But why is 'Ranch' BLUE? Huh? Can't answer that one, can you?"

" 'Chaos'—there's another one. Really bad name. Like I said, 'sthe *opposite* of chaos. At least it was. But now that everyone thinks it's about unpredictability and dinosaurs, who knows? Better take out raptor insurance. . . ."

"I should 'splain about Werner. He's my cat. I haven't heard the little fellow tonight. Have you?"

"Nothin' wrong with Black Russians—nuthin'. I know you want some milk left for breakfast tomorr'. What? Are you sure? I'll wake up early and get you more. . . . No, I *will*. Sweartagod . . ."

". . . still can't explain why the universe weighs so much. . . . 'Sgot all this extra weight, 'dark matter,' whatever they're calling it. We don't know where it is. 'Slike the universe weighs a lot, but it carries it well. . . ."

"Wait—turn it UP! This is the best, the best song ever. . . . Turn it up. . . . *Baby you're much 2 fast. . . . Little red corvette . . . humma humma love that's gonna la-ha-hast . . .*"

Shortly after this last quotation, Dr. Schrödinger finally slumped forward, snoring as his head hit the table.

We sat there, drinking, idly watching the labored breathing of our peculiar houseguest. Sometime later, the phone rang, and we allowed our answering device to receive the call. We heard the voice of Dr. S.'s floozy, informing the doctor that she'd synthesized an additional three thousand Humdingers, that she was going to sleep, that they'd meet at the "usual spot" at 11 A.M.

When she'd hung up, Dr. Schrödinger spoke, his voice muffled by the table. "You oughta call 'er to conf—confirm that. . . ." We pointed out that it was Dr. Schrödinger's responsibility, not ours, to deal with the young acolyte/lover.

". . . still don't get it, do you?" muttered Dr. Schrödinger. We demanded an explanation, but he was already snoring again. From a distant corner we heard a *meow*, lonely and sad. We looked around, but couldn't find the source.

The bus rolled into South Station, carrying six youths, four mothers, two odiferous vagrants, five children, and one President.

The President of Montana (Which Seems Like a Lifetime Ago) debarks cautiously, testing the ground, half expecting to see a horde of FBI agents streaming from the terminal, guns ready, surrounding the bus. He'd imagined media there, too, cameras and microphones pushing past the barricades, a few somehow breaking through and capturing his words as four men held him down, proud, repentant, conciliatory, unbroken.

He saw himself somehow parlaying his enemy-of-the-state status into a kind of folk-hero position, his complaints heard, a legitimate political career in the making. . . .

So there was a little disappointment mingled with the relief of finding no one in particular there to greet him. Unless you counted the old lady with the roses for sale, who didn't look much like an undercover FBI agent at all.

[Coincidentally, the old woman with the roses *was* an FBI agent. She was waiting for the next bus from New York. So were her colleagues, who were dressed as a driver, a bored teen, and a cinnamon-bun vendor. Twenty minutes after the President left, the station would witness the biggest drug bust of the year.]

He wasn't in a hurry, so he went and looked at the harbor. When the PoM(WSLLA) was here last, just after college, he'd been an environmentalist, marching for Boston Harbor, warning everyone about the despoiling of the ecosystem and the horrifying mutations that would take place beneath the waters.

Twenty-five years and billions of dollars later, the harbor looked pretty good. Smelled better, too. Sometimes, he thought, the Powers That Be actually listen, and life gets better. He walked away from the water's edge, smiling, somewhat guiltily recalling the mutated horror-movie monstrosities that he had imagined would someday rule the harbor, and which the little boy in him had half hoped to see.

[As it happened, about two hundred yards off the shore from the President lay a twenty-foot-long grotesquely mutated shark-toothed flounder, its face, already twisted by eons of cruel evolution, now a nightmare of extraordinarily large fangs, some useful, some ornamental. It skimmed sideways along the bottom, wart-covered and hideously labored, passing other fish just closely enough for its oozing skin to spread the paralyzing contact poison that assured their demise. It fed ceaselessly, its body constantly replacing the rotting, PCB-infested fins and scales that it shed daily.]

The Red Line then, to take what was still America's least expensive subway ride. The President's own alma mater, to the south, had never been all that important to him. Cambridge was where everything that really mattered had happened, and now its pull was irresistible.

Everything was different. The station wasn't as he remembered it, the trains were sleek and new, the people wore strange and complex outfits and were decorated with exotic tribal ornamentations and piercings. But it still felt like a subway system— the tunnels still smelled strange and smoky, the sounds still echoed wildly, and the President still imagined crazed serial killers living deep in the tunnels, waiting patiently for nightfall. It was this kind of phobic imagining, he now saw, that probably helped push him back toward Montana. He smiled at this as he stepped onto the train, drawing benign smiles from previously frightening-looking teenagers. He remained standing as the train pulled away, enjoying the feeling of constantly refinding his balance.

[As the train rattled by, Morris barely looked up from his task in the dank, dim catacombs he called home. Against one wall was a folding chair, surrounded by chains and locks. There were some pipes to wrap the chains around, thoughtfully provided by the MTA. A small kit of surgical instruments rested nearby. A few Hefty bags for parts disposal. A few adorable stuffed animals, which had more to do with Morris's problem than any of the darker instruments.]

The President stayed on all the way to Porter Square—the ride was pleasant, and he wanted to give himself a bit of a runway to his memories. Porter was unrecognizable. The station, which hadn't been there back when, was littered with bronzed gloves strewn about at random. "Art," thought the President, and the presidential part of him whispered to him darkly about his tax dollars. Upstairs was no better—yes, the familiar old multifamily houses were still there, lining every side street. But Porter Square itself and Mass Ave were covered in new, angular buildings with signs advertising things that the President couldn't even begin to classify. "Chai," "Futons," "Shiatsu," "Pilates," "PS3," "Vegan." The President felt old—no, not old, like an *alien*. Like he'd just arrived from another planet. But the sunshine was pleasant, and when he found a vaguely familiar-looking Chinese restaurant he walked in amiably, beginning to feel slightly terrestrial again.

[As it happened, just down the street, on the top floor of a multifamily Victorian home, Qretl Prime was contacting the Homeworld. They were getting impatient—the Hatching was imminent, and they needed to know if he'd found a suitable world for colonization. Qretl Prime already knew what his answer would be; he'd been there for several months, living as a near-perfect facsimile of an indigenous sapient, and he was hooked. No, he'd tell the Homeworld, not a suitable place, not for their kind. But he wouldn't tell them yet. At least not until Christmas. His course was clear, if risky: deny, retire, go home, and get Qretly Prime, blow their savings on a commercial reshaping, and return. Then the two of them could spend their retirement here, enjoying the music, the sex, and the incredible food of this odd little place.]

———

It was no longer fun. Perhaps it was the slight hangover, or maybe it was just that this hideout thing was getting old, or perhaps it was the usual torpor that sets in on Sundays. But, with one notable exception, the foursome was ready to split. And to split.

1) Johnny no longer wanted to play guitar, especially not for the campers out front. He'd done that enough, loved it, was done with it. He wanted to *walk*, and the mob prevented this.

2) Deb was comfortable, happy, and enjoying her surroundings as per usual. But she knew she'd enjoy a change even more. Plus, the Grant thing was weirding her out: It was cool, he was still one of her favorite people (maybe even more so now), but it tugged at her mind in strange ways, making things marginally awkward. Some new scenery, some distance from last night's scene, that'd be good.

3) Grant had things to do. There was e-mail. A project he'd hoped to finish before work tomorrow to make his week easier. The sad release of cyberchat. And let's bear in mind the overwhelming urge to flee from Deb. But as long as Johnny was trapped and weird, his duty was here. Getting out of the house, he thought, was the first step toward some kind of closure.

Arlene hoped this would never end. She sat on the back porch with Deb, answering a thousand indiscreet questions in as demure a fashion as possible. Inside, Grant and Johnny were playing with Legos as Mrs. Decaté perused the paper. This morning's vision was fading fast but was still with Arlene, she had no expectations about what might happen between her and Johnny in the future (well, not *many*, anyway), she was still worried about Johnny's behavior and more than a little scared that their recent exploits had been tainted (not the "real" Johnny, she'd taken advantage, an asterisk in the record book). But all of that didn't even begin to touch her state of grace: She had had a wonderful, intimate experience (several times!); she was with all her friends; the complexities in her world were in her *life* rather than her head for once; *Deb* was asking *her* about *her* new boyfriend. Running the gamut from meaningful bliss to petty satisfactions, Arlene was Happy.

> *Dear Diary,*
>
> *Something's still up, off, wrong-o. Two days of it now—no robots, lots of robots, something that feels like a thunderstorm's about to break but it's sunny. Shaky.*
>
> *I actually went and prayed after breakfast (three kreme-filled extras from Barry, who still remembers when he was <u>my</u> customer, bless him). I used the church next to the Dunkin', not that it mattered. Nobody's got a statue of Saint Ivan anyway, and he's the only one I'll pray to: the patron saint of guilt and schizophrenics, and he's the only man who ever successfully crucified himself. That takes talent.*
>
> *Got to hit the university now. There's a library full of history books that need correcting, and a few more Men of Science who are overdue for a little surprise.*

"We're getting out of here."

"Good with me."

"Maybe we oughta wait until those freaks get bored."

"It's okay. Me and Johnny have a plan."

"Uh-huh. Johnny really looks like he's been doing some *serious* planning."

"John-man, put the Lego down for a sec and help me explain the plan."

"The plan? Hey, look! It's like a little barn!"

". . ."

"Okay, maybe it was mostly my plan."

"No!"

"Ya think?"

"You guys are hilarious."

"Aww, Grant, sweetie. We're sorry. Tell us the plan."

"Now you're patronizing me."

"No, we're not, are we, Arlene? Tell us your wittle pwan, Gwant. . . ."

"Stop it! I'm not ticklish! C'mon! Stop!"

"We need more roof pieces. . . ."

"Just one of the many reasons we need to get outa here."

"I'm sure they'll all need to get lost before tomorrow morning. It's Sunday night."

"Am I the only one who wants to get moving?"

"I do."

"Me, too. I want ice cream."

"Okay, then, let's attempt to do something that vaguely resembles focus here, all right?"

"Snippy."

"Snarky."

"That's me. All right, as soon as it gets dark . . ."

. . . 11. And the Prophet Bernie did arrive at the Place of the Crossing. And lo! There was a Crossing there, as the Lord had foretold. 12. And though the people crossed back and forth, still

Bernie did not cross, for the Lord God had said, "Bernie, thou shalt cross at the Time of the Crossing. Before that, thou shalt crosseth not." 13. And the Prophet Bernie waited there at the Crossing, and grew restless, for the Lord spake not to him. And Bernie did cry out to the Lord, "God, why hast Thou forsaken me? For I have done as thou commanded, and stand at the Place of the Crossing, and behold others crossing, and yet I crosseth not. Why, Lord?" 14. And the Lord spoke to Bernie, and was wroth with him, and His voice was like thunder from the heavens. 15. And the Lord said unto Bernie, "Thinkest thou that thou art the only man upon the earth? Dost thou believe thine God hath no other Work? Dost thou think thyself so important that thou seest fit to nag thine God without surcease?" 16. And the Prophet Bernie was ashamed, and he fell to his knees and begged the Lord for forgiveness. And Bernie said, "Forgive me, Lord, for I did mean no offense, and have transgressed, and beg Thine mercy, and will naggeth not from this day forward, as Thou hast commanded." 17. And the Lord heard Bernie, and His heart softened. And the Lord said, "Feareth not, Bernie, for I do forgive thee. It hath been a long day, but I am not overly wroth. Get up already, for people are staring." 18. "But know thou this. Thou hast not Crossed yet because it pleaseth Me not; the Time of the Crossing is not upon us, and thou shouldst be patient." 19. And the Prophet Bernie did thank the Lord, and did promise to abide there on the appointed side. 20. And Bernie did beseech the people for alms, for, though he was a man of many Talents, and didst possess enormous Potential, the Lord had commanded him to develop these Talents not, and to live humbly, and to beg alms for his bread. 21. And it came to pass that the Prophet Bernie did collect many a coin, and he saw the Time of the Crossing was still not upon him, and he didst go unto the merchants that dwelt there, and did purchase coffee and pastries. . . .

We watched Dr. Schrödinger with something approaching admiration. The old guy really knew how to sell it. For the second straight day, Humdingers were selling like hotcakes on the banks of the Charles. In fact, people seemed to be strolling down to the water just to find the old physicist and his wares.

The wares had improved, we had to admit. "Dori" had obviously been working overtime, and now the World's Largest Molecule (sic) could be purchased in a variety of formats, including pendants, rings, keychains, bracelets, earrings, brooches, belt buckles, "Handi 3-Paks," aglets, cuff links, lapel pins, deely boppers, refrigerator magnets, barrettes, hood ornaments, Christmas ornaments, door knockers, "Economy Size" boxes, necklaces, and "Classic." There was even a new "Mini-Humdinger," which made no sense at all when we thought about it.

In fact, we thought as we watched the crowd huddle around the hastily assembled card tables, just what *is* the appeal of these things? Do they *do* something that we're missing? And is it really safe to market a new, untested molecule even if it doesn't have a use (that we know of)? Though we admired the doctor's entrepreneurial savvy, we couldn't help looking with disdain upon the legions of willing suckers as they opened their wallets to what appeared to be a bit of a chemistry-based *scam*.

Before leaving, however, we bought one, just to determine exactly what this silly fervor was about. We chose the belt buckle, because it appeared to be a sturdy and not unattractive accessory for when we were done studying the molecule itself.

Grant's Escape Plan is, naturally, brilliant. Though perhaps a bit baroque. It is extremely important to Grant that it works, because Grant is starting to feel an overwhelming urge to get away from Deborah Johnstone. Not that he dislikes her company (oh no, not even close), but so much has happened or failed to happen that he very much needs to retreat, regroup, consider, and process.

The root cause of Grant's problem with women is so pathetically easy to divine that no remotely honest psychoanalyst could conscientiously take him on as a patient. Not that any of them are likely to have their honesty tested in this manner; Grant himself is well aware of the cause of the malfunction: familiarity, or lack thereof.

Grant is male-identified. More precisely, he was raised by his father, who is terrible with women in his own right (the root cause of *that*, incidentally, is much more complicated and continues to make a seemingly endless sequence of psychoanalysts wealthy without much strain on their consciences). It was a two-man household, Grant and Dad. They were not a physically demonstrative family of two, but they were a functioning democracy, and no decision was ever made without reasoned debate leading to consensus. Grant's dad's occasional girlfriends never lasted long enough to gain suffrage, not that their vote would've made a difference once Grant and his dad had distilled each issue and arrived at identical conclusions, thus producing the necessary two-thirds majority.

When Grant describes his childhood to friends, the world of his household always comes across as bizarre and even a little cold. But it never seemed cold to Grant at the time, nor does he feel very different about it now. There are, however, certain deficiencies that Grant now recognizes. His latest theory about his dealings with women isn't that he's lost his reason or that women are illogical (Deb, for instance, displays exemplary thought processes); it's just that a certain vital part of the interface between them is strongly encrypted and requires some sort of work-around.

That Grant might be right about this doesn't change the fact that the knowledge is utterly useless from a practical stand-point. Which is why escape is so vital.

Chapter 10

OUT ON JOHNNY'S LAWN, among the faithful are a few opportunists, people who've shown up because there's a crowd, a happening. Money is sure to change hands, and there are a few people there who intend to be among the receiving hands.

Floyd is one of them.

Floyd doesn't discount what happened the other night, the blond kid and great music and the undeniable heaviosity. But after he was woken up by a friend's phone call at noon the next day letting him know about the Happening, it only took a sideways glance toward the unusually generous hatful of money from the previous night for Floyd to figure out where his bread might get buttered.

So Floyd has spent the last day and a half at the edge of Johnny's lawn, toward the street, with his guitar and Mouse amp, filling in the long gaps between Johnny's intermittent appearances with sets of his own. There are one or two other buskers from the Square there, but they keep a polite distance, and Floyd's the one who's getting the crowd. After all, Floyd's the guy who was there when Johnny went nova—he might even have something to *do* with it, for all anyone knows. For all Floyd himself knows, that might be true, but he secretly doubts it. This doesn't stop him from casually referring to his and Johnny's "synergy" during his patter and firing up "Knockin' on Heaven's Door" as often as he can get away with it. The money comes at a steady pace, which justifies his approach.

It's all going great for Floyd until late the next day, when the blond kid comes out of the house, steps off the porch, and comes straight at him.

Dr. Schrödinger is taking us out to dinner on his "Hum-dinger money," and, frankly, we're surprised. The old physicist has done nothing but freeload in the past few days, and even his recent success in molecule-vending shouldn't be enough to change the behavior of a habitual bounder. But he seems sincere, and his "fiery Latin lover" (his words, we assure you) has made herself scarce for the nonce. Apparently, the doctor has a burning need to "impart just a few more quick thoughts," as though he intends to leave soon. Judging by the miniature fort of notebooks, magazines, and snack-food containers that he has constructed around our couch, this would not seem to be the case. But the dinner is appreciated.

As we settle into a cozy booth in a Harvard Square restaurant named for one of Beowulf's most monstrous opponents, we muse that we've come to like the old codger quite a bit in the past day or two. Why this is, why our emotions regarding Dr. S. have swung so violently, is not entirely clear. But as he absently dips his spectacles into our water glass to clean them, we feel a surge of grudging affection. We'll listen. Besides, there're a few intriguing specials to order. . . .

If we'd known then that Dr. Schrödinger was going to contrive somehow to stick us with the check, we probably wouldn't have ordered quite so many drinks and appetizers.

"Now," says Dr. Schrödinger, slathering an obscene amount of butter onto a seven-grain roll, "about my cat . . ."

Grant's Plan for Escape was, as previously noted, far too complicated, needlessly baroque, obviously flawed, required too much effort, and was entirely less reliable than any number of simpler plans to get the four of them out of the house unnoticed. It was straight out of a bad movie, substituting entertainment for sound logistics.

Naturally, they all loved it.

This is how it went down:

Around 6 P.M., Johnny floated out the front door and across the lawn, the crowd parting around him in a reverential manner that provoked some quickly stifled laughter from inside the house. Johnny headed toward the curb, toward the very same street musician he'd accosted two nights before.

At first it looked like the guitar player was going to turn and run, but he seemed to calm down as Johnny put a hand on his shoulder and said something that was inaudible to the rest of the crowd. Moments later, the two of them were heading back up the walkway, the musician toting his guitar and tiny amplifier.

"This is Floyd," Johnny told everyone once they'd reached the front porch. Floyd looked a little dazed. "Floyd is going to play for you," said Johnny. He patted Floyd once on the top of his head, smiled at everyone, and retreated into the house.

Floyd played.

It's entirely possible that Floyd's playing and singing was exactly the way it had always been, that he sounded no different from the slightly embittered street entertainer that most of the crowd had heard at various outdoor Cambridge locales over the past few years, a reasonably talented performer in a city loaded with an unreasonable number of great musicians. It could well have been *that* Floyd up there on the porch, rather than a suddenly blossoming and ennobled Major Talent.

But we'll never know. Music doesn't work that way. What with the surreal setting and the singular benediction of Johnny himself, what the assembled Johnnyheads heard was a one-of-a-kind performance from a man specially selected for them. They swayed and nodded to the Square fare that Floyd offered, and, seeing the reaction, Floyd himself started to believe in its beauty, which may in fact have helped him take his game to that fabled next level.

Or it may not have.

Either way, the grooving faithful were too enrapt to notice four youths emerge from behind the house and look interestedly at the musician on the porch, trying to convey the impression that they were arriving via some nearby shortcut. There were two men and two women.

The women were tall and ungainly and wore far too much makeup for their style of dress, which conveyed a slouchy chic. The blonde was fashionably slim, pretty even, and the bespectacled brunette was obviously overcompensating by swinging her hips convulsively as she walked. The men were shorter, both with a discernible five o'clock shadow. They were grungier than the women, wearing baggy clothes and poorly tied bandannas over their hair, which they doubtless referred to as "drug helmets." Despite the facial hair, they looked distinctly boyish.

The quartet self-consciously ambled through the crowd, trying far too hard to communicate that they were just looking for a good place to sit, making desperately casual eye contact with their peers as they jostled by. If not for Floyd and his unbelievably well-received rendition of "The Hook," they'd have been spotted instantly. Instead, they made their way through the crowd to the street without incident, and soon found themselves in the clear. Twenty minutes later, they were among the trees on the deserted campus of the Cambridge Rindge & Latin School, exchanging clothing in the fading sunlight. Which may have been the real reason for the charade in the first place.

"You guys would get *so* hit on if you went out like that," said Arlene, as she and Deb watched Grant and Johnny wriggle out of their too-tight pants. The girls admired their handiwork—Grant's and Johnny's newly shaved calves looked great, in their estimation.

"Yeah, chicks with dicks are totally in right now," agreed Deb.

"It's nice to be popular, for once," said Grant, making sure that he'd pulled on his own pants before taking off the Gypsy blouse and sock-stuffed brassiere, so that he was only halfway nude at any given time. Johnny, naturally, preferred to strip completely first, even the Speedo (Grant's and Johnny's usual boxers would have been, they assumed, too conspicuous under their womanly disguises), and he stood gloriously naked in the sun, feeling the slight breeze on his still-tingling calves, tiny golden hairs shining everywhere else on his slender frame. Arlene and Deb made no attempt to conceal their staring at either of their friends; they hooted and whistled unabashedly; Grant felt a bit jealous as well as oppressed on behalf of his gender when Deb leered at Johnny and raised her hand to Arlene for a congratulatory high-five. His own body, a bit more compact than Johnny's and unexpectedly muscular, was also the subject of some genuinely appreciative leering, which Grant immediately interpreted as mocking and somewhat cruel.

Having changed, the boys came to the aid of their counterparts, dutifully undoing the clips of the ace bandages that had rendered them (more or less) flat-chested. Their breasts (all four of them now red-marked with their recent restraints) flopped into view, providing an odd counterargument to the scruffy facial hair that had been drawn on the girls' faces.

Two days ago, Arlene probably would have changed in a Grant-like fashion, perhaps even attempting to remove the ace bandage with her shirt still on. But today was different, today *Arlene* was different, and soon she and Deb found themselves clad only in their panties. Their bodies, hers and Deb's, thought Arlene, really weren't all that different. They were both, she realized suddenly and hopefully . . . *beautiful*, though, Arlene still being Arlene, she could not complete the thought without mentally kicking herself for previously being so hung-up on her body image and wasting all that time.

Deb's and Arlene's stripping, it should be noted, was greeted not with raucous catcalls and hooting, but with a deep and uncomfortable silence. Even though Johnny was different now, even though Arlene and Johnny had spent the last two nights together, even though Grant's obsession with Deb had raged for many, many months, even though they all spoke about sex as easily and casually as friends could, *still* there was something unexpected here. Grant realized that, despite all the sex swirling between them and around them, as a unit the four of them had been androgynous. Together, they'd been a group: not two men and two women, but a single entity with its own distinct personality. But that entity was fragmenting, differentiating, going to soil. The last of the inevitably fragile conceit seemed to burn off in the glare of the women's nakedness, and for the first time all the complexity of sex and personal politics emerged into the open and filled the air between the foursome.

Until Arlene and Deb were dressed again, at which point the illusion that creates *any* personality, singular or collective, resumed. Albeit shakily. The four of them brushed the feeling off, talked about nothing, laughed, headed back toward the streets of Cambridge.

Dear Diary,

    Cambridge is emptying of robots for the first time in years. I think they're scared, or maybe they just don't want to be here. You can tell that something very human is going to happen. At least I can.

    I'm nervous, even though it probably has nothing to do with me. I haven't felt this way since I turned in my dissertation. Or turned my first trick. One of those, anyway.

    I'm gonna check the egg one last time and then head for Harvard. Because it's the tip of the arrow. And maybe I can get some work done.

Evening was setting in, and the Citizen Formerly Known as the President of Montana was feeling particularly alive. There was joy—a beautiful warm evening in New England. There was nostalgia—a return to the haunts of his youth. And there was more than a little anticipation and fear—tonight would be the first possible time and place for him and his wife to meet, the first possible rendezvous point.

Of course, it wasn't too likely she'd be there. It had only been a few days since the CFKPOM had fled, and there wasn't much

chance that she was free and clear. She'd only make the rendezvous if it was safe for them both, and she was quite likely
still holed up back at the ranch, trapped in the web *he'd* woven
and Dix had made sticky. The President estimated that three or
four more rendezvous appointments would pass before he
could reasonably hope to see her, but, still, *he'd* be there, and
that made tonight significant.

The President feels like he's teetering on the edge of things.
Though not in a bad way. All the alienation he felt earlier today,
back before the Kung Pao chicken, has vanished. He feels vul-
nerable yet powerful, benevolent toward all as he wanders up
Mass Ave and across the Common. He's a Citizen again, part
of the glorious, cacophonous, ludicrous machine that somehow manages more or less to *work* despite everything. Not just
America—people. There seems to be something about all the
complex interactions between them, something he'd dimly seen
years ago, known was important, and managed to forget. He
thinks about this as he watches the sunset falling on the green.
He sits on a bench.

There's a cluster of people toward the edge of the Common,
and strains of guitar music. The song is vaguely familiar, but,
then, *anything* strummed on an acoustic guitar near sunset is
vaguely familiar. There's a Frisbee in midair, and he follows
its flight to the hand of a fair-haired young man with baggy
shorts cut from trousers. Several dogs, all on leashes at various
points along the paths, watch the Frisbee with interest, each
seemingly hoping that the kid will look at him and say, "There's
an alert-looking doggy, maybe I ought to throw this to him. . . ."
There are four young women on blankets who can no longer
keep up the pretext of sunbathing and are now simply loafing
and considering the night ahead. . . .

And suddenly the sun is completely gone, and the former President of Montana realizes that he is now officially just an old man sitting on a park bench, and who'd've thought it would come to *that*? He gets up, still feeling the buzz of humanity around him, still exalted, but a little lonely now. He heads more or less toward his destination, aware that there is plenty of time, oceans of time, and nothing in particular to fill it with at the moment. Which, he thinks, might not necessarily be a terrible thing.

. . . 7. And it came to pass that the Prophet Bernie wandered in the land on the near side of the Crossing, for the Time of the Crossing had not yet come. 8. And Bernie came upon a Square, where the people there gathered in a Court of Food. And the people there spoke in strange tongues and purchased their goods with coin of which Bernie had none. 9. For the Lord had told Bernie to work not, and earn not, though without this command Bernie could probably have been a rich man indeed. For Bernie was possessed of many unique Gifts and Talents which might have brought him fame and bountiful fortune, but he applied himself not, and took direction poorly, and worked not well with others, in accordance with the Lord's command. 10. And as the Lord commanded, and not by Bernie's wishes, Bernie did beseech the people for alms, so that he might eat and be strong, for the Time of the Crossing was near. 11. And the people of the Square were wicked and knew not the Lord, and they spurned Bernie and shared not their goods. And they reviled the Prophet Bernie and criticized him, as had his mother before them, saying, "Fie! For thou art covered in filth and art smelly withal, and we do detest thee!" 12. For, because the people knew not the Lord, they knew not His command that Bernie

wash not and drink not of water but only of coffee. 13. And
Bernie did despair, and almost cried out to the Lord. But Bernie
remembered the Lord's command that He be not Pestered
until the Time of the Crossing, and Bernie held his tongue and
cried not, though his hunger grew and his Feelings had been
bruised. . . .

"My cat, or should I say 'my' 'cat,' " said Dr. Schrödinger,
making ridiculous "air quotes" with fingers that glistened with
butter, "is made of string. Did you know that?"

We didn't. In fact, we were a bit distracted by the fact that Dr.
Schrödinger was willing to talk about "his cat"—we'd thought
that he wanted to distance himself from that "easily misinterpreted metaphor." But now the doctor, looking relaxed and a bit
tanned from two days out in the sun, seemed eager to plunge
back into these same choppy waters.

"That's right, made of string. And even though I created
him, I didn't know what he was made of back then."

He raised an eyebrow meaningfully, successfully drawing us
in with his artful riddles. Somehow, the old man's inner raconteur had been drawn out, and the manic glare in his eye had become what could only be described as a *twinkle*. We thought,
fairly unscientifically, that we wished *we* were getting laid.

"It turns out that, yes, subatomic particles are the building
blocks of atoms, which are the building blocks of matter. But
the building blocks of the building blocks of the building blocks
of matter . . . are strings."

Aha. String theory. We'd heard of it.

"Think of space and time as one pristine fabric, though a
fabric without mass in its smoothest state. The fabric ends up

with a tiny hairline fold, let's imagine, and thus a single string comes into existence. Local colonies of strings weave themselves into subatomic particles that in turn find their way into atoms. . . . So, really, it's not just my cat that's made of string—it's everything. We're all agglomerations of folds in the fabric of space-time. We're spatiotemporal origami, if you will."

We wouldn't. The metaphors were too horribly mixed. We found ourselves begging the doctor to trim the metaphorical hedges, keep it neat. Perhaps, we suggested, he should give the cat a ball of yarn, which is a bit like string, and leave the origami out of it. Dr. Schrödinger smiled at the idea.

"Very good. But I haven't the time to develop it. Perhaps I'll leave that work to you."

To us? What made the old babbler think that we had any interest in developing his tortured metaphors? And who were we to presume to explain physics to the world at large? Who were we to try to inform a world that would only find a way to creatively misinform itself? Who were we? we asked, perhaps aloud. Who were we?

"Exactly," said Dr. Schrödinger, his smile disappearing as he fixed us with a piercing stare, "exactly." We shivered. We changed the subject. We signaled for the waiter.

The very last shred of daylight disappears as Floyd lets the last chord reverberate. The Dave Matthews tune had been pretty tough on his fingers, but Floyd had felt out the audience and had obligingly fed them a steady diet of jam-band material for the past twenty minutes. Along the way he even threw them an original song from five years ago, the last one he'd ever written. He's never felt so good, so competent, so well liked. At this moment the crowd would do absolutely anything for him, he thinks, and they're all just hanging out there, waiting for his next note.

So he stops playing and drags his things off the porch. Floyd's no Johnny and he's no idiot, and he knows when to cut bait. He's done great, and this is the moment to leave. If he plays it right from this point, who knows? He's feeling those long-suppressed feelings of optimism about his musical career. Maybe it's time to get the band back together, or form a new one, or write some more songs.

It's definitely time to stop, though. He wends his way through the throng, looking as vague, goofy, and distracted as he possibly can without doing a flat-out Johnny Felix Decaté impression.

Dear Diary,

The egg's okay. And dinner was a cinch—a wink at Stan over at the potato place. With Stan, who's tortured by guilt, it's not "for old times' sake." It's a never-ending payment, a plea that his wife never finds out (even though it's been more than ten years since I hung up my pumps for good). So it feels a little like blackmail. But it was hot, nutritious blackmail with cheese and broccoli, so I'll take it.

The robots are in a tizzy—walking around like they don't know what to do next. Strange, but anything that pisses them off has to be good.

But at least this means I can get a table at the Au Bon Pain™. One seat for me, one for the worldly possessions, and a ringside seat to the Show, whatever it is.

The four of them are walking the same stretch of road that they took from the Abbey two nights ago, but that was a fundamentally different world. Tonight the pairings are different:

Grant and Deb lead the way, with Arlene and Johnny wandering behind.

Grant and Deb are talking about being naked.

"It was comfortable. I'd do it all the time if I could be in situations where I felt safe, y'know, not like I was being molested by people's eyes."

"*My* eyes were molesting you," Grant points out. Deb's flattered, though Grant was actually confessing.

"Strangers' eyes, I mean."

"You like being sexy, but you want it to be by choice, huh?"

"I think that's right."

"And, unlike a naked guy, a naked woman doesn't have that choice."

"Slow Deb losing you . . ."

"What I mean is, naked guys, guys in their underwear, are *funny.*"

"I didn't think you looked funny. I thought you looked cute."

A simple thanks, a smile, anything to show he's flattered, and Grant might've had a chance. But Grant's an idiot. So his mind won't process this as a compliment. Which is why he and Deb simply aren't fated to happen.

Instead, Grant presses on with his point. "The point is— a guy in his underwear, even a good-looking guy, can be funny. A woman in her underwear is either sexy or embarrassing."

"So, until we sisters can be laughed at in our lingerie, there's no equality?"

Grant grins back at Deb. "Exactly."

"Maybe you could teach me to be funny naked sometime. For the good of all women, I mean."

This time the opening's a mile wide. There's almost nothing that Grant (who's got an IQ of 168) can say right now that won't move him and the object of all his desires toward a greater intimacy.

"I don't think I'd make a really good comedy teacher."

Except that.

Chapter 11

It's time to meet Lester the Rat.

Lester's name is not, of course, really "Lester." Rats do not have names in any way that you'd recognize. But they do have identities; to other rats they are identified by a smell, a certain signature type of squeak, a generalized shape. And since Lester is indeed an individual rat, and one that is indispensably important to our present concerns, we'll need to remember him for later. He's the catalyst, the instigator, the necessary cog—his actions will change the fate of the very world we've been exploring. We *need* to know this rat if we're going to understand anything at all. So we'll call him "Lester."

Lester was a happy rat, as rats go. He was well fed, large, and in the prime of life. His hobbies were eating, mating, and pursuing opportunities to eat and mate. He also liked to fight, though this was not really a hobby; Lester didn't look for fights, but when they became unavoidable (because someone was interfering with eating, mating, or the free pursuit thereof), his eyes would fill with blood and his lips would peel back and he'd go into another world, a world where all that existed was throats and eyes and blurs of instinctively understood motion. Those were good times, whether the opponent was another rat or a cat or a squirrel or something bigger.

On this particular afternoon, Lester emerged from beneath

the street and stepped into one of his favorite alleys, one that almost always had food and rarely required fighting. The alley had easily torn plastic bags, raidable cans, and a really, really great Dumpster that was always filled with food and featured a couple of rat-sized holes on the underside.

On this day, however, the Dumpster was disappointingly empty. Lester, like most of his kind, did not have a calendar, wouldn't have been able to read one anyway, and so couldn't have known that the Dumpster had just received its weekly Sunday-afternoon servicing. Lester had therefore arrived about an hour too late for the truly magnificent feast that had been there.

He wandered around the alley, dashing from shadow to shadow, finding the pickings scarce and unsatisfying. He was, naturally, hungry. He was always hungry. But if there'd been other food in the alley, he might not have bothered with the egg.

The egg was just lying there, right near the Dumpster. It didn't smell quite right, but it was worth a try, Lester supposed. He'd had some eggs in his time, mostly dregs in broken shells, but sometimes all sealed up and requiring an industrious rat to shatter them. This was one of the latter type, and Lester nudged it, nosed it, rolled it, and finally extended one ratty paw to hold it in place while his front teeth bared and lowered toward the egg's white shell. . . .

Perhaps the shell was weaker than most. Or maybe Lester had put on some weight. Hard to say. But for whatever reason, Lester's teeth had not yet reached the shiny surface when the egg all of a sudden cracked like, well, an egg, and shattered moistly under his paw. He felt the liquid immediately and bent his head further to begin the tiny feast.

Only a split second later, Lester was whacked by a smell so awful, so noxious, so brain-cloggingly strong, that he actually passed out for a moment. He lurched away, ran in a circle, bared his teeth for a fight, jumped spasmodically, circled again. His best senses were stuck in a hallucinogenic overload, and flames rose in his eyes. Soon he gained just enough composure to settle upon one well-tested strategy: the venerable and unfailing "Run Away."

Of course, his paw was covered with the horrible smell, the smell that made him flee, so Lester ran for a very, very long time.

Things Arlene said to Johnny during their walk:

"It's cold."

"Isn't it?"

"I mean, for summer."

"If Furble were alive, he'd have loved this. Furble-friendly weather."

"What?"

"Oh."

"Hey, look out—car! What an asshole!"

"You okay?"

"You know, if we were all killed today, there'd be no one alive who'd ever read a single one of my stories. All four of us are together. For the sake of the future of literature, we all have to stop meeting like this."

"What?"

"You know, I had this dream this morning. . . . Oh, you did? What was it about?"

"That's pretty fucked up."

"Believe me, I had no idea we were ever going to . . ."

"It was great! I mean, I can barely walk, but it was worth it. You're . . . gifted, Johnny Decaté, did you know that? In a lot of ways."

"No, I'm glad to have you! I mean, not that I 'have' you, you know, it was just a, you know, whatever. I'm not gonna go all psycho on you, I promise."

"No, really, fine, I don't know, you know, whatever."

"Right?"

"Oh God, I'm actually blushing. . . ."

"No, it's just that—I guess I was raised as too much of a lady. I can't bring myself to say words like 'fuck' or 'pussy' or anything. I mean, not if I'm actually talking about . . . fucking and . . . See, I can't do it. I'm totally the opposite of Deb."

"I'll work on it."

"What?"

"That's . . . Are you okay?"

"No, I mean, really. We're all a little worried about you, that's all."

"No, you seem fine. Really! Totally fine. Just, really . . . different, that's all."

"So you feel okay?"

"Oh. That's cool."

"Funny, I wrote a story kind of like that once. I mean, kind of like that."

"It was about this guy who had these deformed hands, you know, just like two little hooks or something instead of thumbs and fingers. And he gets this job touring with a freak show as the 'Lobster Boy'—right?—and he makes all these freak friends and he's doing okay. But he's really not *happy*, because he always thought his hands looked more like *robot* hands, you know, like from *Lost in Space*, so he really wished he could be the Robot Boy instead of the Lobster Boy. But the guy who runs the freak show won't listen to him, because, like, every freak show has a Lobster Boy, and there's no real market for a Robot Boy. . . . And I guess a lot of stuff happens, some of it I have to rewrite because it just kind of goes off track, you know . . . but eventually he saves up and saves up and *buys* the whole freak show and makes conditions better for everyone and builds himself this huge tent that says 'Robot Man' and has this huge sci-fi set, and he's got a great new robot costume and everything. So he's in the dressing trailer getting ready for his first show as Robot Man, and he looks at his hands and studies them really closely. He realizes that they really *do* look more like lobster claws after all."

"No, that's how it ends. He's just sitting there, looking at his hands."

"Fuck you. You can write the sequel if you want. Call it 'The Return of Lobster Boy' or something. I don't care."

"I'm just kidding."

"Thanks."

"What? No . . ."

"But you've *read* most of them already."

"Okay, okay . . . There's this new one I'm working on. It's about a girl. She's like fifteen, right? And her family is driving her nuts. She's got this mean, retarded brother who can barely form a sentence, and her mom spends all her time doting over this mangy cat of theirs. And the cat is this pathetic thing that can't even feed itself. What makes things worse is, everybody treats her brother like he's this incredibly great, smart guy who's good at everything. Like everybody's trying to be so kind and PC to this *retard* that the girl ends up totally ignored."

"Funny. Do you want to hear the rest?"

"Okay, so one day the girl gets really sick, and she's lying in bed drinking tea, and she spills it on herself, gets burns like totally all over her body. And she jumps out of bed and gets her legs tangled in the covers and knocks over a lamp and gets a shock, right? So she jumps back from the shock, but her legs are still tangled, so she trips over her chair, crashes through the window, falls out onto the roof above the garage, *rolls* down the roof like totally mummified in the blanket, hits the driveway, rolls into the street, gets run over by a bicycle, somehow stumbles up, walks two steps, and gets hit by a car."

"Yeah, it's a true story. Shut up. So here's the thing. When she wakes up in the hospital, she's had a head injury. But it's like a *positive* head injury or something. Her mom and brother are there, and suddenly she realizes that the brother's a totally sweet guy who's not retarded at all. Right? And she thinks at first that her mom has brought the cat, but now she can see that it's not a cat at all. It's her baby sister."

"That's all I have so far. You like?"

"That's . . . that's incredibly sweet."

"Oh, nice segue, pig-boy."

"No, we're almost at the Square. There's better stuff there."

"Oh, come on, we just ate before we left."

"Wait—okay! Wait. I'll tell Grant and . . . Okay, wait up!"

Dear Diary,

Whatever's supposed to be happening now isn't. So:

1613—Michael Romanov becomes Czar, kicking off the whole Romanov thing. Russia's got everything she's ever wanted in a ruler: charm, good looks, ruthless brutality. An alien comes down and warns Michael that there's a comet coming in about three hundred years, but the Czar doesn't listen. He eats the alien, hoping to gain its "powers." He ends up with a faint green glow, which he considers almost as good.

1621—Elvis Presley is born in Cairo.

1625—Paquizetl, a Toltec haberdasher, invents the "Kabpzintl," an early beer helmet. He spends the rest of his career designing headdresses for the ruling class.

1642—Oliver Cromwell takes over England. The English barely notice, unless visitors ask them, "Who's King now?" When this happens, they get embarrassed and change the subject.

1643—The Egyptian Empire finally collapses in a small hut in Alexandria where it had somehow hung on all those centuries.

In Prussia, a prostitute named Hilda Leibenfroeg invents an extremely efficient engine that runs on semen. Fearing the return of matriarchy, the Freemasons ship her off-world and use the only existing prototype to power their subterranean resort community for the next 140 years.

1644—The Manchus begin their three-century reign in China. When they take over, they assure everyone that they'll only be in the Palace "for a second—we just have to go in and get this . . . thing . . . we left behind at the New Year's party. . . ." It becomes the single most effective political ploy in history.

In India, a baby named Bibu drowns in the Ganges. His mother is very sad and never forgives herself (even though it's not her fault). She spends the rest of her life as a vagrant: wandering, writing, tormented by the cries of her lost infant.

"Start by looking from outside of space and time," said Dr. Schrödinger, "which is of course impossible. I'll have the apple-glazed pork chop with the herbed couscous but no raisins, and a dinner salad with Roquefort dressing. From outside it all, you might imagine space-time as a smooth and slightly rippling sheet. There are, of course, strings, the little tiny wrinkles we spoke of earlier. But there's very, very few of them. And another Balvenie Doublewood, neat. They appear in megabunches in otherwise nearly complete smoothness. These bunches are, of course, galaxies, or clusters thereof. . . ."

Dr. Schrödinger had by this time succeeded in confusing both us and the waiter. His hand was fiddling idly with the bottom of the now-empty bread basket. Occasionally, a crumb would attach itself to the pad of one gnarled finger, which would then start a slow journey to the physicist's lower lip. Perched there, the crumb would await the doctor's next pause, whereupon his overworked tongue would emerge and claim it.

"Now move in closer and observe that even inside these clusters there's mostly smooth, unwrinkly space. Within this there are further clusters—clusters of stars or solar systems. But even within *these*, it's mostly space. Pure, empty space, perhaps a bit more 'wrinkly' than outside the galactic clusters, but pretty damn smooth nonetheless. But now let's move in even closer, to a planet and its atmosphere, and for the sake of argument we'll say we're looking at *this* planet, Earth. What do you think we see, from a spatiotemporal perspective?"

We were mainly thinking about how to attract the waiter back to us (we hadn't gotten the chance to order), so we were not immediately aware that we'd been asked a question. However, the doctor's uncharacteristic silence made us look up; we saw him watching us patiently. He appeared frozen, ready to wait all night for a response if necessary, the one moistened, circling finger the only evidence that he was not a wax figure.

We hazarded a quick guess, suggested that we'd see more spaces and wrinkly clusters. The doctor seemed to smile slightly, blinked once, breathed. . . .

"Wrong!!" he screamed, his open hand slamming the table

hard enough to overturn the bread basket. People were staring, making us more than a little uncomfortable. "Wrong! Inside, the atmosphere is a veritable riot of wrinkles. Large stable hunks of solids; drifting, rolling, wrinkly liquids; and the *air*. The air is a seething, whirring, buzzing mess of jam-packed string clusters, grouped together in lumpy molecules and whizzing little ions, bumping and bashing into one another like soccer fans celebrating a championship in a sold-out stadium. We speak of the 'space' between us, but it may be important to remind ourselves that there *is* none."

Now the doctor is staring at us intently, seeming to get personal again, though we can't imagine what he's talking about, not really, no. "There is nowhere you can go," he says, his finger tapping the table, "nowhere on this earth, where you are not part of the swirling, interweaving knot of shifty stringiness. Nowhere."

The old foop thinks he's getting at something, and we don't know what it is. We don't.

The President of Montana (Yeah, *Right*) marvels and wonders, wonders and marvels. Harvard Square is the same as it was but very, very different. Cleaner, filled with more stores, some new buildings . . . but still the same old place. What's missing is the blight, despair, and lawlessness. At least, there's no more of it than he saw back when. Back when he thought that physical and psychological pollution were going to overwhelm the earth.

The PoM(YR) doesn't feel chagrined anymore—just amazed and impressed. Maybe a little left out, at first. But even this feeling doesn't last—it's a beautiful, warm evening, and there are smiles and glad comments coming his way from everywhere.

It's not until he sees his face in a darkened store window that he figures out why—he's got a perpetual, moist-eyed, idiot's smile on his face. Well, fine.

The bars welcome him in, give him beers, wish him well as he leaves. Ice cream falls into paper cups for him. Guitars play him tunes, windows show him miracles, restaurants offer him fragrances, and everywhere he goes there are smiles.

And people! They're everywhere, mostly young, all beautiful. He's no longer looking on with grandfatherly detachment—the parade of sweet-faced women throw hips and breasts and legs directly into his eyes. It's not like his libido's been dead all these years, but it's definitely been taking it easy. He now has one more reason to wish for Tammy's presence—she'd like this new . . . *vigor* of his, that's definite. She'd even be amused at the cause of it, the way she was that night after Dix brought his niece over for dinner. Tammy'd understood, taken advantage of it, trusting him and their marriage enough not to be put off.

The President wonders if finding the absolutely most perfect woman in the universe might've made him less of a man than he might've been. Like maybe he'd known he never needed anything else and just ran away from it all with his take. And he wonders how fair that'd been to Tammy, and why she put up with it, etc. . . . . On top of that comes the realization that they're not old yet, at least not really. That there's time and a million places to go and thousands more warm, friendly evenings.

As long as Tammy's all right, that is.

He absently follows a pair of feminine buttocks into a gigantic record store. There are racks and racks of headphones where you can listen to music for free. He listens, and it's yet another revelation. It all sounds like *hope* to him, even the stuff about "smacking bitches" and "popping caps" and "crazy niggaz." It sounds hopeful somehow, like at least the world's ready to admit it has a problem. Or something. It's a great beat, though.

The President smiles and bobs his head to the rhythm that's pounding through his headphones. There's a teenager of indeterminate race at the station next to him doing the same thing, and they turn toward each other at the same time. There's a moment of communication there, a split second of smiles widening followed by a grinning acknowledgment of how incongruous the image is, how it's the stuff of after-school specials and public-service announcements from religious organizations. They turn back to their respective stations, still grinning.

Inside the President's head there's: the music, the afterimage of his notions about hope, the desire to put his arm around the boy, the growing lamentation that he and Tammy hadn't trusted the world enough to have kids, the ever-present worry about Tammy, the lingering buzz of alcohol, the awareness of a slight chill from the air-conditioning, the ignored perception of the album cover and console in front of him, the lingering taste of that slice of pizza, and the automatic picture of himself which includes the position of his body, what he knows about the store's layout, and his location in reference to the Square, Boston, the United States (and Montana, of course), and the world.

Lester ran. Powerfully, desperately, he ran. He'd dashed out of the alley, found a route to the beloved underground, and now he was streaking through the dark, fleeing the *smell* and the sensory overload. He still hadn't clued in that the odor was now emanating from his front paw. He didn't have enough of a brain to realize that a simple rinsing of the paw in the fetid sewer water around him would've alleviated the problem. Had he realized this and acted upon it, things would have turned out very, very differently.

Instead, Lester ran. He ran past Melanie, a slender young rat (who was, as a point of fact, his sister), without even noticing her. He couldn't smell a thing, not with that acrid, sickly aroma filling his brain. He veered slightly as he ran, not knowing exactly where he was going, his sense of direction (so very dependent on smell, like everything else) also offline.

Melanie, for her part, didn't recognize Lester, either. Her brain registered "ratty shape" and "ratty sound" and "really bad smell" and nothing more, so she shrank back from him as he passed. Not that she would've intervened if she'd been able to tell that it was Lester. She was, after all, a rat.

Chapter 12

. . . 4. And the Prophet Bernie did pass from place to place, but at every inn and way station he was denied. 5. For the people there would say unto Bernie, though they knew him not, "Lo! Begone! For we see that thou art a beggar, and our facilities are not for thee." 6. And Bernie was sore pressed to find some comfort, for his loins did ache with the pressure, and he wast almost like to cry out to the Lord for succor. But Bernie remembered the Lord's command that He be Pestered not, and Bernie held his tongue and clenched his bladder and sojourned on. 7. And at last Bernie did come to a room of rest that was Public, and existed for all Men, and Bernie did cry out with relief and thanked the Lord and thereafter took comfort in the providential plumbing. 8. And whilst Bernie was voiding himself in accordance with the way the Lord had made him, the Lord's voice spoke unto Bernie once more. 9. "Bernie!" quoth the Lord. "Where hast thou wandered to? I have need of thee!" And Bernie didst reply, "Lord, I am here. Behold, for I am in this booth, doing as my body dost demand." 10. And the Lord beheld Bernie, and He did speak again. "Oh, I am sorry to interrupt thee, good Bernie. I can come back when it is more convenient. . . ." And the Prophet Bernie said, "Not at all, Lord, I will be but a moment, and Thou mayst speak unto me as Thou dost desire, for my ears are open and unoccupied for the present Task." "Art thou sure?" asked the Lord. "Indeed, good Lord," quoth Bernie, "for I am even now ever Thine servant." 11. "Then know, Bernie," spake the Lord, "that thine Business here must end quickly, for the Time of the Crossing has come, and thou must make thine way to the Place of the Crossing." 12. And Bernie did gather up his garments and bathe his hands in accordance with the Lord's command, and he said unto the Lord, "Lord, what is it You would have me do in the Crossing? For Thou hast told me nothing of it save that I must Cross." 13. And the Lord God replied, "Thou needst not know, for thine actions will be dictated by what thou dost see there at the Crossing. But be there thou must, for events do run apace, running on the feet of men and rats, on birds' wings and worms' bellies. The design hath been assembled lo these long years, though the design knows it not. But I do know it, good Bernie, and I see that it doth require thine presence." 14. And Bernie did ponder this, and asked the Lord, "God, if the design is set, then am I not part of the design?" "Indeed thou art, Bernie, as I have told thee, thou art bound up in the Machinery of Fate," spake the Lord. "Then," said Bernie, "why dost Thou *command* me to do what Thine design hast made inevitable? Why dost Thou not simply allow me to take part in the Crossing unknowing, as Thine other Creatures do? Why dost Thou tell me this and command me? Doth this telling me really accomplish aught but the calling of attention to Thyself and Thy name?" 15. And the Lord did take a moment and spake not as Bernie dried his hands. And when the Lord did speak again, His voice was like the thunder and did echo across the tilings. "Dost thou question Me, the Lord, your God?" came the angry voice of the Lord, for He was wroth. "Dost thou, a mortal, who knows naught of My Design and does naught but eat and sleep, think that thou couldst perform better the Considerable and Taxing works of the Lord? Perhaps I should step down from My Place in the heavens among the Angels, and allow *thee* to take My place. Would thou likest *that*?

Oh, verily, perhaps *that* is what I should do if thou art Dissatisfied with My Works." 16. And Bernie did cringe at the Lord's mighty sarcasm, and he spake naught but apologies, for he did know how Difficult the Lord was when He got like this. And in time the Lord did hear Bernie's prayers, and His storms did calm, and He spake to Bernie in Quieter, more Civil tones: "Go, then, Bernie, for it is the Time of the Crossing, and I am not wroth with thee any longer." 17. And Bernie, who saw that the Lord had smote him not despite His righteous anger, strode out with a glad heart toward the Place of the Crossing.

THEY WENT TO HARVARD rather than Central. For cover, Grant realized. Central Square was their place, the place where they knew everyone. Harvard Square belonged to everyone, and was both familiar and marginally more anonymous. They stayed close to one another, briefly waving to or high-fiving people they knew. Their acquaintances dimly perceived the bubble of privacy that surrounded the foursome (it wasn't the first time, though it was the first time they'd ever needed it so badly) and more or less respected it.

Grant saw that, whatever was going on, it was almost over. In the morning, he'd go to work, and this would shatter Johnny-Watch, and whatever was wrong with Johnny would be Johnny's to resolve or not resolve. Grant felt vaguely guilty about this, as though he were abandoning a drowning man, but he reasoned that there was nothing demonstrably *wrong* with Johnny, that this "situation" (whatever it was) might continue indefinitely, and that they all had lives to lead in the meantime. Besides, Arlene, given her new carnal entanglement with Johnny, could be counted on to keep an eye on him. Definitely.

None of this flawless reasoning made Grant feel much better.

Even Grant, with his grandmaster-level cluelessness, couldn't avoid the notion that he'd bypassed an opportunity or two with Deb. He needed time by himself to process everything, fantasize about what he'd seen and done, and somehow find a way to reconstruct the shabby illusion that if the "right opportunity" arose he might just Do or Say Something.

"Now, let's look at what we've got. Let's, shall we say, put it all back together."

Dr. Schrödinger had devoured his entire apple-glazed pork chop while waxing romantic about "superstrings" and such. Now we were watching helplessly as his fork casually roamed the table, dipping into our plates, casually snagging bits of salad and pasta primavera without asking our permission. Apparently, the doctor's new thoughts about the fundamental interconnectedness of all things had erased his ability to differentiate between what was "his" and what was "not his." If he'd ever had that ability.

"See, we have several seemingly competing worldviews here. Yet they're all scientifically valid. We've got the hard physics of atoms and molecules, the uncertain world of quantum mechanics, the wrinkly, interconnected space of string theory, and the grand design of chaos math. Obviously, we're talking orders of magnitude here. Our string-riddled world forms those shifty particles which make the hard molecules . . . like this one," he said, producing a Humdinger from his breast pocket while using the gesture to cover his other hand's foray into our garlic bread. "And this little baby will interact with the world in a seemingly chaotic pattern whose rules are nonetheless discernible. So where, you ask, where is *human thought* in all this? What level do we look at it on? What does it DO, physically, besides issuing commands to its body? These are your questions."

No, these were the doctor's questions. Our own concerned our rapidly dwindling food supply and the need to speak up about the check before the old physicist stiffed us again.

"When I first took on Heisenberg's uncertainty principle, when I first gave birth to my Cat," said the doctor, conjuring up an image that we tried desperately to push from our minds, "I was flying blind to some extent. I still am, but less so. See, it's one thing to know that a particle or wave's very nature is determined by the presence of an observer, but quite another to understand exactly *why* that's the case. I wasn't concerned with *why* when I invented the Cat; I just wanted to explain *how* that breaks down under scrutiny. Of course, it turns out the power of the observer works on so many levels, so very many levels. As does the *understanding* of the observer. One's thoughts do not have to be *right* to influence the very nature of reality. So we men of science must be careful with our explanations, lest a world of semicomprehending clods end up changing the very laws we worked so hard to discover. Reality is permeable from both sides. It's all give and take. Give and take."

In reality, there was a lot more "take" going on with the doctor at the moment. Our meal had unmysteriously vanished right before our ever-observant eyes. We were not pleased. Not that we weren't listening. One of the world's preeminent physicists seemed to be on the verge of validating witchcraft and voodoo and spoon-bending and the like, and this was a matter of concern. He was also on the verge of ordering several expensive desserts.

He scanned the little dessert menu, bouncing the Hum-

dinger on the table as he did so. Individual molecules, we we
pretty sure, should not *bounce*, should they? "To think, just to
think, that, after all this time, a lifetime and then some, devoted
to science . . . that I'd find myself speaking like some sort of
neo-Jungian, advocating some kind of 'collective subjective'
model of reality—it's quite humbling, really. In some ways,
Heisenberg opened the floodgates—he let the psychological
contaminate the immutable physical world we'd worked so hard
to nail down. But the psychological is right at this moment a
more pressing concern. Wouldn't you agree?" The old man gave
us that hard stare once more. We were sure he was going to dig
into us, start getting too personal more. Looking right at us,
right through us, he parted his lips and intoned . . .

"An apple tart, a slice of the Black Forest cake, lime sherbet,
peanut-butter pie, and a cup of coffee, please."

Lester the Rat was far from home. His unthinking, panicky
flight had taken him a great distance underground, and he was
in unfamiliar territory.

Now that the stink had more or less washed off his paws and
his nose was starting to clear a bit and fill with the more palat-
able aromas of waste, mold, and other rats, Lester felt a lot better. He began to think again, as much as rats think. His first
thought was, of course, that he was hungry.

He'd been hungry in the alley, and that had been a long time
ago, back before that . . . thing . . . happened (rats do not have
extremely good memories; Lester wouldn't recall the egg incident until the next time he came across an egg, and even then
it would be a general and vague warning that can be roughly
translated as "Oh, hey, this is one of those things that might be
very good or might be very bad. . . ."). Going all the way back to

ants was out of the question. He knew the way
eneral sense, but he was hungry *now.*

hurried around in the dark, finding nothing but paper,
, and a few unfamiliar rats (or evidence thereof). Instinct,
perience, and some tantalizing smells told him that the world
above held much better feeding prospects. Up he went, toward
a fresher breeze and a faint light.

It was a sewer grate in a curbside that Lester's nose eventually poked through. Being a fairly competent rat (rotten-egg fi-
asco notwithstanding), he knew not to emerge any farther until
he'd checked out the situation. The situation was a street, night,
many humans, cars, the usual . . .

. . . and a piece of meat.

Right there, about twenty feet away, visible in the lamplight,
a small but appreciable slab of bona fide, only slightly rancid
meat. Unattended, unnoticed, suitable for immediate rat con-
sumption. Lester began to salivate. Well, to salivate *more.*

It was too crowded to go out there. But it was *meat.* And he
was so very, very hungry.

The bar at the Charles Hotel is not the kind of establishment
that is frequented by postcollegiate, indie-rock-and-vintage-
clothing, liberal-minded, somewhat unfocused youths. But it
seems appropriate on this night.

The room, a spacious yet cozy symphony of golds and browns,
is dimly lit and speaks unabashedly of *class.* Speaks a bit too
loudly of it, in fact—it seems to be the watering-hole equivalent
of a New Money couple trying too hard to be mistaken for Old
Money, a room very self-consciously at ease with its splendor.
Still, it's comfortable and quiet, and the overpriced drinks are
at least generously sized.

Johnny, Arlene, Grant, and Deborah are there because they're celebrating their escape. Or celebrating something else. Mainly, they had silently agreed to go somewhere that would contain absolutely no one they knew. They've found a comfortable table, they've ordered drinks, and somehow Johnny has snagged a box of those small red plastic swizzle sticks, which he's playing with as they talk.

They are having one of those earnest, open conversations that Johnny's been increasingly fond of lately—sharing their thoughts, dreams, desires, problems, and ambitions, each taking a turn, with very few humorous interruptions, going around and around the tiny table that holds their drinks. They're being particularly honest, partly because they're not really listening to themselves or one another.

Grant would like to fly a plane. Deb would like to skydive. Arlene would like to visit China. Johnny would like a sundae that always replenished itself so that it was never empty.

Arlene needs to stop thinking about herself all the time— self-awareness is killing her. Grant needs to say what he's thinking. Deb needs to find new strategies to avoid hurting people. Johnny needs to learn how to do magic.

Grant thinks the world can be completely fixed by erasing all religious and ethnic identities. Arlene favors complete and total disarmament (moments later, she recognizes the paradox of trying to enforce this, and she badly wants to take her answer back). Deb advocates the massive worldwide distribution of (good) food, (attractive, figure-flattering) clothing, and (airy, livable) shelter. Johnny doesn't understand the question.

Deb's ideal partner would never lose interest—obviously, she doesn't mean in *her*, just in general. Arlene's looking for perfect mutual admiration and an unfailingly cute ass. Grant . . .

needs to say what he's thinking. But doesn't. Johnny doesn't particularly care who the person is. Arlene hits him for this. Johnny likes that.

And so on. Grant notices that his martini is remaining very cold. Soon he sees that stuck at the bottom of the glass is a "Schrödinger's Humdinger," the giant molecule that Leonora had shown him. It is apparently keeping the drink cold. Grant wonders how that could possibly work.

Their discussion is lightening up a bit. Deb chafes her arms and mentions that the air-conditioning is turned up too high. Grant, breathing deeply, idly says, "I like it."

"Of course you do—it lets you see Deb's nips," says Arlene. At the moment she says this, Grant is indeed staring directly at Deb's blouse. He's busted, big-time, and somehow he's able to laugh along with everyone, raising his hand to acknowledge the foul. He takes in Deb's friendly wink, Johnny's helpless laughter, Arlene's happiness at having scored such a big point. The room is brighter, the overly serious air of their discussion dissipates, the conversation easily passes to a recapitulation of their Great Escape complete with embellishments, accusations, and insults, and everything is momentarily loud, kinetic, and hilarious.

Deb falls suddenly silent, a quizzical expression on her face, her head tilted to the side. When Grant and Arlene notice this, they follow her gaze to Johnny. In front of Johnny is a fantastic wire-frame figure he's idly constructed out of a few dozen swizzle sticks. It looks like a simple house, or maybe a church. But after a moment they begin to see the truly odd thing about it: The tiny straws don't appear to be threaded through one another. They just appear to be balanced.

Grant's first thought is that the swizzle sticks have been joined by melting the ends and sticking them together before they cooled. That's how he would've done it. But it doesn't look that way. Acting for Arlene and Deb, he slowly extends a finger toward the construct, just barely touching the north side of the miniature, elegant steeple. . . .

Instantly the church collapses, the sticks falling to the table as though they'd been hovering in thin air. A messy pile of swizzle sticks lies on the table in front of Johnny. Johnny giggles and raises his hand, as though *he's* been caught staring at somebody's nipples.

The others don't laugh. The room is suddenly cold again. The voices from other tables, the smell of food and smoke, the shadows that move around the room are all assaults from Outside, unwelcome reminders of how porous their little world is. They're suffused by the feeling of waking up too early in an unfamiliar house, hearing inchoate voices and activities downstairs, trying to get back to sleep, and knowing that it's impossible.

The President of Montana (hehe) couldn't believe the Bow and Arrow was still there.

Always an anomaly, the bar was somehow necessary to the life of Harvard Square. It was downscale to the extreme: a place that steadfastly refused to take on any piece of pretension or chic. A *bar* bar, a place to drink cheap beer, catch the game, play darts or pinball, or just watch an alcoholic in the corner pissing away what remained of his life. In short, a bar that would have been completely unremarkable almost anywhere else in the world.

It was full of bikers and locals, mainly. A few students who'd come to Boston without any desire to have their ideas about bars redefined. The universal rules of American bars applied here as nowhere else in the vicinity. As such, it made both components of the PoM(h), the Montana one and the recently reawakened youth, very comfortable.

He watched a silent broadcast of the news as he sat at the bar. The standoff back home did not appear to be making headlines anymore. The last time he'd seen the news (back in Elmira, New York, forty-eight hours ago), his rebellion was still a somewhat hot story. Had something happened? Had nothing happened? He felt a slight surge of relief—he'd've heard if there'd been a Waco, it'd still be a hot topic. And the lack of a story meant that nobody at this bar would see that photo of him they'd been using. Sure, it didn't look too much like him anymore, but it still had made him worry, and now he sank into a grateful feeling of deeper anonymity. Just an older man at a bar, having a drink, half watching the Red Sox cling desperately to first place as the inevitable fall fall approached . . . a guy nobody knows, soaking up the atmosphere and moving invisibly along . . . removed from the world of emotional and circumstantial attachments that turns a two-legged hairless ape into a storytelling drama machine . . .

"Earl?" said a voice to the President's left. "*Earl!?* Is that you?"

Act v Scene i—A tavern near the college

(*President, Muldower, Innkeeper*)

MULDOWER: Earl, I say. 'Tis thee, is't not? 'Pon my life! Gentle Earl!

PRESIDENT: No earl am I, good sir, but a man of common blood.

MULDOWER: Nay, sirrah; Earl thou art, and President, too.

PRESIDENT: Marry, sir, but 'tis a paradox! For the titles do conflict, blood and ballots, and thus offer proof of thy confusion.

MULDOWER: You make sport of me, sir.

PRESIDENT: And why not? If thou wouldst make an earl of me, then 'twould be impolite to make nothing of thee.

MULDOWER: Ah, I see it now, your wit doth serve as cover for your fear.

PRESIDENT: As your wig doth for your pate, sir. Though more subtly than that.

MULDOWER: Another barb! Could it be thou knowest me not? 'Tis I, good Earl!

PRESIDENT: Your visage has no twin in the catalogue of my thoughts, sir.

MULDOWER: Ah, but if thou searchest amidst catalogues, thou dost search aright, for 'twas 'twixt tomes that we did meet!

PRESIDENT: 'Twixt tomes? A curious phrase indeed, and cumbersome withal. Dost thou mean we met 'mongst books?

MULDOWER: Just so, m'lord. Though an age hath passed and cruel Time hath pinched our faces and stretched our middles, still I remember thee. For oft thou didst sing, "Hope I die afore I get old," and I with thee, and yet stand we here, those insolent bars blessedly unfulfilled.

PRESIDENT: Muldower? Gentle Muldower?

MULDOWER: Twice true, good sir, 'tis I.

PRESIDENT: Zounds! Twenty times has our blue sphere made full orbit round Apollo's bright bauble ere I saw thee last!

MULDOWER: More, m'lord, still more. How do you fare?

PRESIDENT: How do I fare? Fie! Thou knowest that from others, I'll warrant.

MULDOWER: Aye, there has been much said.

PRESIDENT: And more shall be said here. But stay! I'll buy ye a pot of ale and learn of thee as well. Innkeeper! Fetch this graying cur more of his meat, there's a good man. So how now, gentle Muldower? Whither hast thou traveled?

MULDOWER: Everywhere and nowhere, my good companion. For, though I have like a morning sprite skittered o'er dewdrops to greet all the world's dawns, always hath my compass led me here, to this place, where still I pore 'mongst the texts, though now the pupil hath become the master.

PRESIDENT: Thou teachest? I should have guessed it. Lectureth thou 'pon the high arts or the low law, noble Muldower?

MULDOWER: A law of sorts, if you will, though a high one. And small.

PRESIDENT: You speak in riddles.

MULDOWER: Precisely, thou hast it!

PRESIDENT: A lecturer in riddles, then?

MULDOWER: Verily, though the riddles be all of a kind.

PRESIDENT: In what sphere?

MULDOWER: That smallest of spheres, m'lord. The atom. For I have made of my days the study of that which is unseen, yet seen by all.

Through this tiniest of doorways have I sought entry into heaven, and have been rewarded with some small glimpses.

PRESIDENT: Thou lecturest upon physics! A scholar! Bravely done, good Muldower.

MULDOWER: Aye, 'tis a living and doth offer some rewards. Some most curious, in fact, if this very afternoon be counted 'mongst them.

PRESIDENT: What reward didst thou receive this day?

MULDOWER: A questionable one, my lord, and one which I am loath to speak of, for its providence be uncertain and passing strange.

PRESIDENT: Nay, shy thee not from the tale, friend. Though we have long been apart, mark you; we have trod the streets hand in hand, and together oft did suck smoke from Pan's other, unmusical pipe. Speak thee, I pray!

MULDOWER: I will tell thee, tho' a strange and sordid tale it be:
  This weekend day did dawn so bright and fair,
  And lacking work did I thus venture out
  'Pon that two-wheeled chariot so favored in these climes.
  Thus my day I spent in idle thought,
  And rested 'pon the grassy, sheltered lawns
  Where soon the urgent students shall return;
  They now lie richer for their fallowness.
  And there, with lids drawn o'er my weary eyes,
  Did I feel two eyes upon me on the Quad.
  And, gazing there toward this prickling feel,
  Did I behold the sight I now report:
  'Twas a woman, though not one known to me.
  She was clad in vile rags of garish hues,
  And her eyes alight with humors mad and strange.
  She did know me, I know not how this was
  (Though, certes, in certain circles I am known).

Her voice, cracked and agèd, called my name,
Which sounded on her lips too familiar
By half. No sooner had I met her eyes
Than did she hoist in hoary hands her filthy skirts
And reveal neither bloomer nor petticoat,
But the naked folded proof of womanhood
That 'twixt less ruined limbs would stir one's lust.
Then, waiting not for my reeling mind to unbend,
The cackling crone did crow and drop her skirts
And flee, vanishing like the very ghoul she seemed.

PRESIDENT: Gads, good sir! But what a tale thou hast told!

MULDOWER: Verily, my friend, would that it were the tale.

PRESIDENT: There is more to't?

MULDOWER: Aye, the tale's tail, though it wag the body with its import. And yet I am loath to speak of what I did see there betwixt her thighs.

PRESIDENT: Wherefore, good Muldower? Surely thou hast come this far—unburden thyself! What didst thou see there?

MULDOWER: Her nether hair, m'lord, or its lack, did disturb and puzzle me. For 'twas shavèd, m'lord, though not gone. Rather, it did present to the world . . . a shape, if this thou canst credit.

PRESIDENT: Gentle Muldower, though I have passed many moons in Montana's mundane milieu, am I not still a man of worldly knowledge? Shy thee not from 't! For e'en I have heard of "Cupid's Topiary," long favored by the decadent and fine. Come! What form did it take? A heart, mayhap? A devil's horns, perchance?

MULDOWER: No, m'lord, but stranger still.
For there upon the low-peak'd mount of Venus
Was there carved in detail beyond precedent

A spiral, lord, seemingly alive
And wound around another spiral still.
This twisting shape I'll guess you know is one
That we of science call the helix doubled,
That form 'pon which life's race is run,
And thus the sight did leave me pale and troubled.

PRESIDENT: A double helix, you say? How bravely done!

MULDOWER: And skillfully, good Earl! For the job could not have been easily done!

PRESIDENT: True, true.

MULDOWER: Why, e'en down as low as sight could see, still did the serpentine shape assert itself.

PRESIDENT: Thou shudderest, Muldower.

MULDOWER: And yet I am impressèd. And, yet again, confused. Her meaning, if there be one, doth escape me.

PRESIDENT: Lookest thou not at me, good friend, for I fathom this not. But this I know: We men do circle round women all our lives, and they round us. And yet Time moveth on, bearing us with it. And so are our circles never closed e'en as we make 'em, but instead describe that same spiral, doubled.

MULDOWER: Wisely said, m'lord, and graphable withal. Yet as devoid of apparent meaning as was e'er your wont.

PRESIDENT: Fie upon thee, knave! Ho-ho! But it is good to see thee! Innkeeper, why laggest thou? Seest thou not that we die of thirst?

INNKEEPER: 'Tis 'gainst my judgment. . . .

MULDOWER: Then keep thy judgment sealed along with thy lips, saucy servant! Serve on!

PRESIDENT: Well spoken, gentle friend!

MULDOWER: I thank thee. But what of thee, m'lord? Thou didst disappear from men's sight lo this sevenday, and are hunted by many, yet thou seemest well.

PRESIDENT: 'Tis true, 'tis true. For 'pon my escape 'twas as if my clouded mind, once fraught with fear and heavy suspicion, did clear like the sky after a March squall, and all that had seemed devilish and dire did lose its particular terror.

MULDOWER: How now, then? Hath our mutinous Montana man recanted?

PRESIDENT: E'en so. At the very fruition of my goals did it all seem a sudden folly, the rebellion 'gainst my rebellion a welcome one, and now my dearest wish is but for the safety of those unfortunates who didst follow my unlawful lead.

MULDOWER: Thy wish? Could it be that thou hast not heard?

PRESIDENT: Heard what, good friend? Is there news from the west? I pray thee, if thou knowest, speak!

MULDOWER: Why, 'twas a story of the greatest significance, sirrah, but a sunrise ago. 'Twas above the fold. Thou sawest not?

PRESIDENT: Nay, I have told thee, knave, for I have been in flight! Speak, I command it, speak! How fares my lady? Has dire calamity lowered its hand 'pon my flock? Speak!

MULDOWER: Gentle, my Lord, and I will tell thee as I heard it. . . .
　'Twas yesterday, when all seemed darkest for thy friends
　And the very wind did whisper "Waco" withal,
　That the doubled rebellion was of a sudden trebled,
　And your usurper did find himself alone.

PRESIDENT: Alone? What massacre led to that turn?

MULDOWER: Not a massacre, m'lord, but an exodus!
>For his unyielding resolve extended not
>Beyond his own hand, and your erstwhile
>Friends did beg surrender, yet he would not yield.
>Yesterday did dawn so clear and cool,
>And thy usurper Dix awoke alone
>To find no soul within your rough-made home.
>In darkness fled the throng he had commanded
>To find succor in the bosom of the law,
>All broken their rebellion and resolve,
>And happy yet, they seemèd, to the man.

PRESIDENT: The Lord be thanked for that. That blood was not spilt doth warm my thawing heart.

MULDOWER: Ah, would that this were true, m'lord.

PRESIDENT: How now? What transpired? Tell me, knave! How fares my lady?

MULDOWER: Gentle, good m'lord, for she lives. The blood that spilled was not hers. Rest, I shall inform thee:
>'Pon discovering betrayal in his ranks,
>And finding naught but shadows in his corps,
>Still Dix did not a swift surrender make.
>E'en still he held himself against the tide,
>And struggled there alone upon thy lands.
>E'en I, who loveth peace as much as breath,
>Was compelled to admiration for his stand.
>Full twenty minutes did he fire and fume
>'Midst gases that brought tears into his eyes
>And filled his lungs and stained the very air.
>Yet still held his bold resolve unbreaking,
>Till all at once through smoky air there came
>A whizzing missile fired from a gun.

It seemed the very arrow of fair Eros,
Yet with purpose dark and black intent
It pierced thy lieutenant's aching breast.
He teetered briefly, screaming 'gainst the smog,
And, falling then, he clattered to the ground.
So dying there his blood spread like a rose,
And thus brought thy rebellion to its close.

PRESIDENT: Ah, fair Dix, I did love thee once. Foul was the day that thou didst come under my sway, for it did bring thy downfall.

MULDOWER: E'en still, good Earl? For did he not depose you?

PRESIDENT: Aye, but washèd was his brain from my declamations, and his bullish mind once set 'pon a course did lack the sense to turn aside. Fell were his deeds, and fevered was his angry brow, yet do I regret his demise.

MULDOWER: And yet thou livest, m'lord, as do thy friends and thy fair mistress. Keep this glad news close to thy breast.

PRESIDENT: This I will—and in that vein—ye gods! Look upon the hour! I must away!

MULDOWER: Away? 'Tis early yet, old friend. Come, drink ye more, for 'tis the Hour of Happiness, and small silver will it cost thee to imbibe.

PRESIDENT: There will yet be time for such a night, gentle Muldower. But this night, with thy news, has been renewed, and so must I away to see its close.

MULDOWER: Then take thee my card, and wait thou whilst I gather my effects; I'll walk with thee awhile.

PRESIDENT: I thank thee, kind friend, let us away, and afore our parting will we many things exchange, names, numbers, and notions, so that future congress will not rely on chance. Come, gentle friend! For though we age there may yet be deeds ahead. The moon be old itself, and so smileth 'pon the agèd, and smoothest e'en the most furrowed countenance. Come! For live we yet!

MULDOWER: Lead on, lord. I'll follow awhile.

[*Exeunt*]

Chapter 13

JOHNNY'S STARTING TO FEEL lighter and lighter. He's playing with things now, seeing how far things will stretch around him. Everything feels warm and semisolid, like he's moving through a dry liquid. Colors radiate from everything, reminding him of particularly good acid trips. He's been speaking less and less. There are no words for the things he can see and hear, which makes language a little confusing and inadequate.

He's leaving the Charles Hotel now with his friends, aware that he kind of freaked them out with that swizzle-stick thing. He didn't mean to. It makes the gulf that's growing between them even wider. This isn't what Johnny wants, and he resolves to keep himself from doing those kinds of things again. At least not in plain view.

Idly, as they walk out the door, Johnny considers the ground beneath his feet, notices how much air is displaced by each step, wonders if that displacement could be prevented . . . thinks indescribable things . . . and decides, yes, it could be done, perhaps like *this*. Carefully, subtly now, so as not to freak out his friends, Johnny arranges things so that the displacement isn't total. A quarter of an inch or so beneath the shoes . . . no more . . . It seems to work!

His feet don't quite touch the ground, and he smiles broadly, secretly enjoying the spongy feeling of his strides, tinkering with the resistance and resiliency . . . finding ways to make this easier on his legs and back as well, creating unseen cushions and massaging tendrils all around him. . . .

"John-man, what is it?" comes a voice, slightly muffled until Johnny thinks to thin the atmosphere around his ears (hadn't thought of *that* . . .). It's Grant, still a little freaked but obviously happy to see Johnny's grin. If Grant has noticed that Johnny is now a quarter of an inch taller, he doesn't let on. Johnny's thrilled to be singled out for conversation, no less so for his difficulty with words, thrilled to see Grant (as though he'd been gone for weeks), just thrilled in general.

"I'm walkin' on air, Grant-man," he says, "just walkin' on air." Grant smiles, and Johnny giggles uncontrollably at the perfect (if lonely) joke.

Dear Diary,

Another beautiful sunset. Bibu would've loved it. It sounds nuts to say what a baby would've loved, but I __am__ nuts, and I know.

Walking by all the dorms is always a stroll down memory lane. How many girls can say that they've turned tricks at their own alma mater? Very few, I'd guess. Two lives—three now, if you think about it—all in the same place. I walk by a building and there's three sets of memories. For instance, "Hey, that's where I [studied organic chemistry / took it doggy-style from a terrified freshman on his birthday / snuck in for a muffin last Thursday]!" All of the above were difficult and rewarding in their own ways, by the way.

So now I'm sitting by the river (not __too__ close, mind you, not anymore, not ever again), playing with one of these trendy giant

molecules someone left behind. Damned if the thing doesn't vi-
brate just a little. Should it do that? Maybe I'll keep it in my
panties. Ha!

Been ridin' fifty-eight hours straight now, man and boy, up
the ramps, down the innerstates. Buzzin' like a beehive. Goddamn radio show won't take my calls anymore, and everyone
calling in is a fucking idiot anyway. I should just listen to the
music anyway, get me movin' a little bit in the seat for the next
hour or so, so I can make the dropoff and then the pickup and
then just park it and get some goddamn sleep. Lessee . . . talk,
talk, Latin shit, talk, rap . . . *There* it is—*Workin' for the man*
evry night an' day. . . .

Got nuthin' but buzz and road now, right down to th' mcgin-
lies. *A big wheel keeps on binin', Proud Mary keeps on tinin'.* . . .
Shit, but why the hell din't I stop at the Arby's? Coulda had a
road beef n' maybe used a men's room 'stead of the goddamn
Coke bottle. Coulda got a little somethin' with extra jaspers on
my collup. . . .

WHOA! Almost lost it there, fell asleep, yes I did. Gotta
admit it, keep me sharp, keep on truckin' . . . Where the hell is
495? I passed it, maybe. Fuck. Same song, though; I'm okay.
Rollin', rollin', rollin' onna rivuh . . . Okay, no big, 95's as good,
just take 95, or maybe skip that and come straight in on 90, why
not. Past the bowlin' alley with the fagpins they like up here, go
straight as piss into the migilicuddy.

Got some kinda dagnab makin' my bungleys itch somethin'
awful. . . . Don't scratch! Don't scratch. *Rollin' rollin'* . . . Itchin's
my friend, itchin's gonna keep me sharp, itchin' away as I cruise
inta the heart of the goddamn . . .

Boston, godfuckingdamnit. Worst goddamn streets I ever except for Frisco, with all the steep bullshit making the brakes get all frungy. And that crappy Super 8 or 6 or something, with no shower curtain and the radiator spusterin' like a lungshot deer—

WHOA! Back in the game, bro! Stay with it! Never shoulda scratched that thing. Where th'—? Missed 95, no doubt there, but I guess 90's what the good Lord wanted for me. *Gotta be a juke. Box. Hero. Got scars in his size.* . . . Straight down 90, right down the chute, no fuss, no muss, and damn th' tortillas, like they say. . . .

"God died a cartoon death, you know."

Dr. Schrödinger, we noticed, had taken to introducing topics as though composing a tabloid headline or providing catchy buzz-phrases for a movie preview. He was also, we observed, knee-deep in his several desserts.

"Look, God cheerfully led us to science, right past the cliff's edge of his own plausibility. Then, sometime in the middle of the nineteenth century, he looked down, saw he was standing on empty air, did one last double take to the camera, and plummeted to his death. If there ever was a *deus ex machina*, the *machina* was built by the ACME Corporation."

We were entertained, but a little unnerved. What had happened to Dr. Schrödinger, who now seemed a hip avatar of mod science? Was it Dori? Was it the pressure of the success of his Cat that finally turned him into the raconteur we all wanted? He was still, in some ways, a pedantic and occasionally gross old man. But more often than not, he now seemed increasingly urbane. Obnoxiously so, we thought.

"There was a sweet spot, you know. Back about a hundred years, after God had walked the plank but before Planck had walked all over us—ha-ha. We'd briefly, beautifully eliminated the unknowable and incomprehensible. And people would've been much happier if we'd kept it that way. That's what we want. People want electrons to orbit atoms like tiny planets, hard and regular. They make *sense* that way. People like that— they don't want their electrons to exist only as a cloud of poten- tialities. But that's what we've got now, and we're stuck with it. Quantum mechanics isn't going to roll over and die as easily as God did."

The old doctor was obviously enjoying himself, unaccount- ably amused at mankind's spiritual dead end. He ran one long finger through the patterned syrup that had adorned the plate for his Black Forest cake.

"So, yes, as people like to say, we can consider ourselves the end product of history. But you have to bear in mind that his- tory is more or less a digestive tract."

Ugh.

Lester the Rat watched the meat. It was now definite in Lester's mind that it *was* meat. No doubt about it. Now Lester prepared himself to go and get it, all his senses extended toward the meat and the space between it and his ratty presence.

It seemed safe. Yes, there were large moving objects semi- nearby, but they were cars, not predators (not that Lester could have told you what a car was, but they'd never gone out of their way to eat him). There were humans around, but not always near the meat—there would be opportunities. There was also a bird.

The bird, a sparrow, was out a bit late. It would be useless to name the bird or try to get too deeply into its thoughts, since birds have even less going on upstairs than rats do. Suffice it to say that this bird had discovered that the meat in the gutter had a small but significant quantity of bread attached to it and had been picking away at it as the sun set. Hungry birds sometimes stay out late, one might suppose. Or perhaps this particular sparrow was a bit of a night person, as it were. For whatever reason, the bird was there. On the meat.

Lester was not above trying to eat the bird, but that wasn't Plan A. Plan A was simply to scuttle over to the meat and eat it. Frightening the bird away from the quarry would be good enough.

And so Lester watched, waiting for the opening. And suddenly, with the passing of a lone pedestrian, the time had come.

On a street in Cambridge, just after sunset, a furry gray shape in the gutter suddenly leapt to life and began to dash furtively along the curb.

The President of Montana (Just Call Me "Earl") was alone again, walking aimlessly, his head a riot of emotions. He was elated (*Tammy's alive!*), concerned (*Tammy might've been arrested!*), hopeful (*Tammy might be on her way here!*), melancholy (*Dix is dead*), and touched (*Muldower is still my friend*).

After walking Muldower to his enviable Victorian house, the PoM(JCM"E") found himself wondering if he (the President) actually had any backbone at all. Sure, he'd been a natural "leader" all his life, but his convictions seemed . . . *environmental* in origin. He'd been a left-leaning activist years ago here in Boston, found himself increasingly conservative and isolationist in Butte, and had become a bit of a fanatical conspiracymonger once he'd moved back to the sticks. And now that he was back in Boston, here was all the dewy-eyed humanism he'd left behind, as though it'd been waiting here for him like an eternally patient Irish setter. All these serial belief systems had *felt* real, but the President couldn't completely discount the idea that he was a bit of a windsock, ideology-wise. Perhaps, he thought, he ought to stop being so *convinced* about things for a while, though it'd be a hard habit to quit cold turkey after all these years.

Right now, all he wanted was Tammy. He knew that even if she was free there was a strong possibility that she was being tailed by spooks who would arrest him the minute he showed his face. Or maybe not—he didn't really have enough information as to where he stood, law-enforcement-wise. Either way, he was going to go to the appointed place and hope Tammy was there, with or without the Law. He was tired, he missed his wife, he was eager to find out what was next, whatever it might be.

The little park was just a block away, just a tiny little path-and-bench-strewn green place on JFK, not far from the center of the Square. The President checked his watch: ten minutes now.

From fifty yards away, the park was heartbreaking. If Tammy didn't show up, he realized, he could happily spend the whole night there, just sitting on a bench and recalling the twenty-one-year-old girl he'd sat there with, the one who'd made his stomach ache, the one he'd married and dragged out to the middle of nowhere.

She wasn't there yet, as far as he could tell. But he was still across the street and couldn't see too well in the lamplight. In ten minutes (seven now) he'd know.

. . . 3. And so the Prophet Bernie did come to the Place of the Crossing, and saw the people there, yet he did not cross. 4. For the Lord had said unto Bernie, "Bernie, when thou dost come to the Place, thou shalt not cross until thou seest the Sign." 5. And Bernie had replied, "Lord, what is this Sign of which Thou speakest? Dost Thou mean 'Walk' and 'Don't Walk'?" 6. And the Lord had answered, saying, "Nay, Bernie! Would the Lord your God be so small? Thinkest thou that I concern Myself with foot traffic? Hast thou ever known Me to *literally* post a sign?" And Bernie was ashamed, and begged the Lord's pardon, and thought it best not to mention that "MENE, MENE, TEKEL" business from the book of Daniel, and rather abased himself until the Lord did cut short Bernie's mumblings, saying, "Cease thine endless apologies, Bernie, for thou talkest too much! Go as I have commanded thee, and seek ye the Sign." 7. And so it was that Bernie had come to the Place of the Crossing. And there at the Place of the Crossing Bernie did stand, and did not cross, for he saw not the Sign. 8. And the Prophet Bernie wondered again what the Sign might be, yet he did not cry out to the Lord, for he was acting in accordance with the Lord's command, and besides, the Lord had been Curt and Pissy of late. 9. And so the Prophet there stood as the night fell upon him, and yet he did not move, saving only for his hand, with which he did beg for alms of the people there, as the Lord had commanded.

Leonora Decaté rose, shrugging on the blue policeman's shirt that lay at the foot of the bed. It came down past her knees. She went to the window and saw that her nap had turned the day into night. She felt abruptly disconnected from time—it could have been anytime between sunset and sunrise.

She'd been napping because Officer Jack Kennedy was possibly going to drop by after his shift. Or was that his "rounds," or his "patrol"? She wasn't sure.

Leonora briefly considered that he was, of course, too young for her, reminded herself that she was not the sort of person who thought of such things, and felt her well-tempered self-image click back into place with a satisfying and secure thud. This wasn't self-deception, just the mental calisthenics of a woman who knew in her bones that personality was a construct and was careful to construct her own creatively. She liked Jack, liked his sturdiness, his sweet interior, his muscular frame, and his obvious good taste in women. Not to mention the cachet that dating a younger man (and a *cop* at that!) brought her within her circle of staid but admiring fellow faculty members, the way it shored up her already invincible reputation as a remarkably active, wild, exciting, eccentric scholar. Leonora was not so shallow as to think that such shallow satisfactions didn't matter.

That she wasn't "in love" with Jack, that she didn't think the relationship would last any longer than had the past few, that he'd eventually abandon this adventure and opt for a younger and more suitable mate, that she wasn't any closer to finding true companionship—these all seemed like positives to Leonora. What good would it do to go through all *that* again?

Outside, the lingering gang of children was still making noise, and she realized with some annoyance that this was what had woken her from her nap. She thought of the shotgun in the basement, and she smiled broadly at the image of *her* standing on the porch and brandishing it, dispelling the crowd. What a story *that* would make at the dining hall tomorrow!

Leonora padded out of the room and down the stairs. She thought of her peculiar grandson, the assembled throng, the warm evening, and she found herself filled with immense gratitude as she reached for the basement door. . . .

———

Deborah Johnstone is walking silently next to Johnny, idly listening to Grant and Arlene, enjoying the warm evening. Johnny seems taller, she thinks in passing.

Her head is filled with pleasant things: the faint blur of alcohol, the nearness of friends, the beauty of the Square, the breath in her lungs. There's also an undeniable buzzing—something is afoot. It may be Johnny, or Grant, or both, but there's that feeling of things in flux. The air itself is humid, breezy, warm, crackling. Anyone with even the faintest sensitivity could tell you that there is a thunderstorm coming. Deb has known it for hours and is hoping it will break while the four of them are walking.

You have noted that Deb is happier, prettier, better adjusted, and more joyful than yourself. You have, perhaps, speculated that there is a darker underside to this, that no one can sustain such ongoing bliss in an imperfect and ever-changing universe. You suspect that events will lay her low, or that her state of grace will come to a crashing end. You likely do not believe that happiness, true and nondeluded happiness, is sustainable at these levels over the long haul. Perhaps Deb feels like a fictional construct to you, or an exaggeration seen through the eyes of an adoring Grant, a Platonic ideal only dimly seen as a shadow in the real world. In short, you don't buy it.

You do, however, believe in chronic *depression*. Don't you?

So, whether you like it or not, believe it or not, Deb is moving through the thickening air in her state of perpetual and vastly unfair grace. Storms, both actual and metaphorical, are brewing all around her—a vast and improbable mechanism has assembled itself and is rattling to life, the winds will rise, thunder will crack, lives will be made and ruined and lost and found, and everything that we are concerned with will change, includ-

ing the life of one Deborah Johnstone, which will be shaken
and altered along with everything else.

But, really, don't waste your worries on her—plenty of others
need you much more. She'd tell you that herself, if you existed
as anything other than an imagined observer.

Chapter 14

LIKE A GRAY DART, like a windblown cloud, like a tiny, hairy tumbleweed, Lester the Rat is streaking toward his goal. His movements are alarmingly swift and smooth, like a spider on a bedspread. He's meatward bound, full speed ahead, and damn the torpedoes.

Lester is moving, closing distance, completely focused. He's within two feet of the generous morsel when the bird that's been pecking away at it notices him. It startles, leaps, panics. By the time Lester has actually reached his goal, the bird is airborne, fleeing, frantic. Lester descends on the rapidly decaying prize, grabs it in his pointy yellow teeth, jerks his head upward to lift it off the ground.

By this time, though he of course doesn't know it, Lester is no longer strictly part of our story. He has served his purpose. He's done, as far as we're concerned—his necessary though inscrutable task fulfilled. Of course he's not *dead*, nor has he done anything extraordinary in and of itself. But he's not our concern anymore, and it would be kind of strange for you to continue to worry about him—after all, he's just a *rat*.

In case you're interested, however, this is what happens next: Lester wolfs down the meat, turns, and runs back to the sewer grate, still chewing. He pauses there a moment, sniffing the air, and then vanishes into the underworld. There, slightly less ravenous than before, he sets out to retrace his steps toward more familiar territory.

His name is no longer "Lester." It never was, really.

"I'm afraid I'll be leaving soon," said Dr. Schrödinger as we strolled out of the restaurant. "I have to be going."

He obviously wanted us to voice some sort of objection to this. And, as unthinkable as it might have seemed a few days before, we were somewhat inclined to do so. Still, the thought of reclaiming our living room and getting a break from his increasingly personal remarks was appealing, so we only inquired casually about the nature of his obligations.

"No obligations, per se. Not at all. It's only that I can no longer stay here, that's all. I've been observed as matter, but now I must 'wave' goodbye—ha-ha-ha." It was a lame joke, but we smiled politely. The old physicist had seated himself on a bench in the little park that abutted the restaurant. He patted the bench next to him invitingly, his eyebrows raised in an expression of such fervent hope that we had to laugh and join him. "You'll have to take care of Werner, of course." Werner, his cat. His *actual* cat, who dwelt somewhere within our house. We told him that we didn't have the foggiest idea how to even *find* Werner.

He sighed deeply. "The life of a scientist is not easy, is it?" he asked, presumably rhetorically. "We find ourselves so enrapt by our studies that we hardly notice the Byzantine structures our psyches are constructing in the meantime. Frustrated by the lack of daily attention, our personalities twist and turn themselves like forest trees straining toward the sunlight. So, if something goes wrong and we suddenly *have* to pay attention to our lives, the most bizarre things can occur."

We were not sure why he was saying this, though he seemed to have a very specific thing in mind. We were more than a little worried that some ghastly and distasteful confession was forthcoming from the old man. Perhaps, though, he was merely saying that scientists were crazy.

"Scientists are crazy, is what I'm saying," he went on, "and that craziness often comes in the form of self-neglect. A failure to build and maintain a connection with oneself and one's social life. But the personal side of a person can't be denied, and it will grow and change and mutate, whether noticed or not. Hence the bizarre delusions, the psychotic breaks, the absurd yet sometimes therapeutic neuroses. They're not necessarily bad—sometimes they crop up to get us through difficulties, trauma-induced. But they're just stopgap measures really."

The "Wise Old Man" look on his face combined with his ever-more-direct glances had become infuriating—he was clearly not about to confess something about *himself*. We were livid, suddenly, and we demanded that the doctor either come right out and say what was on his mind or leave *immediately*. He remained calm, the very picture of the emotional detachment he was just prattling on about.

"As I said, I will leave quite soon," he said quietly, "but let me ask you one deceptively simple question, if I may." He cleared his throat. "When I get up from this bench and leave, how many people will remain? Count carefully, mind you. Who will be here?"

With that, he turned to face forward, gazing out into the park and the street beyond. We could not for the life of us understand what he was talking about. What kind of airy-fairy question was that? Did he expect an answer? What did this have to do with physics, anyway?

We, too, stared into the middle distance, fuming, determined not to answer the old coot, who didn't seem to mind.

The bird, startled beyond sense, took off and fled in a state of panic.

As we said, it was out rather late for a sparrow. It was, therefore, immediately confronted with the night sky and headlights and lamps and all sorts of things that it generally preferred not to encounter. Not only that, it was as near to hysterical as a tiny bird's brain can become; the sight of a rat suddenly appearing out of nowhere in the lamplight a mere few inches from its beak—it was too much.

So it flew erratically, trying to stay high enough to avoid the rat, low enough to have some sort of bearing on its position. It crested a building (vaguely familiar), swept down into an area with some trees (though not its own personal tree), thought it saw a shadow moving, swooped back up through the branches of the tree toward the black night sky.

It's only natural, then, that the agitated sparrow did not notice that the particular gap in the branches it flew into wasn't a "gap" per se, but a black plastic bag that had been caught there.

Like a game-winning hockey puck, the bird found the small aperture of the bag and flew directly inside; the bag detached itself from the branch; the bird, now thoroughly panicked, desperately tried to get away from the strange substance that surrounded it.

It was a losing cause for the bird. The airborne bag zigzagged crazily, contracted around its prisoner, lost altitude, and then abruptly collided with a street sign, which further accelerated its descent to the pavement.

There, in the middle of the road, the bag lay, fluttering slightly, not more than ten yards from where a few seconds before there had been a piece of meat, the bird itself, and a very sudden rat.

"Maybe it's just my brain trying to protect itself from possible rejection, you know? But that doesn't really make sense, does it? I mean, it would explain me dreaming that Johnny was all dead and bloody on the bed, but what about the fire thing? I was *awake* there, Grant. And, besides, that was before we'd done anything. I mean, maybe I'd been picking up that it was *going* to happen or something, but that'd be one overactive defense mechanism, wouldn't it? I guess what you said yesterday could be it—you know, I've been so upset about Furble that I've been repressing it, and it's been coming out in all kinds of weird ways—but I don't think I've really been repressing it, you know. What with all the crying and talking about it and thinking about it, I'd say that I've pretty much begun the grieving process in a proactive, healthy way, right? And there's no denying that Johnny's been weird, right? I mean, it's not that bizarre to want to sleep with me, I guess—shut up, don't even . . . But the other stuff, you know? He's just been weird, we all know that, right? And there's been other weird stuff, too, stuff that only I'd know that I *definitely* won't get into. . . . I know this sounds classic, and now that I've slept with him I'm even more totally unreliable, but there's something *wrong*, isn't there? I mean, it's not like I'm asking you if he's said anything about me, because that would be, like, pathetically girly, and it's not the point. Though of course, if he *has* said anything about me, you'd tell me, right? Just kidding. No I'm not. No, really, this isn't an obsessive-girlfriend thing; Christ, it's not even like I'm his *girlfriend*. I know *that*. It's not about that. So, you know, what *is* this about?"

"I'm not sure. I think I'll just have to wait to read your short story when it comes out."

"You suck."

"Make me handsome, okay?"

"You'll be a retarded circus clown."

"That works for me."

. . . 18. And, abiding there, the Prophet Bernie did begin to think that the Lord had once more beset him with a Practical Joke, though He had promised never again to behave thusly. 19. All at once, Bernie beheld a wonder, and he repented having questioned the Lord. 20. For from the heavens there did fall a black sack, which did plummet from the sky and fall through the air, and did come to rest in the center of the Crossing. And the people there were amazed, for they had heeded Bernie not. 21. And the Prophet Bernie did say unto them, "Behold! For it is as I have told thee. The Lord has produced a sign, and thus has the Time of the Crossing arrived!" And the people beheld in wonder as Bernie strode forth into the Crossing, and they were amazed, and they shouted at him, "Beware! For, though thou hast foretold aright, the light doth flash that thou shouldst not walk!" But Bernie heeded them not, and set out upon the Crossing. 22. And Bernie did come to the Center of the Crossing, and there beheld a wonder. For lo! The sack which had fallen from the heavens did move, though the wind bleweth not! And Bernie did bend there in the Crossing, and did apply his eye to the wondrous sack. 23. And the Prophet Bernie beheld that within the sack there was entangled a small bird of the sky, whose wings were fouled 'midst the folds of the sack. 24. And the Prophet Bernie did cry out to the Lord in thanks, saying, "Lord, I thank Thee, for Thou hast made to me my purpose clear, and here in the Crossing shall I free this creature, or sacrifice it to Thee as Abraham did the ram in the place of his son, whichever that Thou dost require of me." And the Lord did not then reply to Bernie, but left him to decide the matter unto himself, which was indeed the Sort of Thing the Lord was wont to do to Bernie from time to time. 25. And so the Prophet Bernie knelt there in the crossing and set about the freeing of the bird of the sky. 26. And as Bernie knelt, the strange talisman that had been his gift did fall from his pocket and rolled from his side, yet Bernie heeded it not. 27. And so rapt was he in the Lord's task that he saw not the changing of the lights. . . .

himme with yer best shot! Why doncha himme with yer best shot. . . .

Damn the goddamn red lights round here! Got nothin' left from the six of Mountain Dew and no more pinks or blues, neither, just a man and his machine, stop and startin' all the way through. Two fuckin' miles on the map, but I'll be sittin' here till my kebabs rot, 'cuz I missed that frickin' turnoff. Good thing I got all kindsa grit, only a pro could see this one out, no doubt, no bout. "Bout?" Dunno what I'm sayin' there. . . .

WHOA! Who's honkin'? Fuck you! Oh. Green light. Musta taken a quick one there, twenny winks at most, no biggie. Okay, back on it. Man in motion. Pedal to metal. Oh, man—Zep! *When she gets there she knows, if the store's hours are closed, with a word . . .*

Lookit all these kids. Damn good-lookin', some of 'em. "College girls," like on the Innernet. Or is that one a boy? Goddamn blurry. *An she's buy-eye-ing a stairway to hea-eh-vun. . . .* Ivy

League girls, they know all about it. Not that I could get anywhere near 'em now, not with the beer gut and the lines and the weird-ass mcgumly on my neck n' all. . . .

If they're a-bustlin' yer hedgehog, don't be alone now, it's just a sprinklin' for ol' Nadine. . . . Hey! Another green light! That never happens here. Good karma, like the hippie kids say. Right through the center of the square, though there's nothin' square about it. Pedal to th' metal! Might be at the drop before nine now, straight as nun piss over the river and along the whatever, I'll know it when I see it. Kinda sad to be leavin' all the college girls—best view in Beantown. "Beantown"—why the hell? Oh yeah, the baked beans—

SHIT! Who's that?! Get outa the road! It's *green,* ferchrissakes! Brake! Brake! Turn it! Can't stop this fast—not my fault—he's just standin' there—not gonna hit him—gonna go off the fuckin' road!—Right inta the park—can't stop—FUCK! What's that bump?—kids!—outa the way!—Move!—Can't stop!—'Slike slo-motion—M'I gonna die?—Look out!—SHIT! SHIT!! SHIIIIIT!!!

. . . *An' she's buy-eye-ing a stair-air-way to heh-vun.* . . .

Johnny Felix Decaté was glad that Deb didn't want to talk. He was discovering things at an unbelievable pace, things that were obvious yet always hidden from him, things he could do or not do.

For instance, he realized as they walked through the tiny park on their way to still more ice cream, he could stop his own heart. Just for a second or else it hurt, but he could do it. Johnny looked into and through things, right down to the small parts. He could see light moving like liquid, and he could slow it down if he wanted to, and it all made a kind of obvious sense that it never had before. Like what he'd done when he was on fire, but now he understood *how.*

It was all incredibly, complicatedly simple. And beautiful.

He saw that he now could fix a broken bone with a touch. He saw that in time, with the right couple of adjustments, he could learn to see through women's clothing, which was something he'd always wanted to do as a kid. He could make plants grow faster. He could— Well, it was easier to consider what he *couldn't* do, because the list of "could"s was suddenly far too big to conceive of. He understood the question now: He could, he realized all at once, fix the world in ways he'd always dreamed of doing.

And almost immediately he decided not to do anything.

Because, once his hands were off something, it would continue about its business, doing whatever it did, with no way for Johnny to know whether he'd made things better or worse. It was all too deeply interconnected—he could *see* the . . . *strands* of everything, some sort of ghostly strands, reaching out of things and into things and winding around other things. And he was part of it. When he moved his arm, a thousand million of the milky, translucent tendrils were tugged and pulled along with it, and they in turn pulled at others, each action reverberating endlessly through a tightly woven web. . . .

No. Best just to breathe and move and try not to disturb things too much. He wanted to see how one strand pulled on another, how it all worked together, and he became aware that he couldn't do that unless he was very, very still—more still than he'd ever been—so that he didn't disturb the patterns he was trying to watch. *That,* he decided, would be his new hobby. Watching and understanding the pattern of things.

Part of that pattern, he saw with a start, was a big truck that had swerved out of its lane and was now heading for him and Deb and the old lady behind Deb and the tree behind her, which would be strong enough to stop the truck. Johnny saw the truck try to right itself, saw its course made inevitable by its front tire's almost imperceptible slide upon an unnaturally large molecule underneath its tread, saw what now must necessarily happen. Grant and Arlene were safe, because, ironically enough, Arlene had shoved Grant playfully, and they were now a little ways out into the street. But he and Deb were directly in the truck's path, him first, then Deb, etc.

The face of the truck's driver, over the headlights, was gorgeous. Johnny saw the look of panic and fear, and he wished there was time to explain to the man that it was okay, that the accident was so inevitable as to make the word "accident" meaningless, that everything would work out. He also wished that it wasn't happening, because he had just made plans to sit very still and watch everything and figure it out, and now there wouldn't be enough time. This was somewhat frustrating, if inevitable.

Moments before the truck reached him, a second or so really, Johnny realized that he could in fact stop the truck before it hit them. Instantaneously. He saw that he could do it, and then cradle the driver in a cushion of slightly hardened air, and prevent any of them from getting hurt at all. He saw, with just an instant left, how he could do this. There were good reasons to do it, and no reason *not* to, he thought.

Until he saw what was going to be the first thing to hit him. There on the truck's front end, on a collision course with his abdomen, a frayed black bumper sticker with yellow block letters bearing a familiar and ageless message: SHIT HAPPENS.

Yes, thought Johnny Felix Decaté as his lips began a movement that would never get the chance to become an actual smile. *That's about right.*

The President of Montana (Oh, Get Over It Already) was watching the park, getting ready to cross the street, when he heard the screech of tires next to him. He turned and saw a massive tractor-trailer turning and braking at once, trying to avoid something in the crosswalk. It sped by him, decelerating, not moving fast enough to jackknife but not slow enough to stop in time.

The PoM(OGOIA) turned to watch the truck slide across the intersection, heading right for the park. It was barreling down on some *people*, the President realized. Just before the bulk of the truck cut off his view, the President identified the potential victims as a young man, a young woman, and someone who might very well be—

—Tammy.

By the time the truck collided with the tree, the President was already dashing across the street, his head filled with a cold, nutrient-free liquid that felt nothing at all like blood.

Grant was closer than that, and had a better view than anyone. He saw the old bum kneel in the street, saw the truck bearing down on him, saw it swerve first, brake second, and then straighten out just in time to head directly at Johnny and Deb and some old lady behind them.

Everything about Grant that was rational knew that there would be no time for him to do anything. Still, his legs were moving, his eyes focused on Deb. By the time he saw *her* eyes widen as she took in the fact of what was about to happen, he realized that the best he could hope for was to reach her just in time to get killed with her. Still, he was running, propelled toward her on legs that didn't exactly feel like his own. By the time that there was no time left at all, he was off the ground, leaping toward Deb, taking in the old woman behind her, reaching out across a space that was just too wide, but then, suddenly, feeling contact—

There was an impact, and a noise so loud that it sounded very faint in his ears.

At just about that precise moment, Leonora Decaté opened the basement door, flicked on the light switch with an automatic motion, looked down at the bottom of the stairway, and screamed.

The sparrow, startled back to awareness by the sudden noise, found its wings free and launched itself skyward from the man's hand, flapping exultantly through the night air, over the loud and incomprehensible scene below it, above the treacherous treetops, toward home. It did not look back, not once, mainly because birds never do.

Chapter 15

Dear Diary,

That's why the robots had cleared out for the evening—the whole Square reeked of humanity. Crazy, clumsy, random humanity. It smelled good. It had been a while. Gives a girl some hope.

Bernie was just sitting there in the street with a dazed look on his face. I heaved him up to his feet and he came to, more or less. Bernie's always like this when he's done doin' some "task for the Lord." He kinda takes a day or two to reset. I guess the Lord really takes it out of him. But who am I to talk?

Bernie needed to get back to Central Square. Took me an hour to drag him through the downpour, but it was okay. Speaking of crazy, some kid threw himself in front of the truck that Bernie diverted at the last second, trying to save his girlfriend or something. Heroic, maybe. Stupid, definitely. Now:

1650—French comedy duo La Fontanelle & Claude finally retire their literary alter ego "René Descartes," bringing to an end their most elaborate prank. Inscrutably, young Louis IV orders all record of La Fontanelle & Claude destroyed, which pretty much removes all the fun irony from some of their best stuff.

1659—Aurangzeb, last of the Mogul emperors, starts more trouble with the Hindus and confiscates a lot of their valuables, this time mostly to fund an early production of "No, No, Nanette."

216 · Adam Felber

He suspects, correctly, that this will come back to bite him on the ass.

1666—The final remnants of the Australian Empire launch a last-ditch full-scale assault on London and are wiped out in the ensuing holocaust.

America is filling up with white people, which forces the Atlanteans to impersonate Native Americans, whom they'd conquered and wiped out only a few decades before. It's all pretty awkward for everybody.

1676—Nuar Fazib al Bernstein, the famous Turkish courtesan and inventor, loses her first and only child to a nursery accident. Burying herself in her work, she builds the world's first fully autonomous self-replicating robot, the Mark 1, and the modern world is born.

Grant opened his eyes and saw that he was in heaven.

Heaven was a place where the grass was soft, where a warm, clean rain fell, and where—most important—he was eternally embracing Deborah Johnstone.

And some old lady.

It was the old lady's presence that made Grant suspect that this was not the afterlife (which he'd never actually believed in, anyway). He lifted his left arm so that the stranger could roll away while he replayed the events of the past few moments.

He'd jumped in front of the truck. Arms outstretched. He'd reached for Deb. At the last moment, he'd widened his arms to encompass the terrified old lady (not that old, really) and let his momentum knock them all to the grass. He wasn't sure how he'd managed to make that decision in such a short time, but he'd done it. So, if his memory was accurate, there'd be a park around them and a crashed truck very nearby.

He looked up. It checked out.

Strangely calm, he returned his attention to Deb beneath him. She, too, had been looking around and was now returning to the body on top of her.

"You . . . It . . . *Wow*, Grant."

"Yeah," said Grant, just as the calm he was feeling turned out to be an extraordinarily short-lived stage in his state of shock. He began to shake. He looked at Deb beneath him, alive, unhurt, beautiful as ever. Grant couldn't believe it—there, laid out beneath him, perfect, complete, was Deborah Johnstone, the Undiscovered Country. He fought a sudden feeling of déjà vu BUT HE COULDN'T REMEMBER WHY [BK SYS OP 311117]. His eyes blurred.

"Are you all right?" she asked him.

"I'm—I'm . . ." he said eloquently. He then found that he didn't have the strength for self-censorship at the moment. "I love you," he said, nullifying six months of careful footwork and ineffectual strategizing. And because he'd *blown* it now, he kissed her. Her lips were as pillowy soft as he'd imagined so often, but the difference between the thought and the deed was startling.

The rain, warm and soft, began to fall more steadily.

He lifted his head again, awaiting the inevitable judgment. She was trembling a bit, too, though that was kind of par for the course when you've just been a few inches away from bloody extermination. "You realize," she said, her voice shaking a bit, "that you doing this is the moral equivalent of molesting me when I was drunk the other night."

"*Last* night," Grant pointed out, unable to control his idiotically didactic tendencies any more than his bare emotions, "and, in retrospect, I wish I'd done that, too."

Deb stared at him, considering, biting her lower lip in the

way teen movie actresses are universally coached to do. Grant found himself holding his breath.

A few inches away, inside Deb's head, the action was no less intense. She'd almost died, yes, but that was taking a back seat to the current situation. Grant's declaration had been startling, though in retrospect she realized it shouldn't be. And that three-word bomb had been dropped on her many times before, as one might expect. But not by Grant—not by goofy, brilliant, unwittingly lovable Grant. Had she ever been in the position of needing to *look* for opportunities rather than merely considering various offers, she might have thought of it herself. She might, in fact, be in love with him, too. *It could be,* she thought, *reasonable. It might not be just an artifact of having my life saved and being in an incredibly powerful and sudden thunderstorm and being pressed up against a male body.*

Or, of course, it might be *exactly* that. Or partly. Shit Happens: That's the guiding principle behind why theory and practice are separate things, why sports teams actually *play* the games, and why no one has any idea what they're talking about when they talk about love. In any case:

"You know, I think I love you, too."

"You—you're kidding me."

"Nope. Pretty sure of it, now that I'm saying it."

"Get outa here."

"I might, if you'd get your big ol' carcass off me."

"No chance of that, then."

What followed was slightly hysterical laughter, a warm and torrential downpour, and more kissing.

Earl Anderson dashed around the tree with the truck partially embedded in it. The driver seemed to be okay, which meant that Earl could kill him when he had the time. But he didn't now. Tammy might be twenty yards off, lying broken near a park bench, or brutally crushed between the fender and the tree, or—

—lying on the ground right next to the kid who had saved her.

Earl just stood there a second, catching his breath, feeling the icy liquid in his temples subside. As he watched Tammy roll over, get to her feet, and brush herself off, he found himself checking again and again that he was indeed seeing her. Yes, he kept saying to himself. It *is* Tammy. And she's okay.

It took him quite a few moments to remember that he was there, too, that he could actually go over to her.

"That was quite an entrance, lady. Welcome to Hahvahd Squeh."

She looked up at him, jumped a little, smiled, looked at the truck, started to say something clever, began to cry, and then opted just to throw her arms around him.

She had a lot to tell him: the outcome of the siege (he'd heard), his legal status (he was, by and large, okay), what she'd gone through (he had no idea), how much she'd missed him and worried (he knew, he knew, but of course he needed to hear it). For now, though, just standing there in the new rain pressed up against each other was more than enough.

At last Earl turned, his arm still around her waist, and moved toward the kid, who was grappling passionately with the other girl he'd rescued.

Earl bent down a bit. He began to hear sirens in the distance, so he didn't have time to wait. " 'Scuse me. . . . *'Scuse* me, young man." The kid looked up. The girl beneath him was a stunner. Good for you, kid, thought Earl.

"Listen," he said once he was sure the kid was listening, "I have to get going, but I want to thank you for saving my wife. Not that there's any way to thank someone for that, but, still, a man's got to try. . . ."

"Yes, *bless* you," added Tammy.

The kid looked at them for a minute, perplexed, and then seemed to recognize Tammy. He smiled, embarrassed, gleeful, distracted. "Anytime," he said. And just like that, he went back to kissing his girlfriend.

Earl and Tammy looked at each other. There was nothing else to say, really. And they were getting really wet.

"I found this little Tex-Mex place where that coffee shop used to be," he said.

"Sounds lovely. I'm half starved," said Tammy, and ten minutes later they were ordering margaritas.

Chapter 16

WHEN DR. SCHRÖDINGER suddenly pointed across the park, we watched the whole thing, yet we had the sense that we were seeing only the end of the process. We were sure Dr. Schrödinger would point out that such a coincidence of events, this apparently intentional "machine," is only truly assembled in retrospect, and to speak of the "device's" "purpose" was meaningless, but it was impressive nonetheless: the bird-laden bag, the vagrant's insane rescue, the truck veering away, the youth saving the two women (we couldn't see what happened to the other youth, and feared the worst), the gross but understandable public displays of affection, all of it. *Very* understandable, really—they'd been within a hair's breadth of extinction. They were alive.

There was a sudden pain in my temple, and I turned to see if old Dr. Schrödinger had struck me in pursuit of proving some obscure and lunatic point.

But he was gone. Slipped away in the confusion. I didn't see him anywhere.

"I"?

Indeed. "I." That seemed to make sense all of a sudden, and when I considered Dr. Schrödinger's last question, I realized that with his absence there was now only one of us on the bench. One of *me*, that is.

One of me. That thought just hung there in my head for a while, not connecting to anything. We—I—felt groggy and strange, unsure of anything for the moment. So many thoughts were trying to get my attention that they'd created an impassable bottleneck.

It began to rain, becoming a downpour almost immediately. That much I was aware of. Automatically I got up, and it seemed that I knew where my car was, and I knew the way home, and going home was the most prudent course of action, and that would suffice for now.

The rain was a torrent now, and laughing youths were running through the sparkling streets. Over at the scene of the accident there were police shouting at the truck driver, who seemed to want to stay in his truck forever. He seemed as dazed as I was by it all. I couldn't imagine what it must be like to be a truck driver, and in that instant realized that I was not, in fact, a truck driver. That was a start, at least, though I hoped I wouldn't have to construct all the details of my life through the process of elimination.

I didn't hurry. The rain felt good, cleansing, and I was utterly soaked already. The rain colored me in, defining all the parts of my (singular) body for me as it touched them. It felt like a shower running down my back, like a massage running down my limbs, like tears running down my face.

No, it occurred to me, there *were* tears running down my face. How very odd, I thought, how very, very odd.

There wasn't a lot that Officer Jack Kennedy could do other than stand around. Leonora didn't want to be held, not by him, maybe not by anybody. He knew the police investigators, he'd helped them, but they were gone now, along with the body.

224 · *Adam Felber*

Leonora had flown into a rage or two, and he'd been unable to offer her much of anything. But now Leonora was quiet, roaming the house without a purpose, inexplicably clutching the wicker duck from the mantelpiece to her chest.

He couldn't pretend he really knew the kid, couldn't even pretend he knew Leonora well enough to know exactly how *she* felt about the kid. And he was at a total loss to explain how a kid they had all been talking to a couple of hours ago, who wasn't even *in* the house, could be lying dead in the basement in a state that even a rookie could tell was a couple of days dead.

"You sure about that?" he'd asked the investigator.

"Sure, lookit him. Blood's dry, cold as a rock, yadda yadda yadda. Lookit, there's some decomposition already—right *here*. Sorry 'bout that, ma'am." Leonora had gasped and excused herself yet again. The investigator continued, "Look, Jack, this kid's been here a coupla days, no matter who you think you saw. He's cold—two days minimum. 'Course, you know that." Jack knew that, of course. But he'd asked anyway, because it made absolutely no sense at all. *Fuckin' kids.* What was this one trying to pull, anyway? Whatever it was, it was over, that was a sure thing. The kid was dead now, a shotgun blast to the head, no matter what had happened earlier. That was the fact that Jack Kennedy was going to cling to, something to keep his head straight. The rest would fade away.

Now, as Jack sat in the kitchen, formulating a respectable retreat from this suddenly complicated relationship, Leonora wandered the house, clutching the duck, which she'd never really liked but had kept in her house because it had fascinated the young Johnny Felix Decaté, who didn't exist anymore. Unlike almost everyone else, Leonora would never completely accept Johnny's death. Or at least she'd remain aware of the contradictions behind it. The fact of it, she supposed, was inescapable. Seeing his mutilated face had the effect of dispelling any doubt in that regard. But she'd seen him walk out, she kept thinking, in *drag* no less. She laughed, remembered the body, gasped, walked into another room again, walked around and around, wandering as erratically as her thoughts.

She couldn't go back to this afternoon and prove to Jack and the coroner and herself what she believed to have been true. This afternoon was gone, and whatever truth it held was gone with it. There was just an aging woman with a dead grandson and a wicker duck, stepping distractedly out onto the porch in her bathrobe.

She sat on the step, only partially shielded from the pouring rain, which had now completely flooded the streets and turned her lawn into a sea, utterly erasing any sign of the kids who'd been there all weekend. She had phone calls to make. Her son and daughter-in-law and niece, of course, needed to know. It was only fair that she call them soon.

Fair. What on earth was fair about this? Johnny had moved in to be closer to his life and maybe spend some extra time with his grandma and save some money on rent, and now he'd accidentally killed himself with her dead husband's gun. In what way could one describe that as fair, when there was nothing but goodwill on all sides as far as the eye could see?

As far as *she* could see. Leonora was bright enough to see that she couldn't see all that far. She spun the duck between her hands. The duck, balanced between two index fingers pressed against its beak and its tail respectively, didn't spin very well at all. Wobbly. Without a head, she thought, a duck would be more or less a feathery football, and you'd be able to throw it in a perfect spiral. Everything, she thought childishly, would run smoother without heads.

A sound made her look up, and she saw Johnny's three friends approaching the house, still thirty yards or so up the street. Even at this distance, even in the unceasing deluge, she could tell that they were bewildered, that they were coming to see if Johnny had somehow returned home (which he had, she supposed, *somehow*). She heaved an uneven sigh and began to rise as she steeled herself to tell them as much as she understood. Good practice for the phone calls.

As she stood, the wicker duck slipped from her hands. It hit the step below her, tail-first, bounced to the step below that, beak-first, and then tumbled onto the flooded lawn. Somehow it landed in the water right side up, and it floated there for a moment, looking for all the world like . . . like a duck.

There was a current of sorts, and the wicker duck was carried a little ways out onto the lawn, where it caught a breeze and was pulled even farther away. There it somehow got caught in the current of the deluge, the current that covered the street and sidewalk and flowed downhill. Sometimes it seemed to submerge or get knocked over, but the head always rose back into view as it was carried away from the house. The three friends and the old woman stood there watching as the duck swam more and more confidently with the current, its head high above the waters, as proud as a ridiculous wicker duck could ever look, swimming or floating, farther and farther away, until it disappeared from view.

Epilogue

I RETURNED TO MY HOUSE, still unclear as to who I was and what exactly had happened to me. The facts were there, but they were coming to me slowly. I suppose I could have stopped moving for a moment and teased all the information out of my brain, but it was more comfortable just to act, to let it happen. Once or twice I found myself thinking in the plural again, but it felt like a shabby construct at this point. Which, in retrospect, it was.

I left the car, got drenched again, and let myself in. I expected to see Dr. Schrödinger there, was looking forward to asking him to shed some light on my current condition, but he wasn't in the entryway or in his customary position of unjustified and intrusive relaxation on my couch. After a moment I heard some movement in the kitchen, so I slipped off my soggy shoes and went to investigate.

It was the girl, Dori. She was wearing one of my shirts and a pair of sweatpants. She was at the stove, cooking something. She looked at me and smiled, then turned back to the stove.

"There you are! I figured you'd be home soon. And I knew you'd be soaked. Because you're an idiot." She said it affectionately, and with far too much familiarity for the friend of a friend. For some reason, though, she didn't seem out of place.

"There's a towel and some dry clothes for you on the couch," she said. Mechanically, I slogged into the living room and began to strip and towel myself off. The clothes, clean and dry, were welcome, as much as the rain had been.

"I'm making you some soup," came Dori's voice, alarmingly close. I turned, half naked, to see her standing in the doorway. She did not seem to find the sight of her host seminude unexpected or objectionable. She was undeniably attractive, too, and obviously older than I'd first assumed she was back at the ice-cream parlor, and at least *I* found the situation uncomfortable.

"Where's Dr. Schrödinger?" I asked desperately as I hastily pulled on the rest of my clothing.

"Who? Oh, you mean the Humdingers? I made another bunch in the lab today, but, you know, I think we're going to have to start making them here, or the university is going to want to get a piece of the action or something. Randy says he can get some equipment, and if you would let me go into the lab in your garage I could start to set things up. . . ."

"No!" I cut her off. She was babbling—none of it made sense and all of it made sense and I couldn't keep up. I went back to where I'd left my mental bookmark. "I meant Dr. Schrödinger himself. Where is he?"

"You mean the guy? The physicist?" she asked, genuinely confused. I nodded. "Well, he died in, like, 1960 or something, didn't he? Are you asking me where he was buried, or something? Is this a pop quiz?"

She was being playful, but her words hit with force. A couple of things clicked into place. Dr. Schrödinger was indeed dead—died in Vienna, in 1961, to be precise. I'd told Dori that myself in class.

Class. Dori. I was a professor. I taught physics. Dori was a grad student. She worked at the ice-cream place, too. She and I had always flirted, but I never did anything, of course, because . . . because . . . Dr. Schrödinger had come to me.

"Are you all right?" She came over to me, sat me on the couch, and held my hand.

"Look," she said, "this has been a really tough weekend for you, okay? And we've all been worried about you, you know, coming back to work so soon. . . ."

" 'We'?" I asked, smiling with a stupid irony that she couldn't possibly understand.

"Okay, well, me *personally* of course, but all of us," she said, and I realized she meant the other grad students, the TAs. She was relentless, forcing truths down my throat faster than I could swallow them, unaware, I suppose, that I'd spent the last week as an ephemeral, plural observer.

"But, you know," she went on, "when you came back and said let's go with the Humdinger thing, we all thought it would be good for you, you know? And it would be an excuse for us—for me—to keep an eye on you, okay?" I nodded. I tried to smile. I couldn't stop her, even though part of me knew what was coming.

"But I gotta say, maybe it was too soon. Hey, not that I regret what happened this weekend, you know, between us. No way, believe me, I do *not* regret that. But I want you to know that I don't expect anything from you, all right? And if you need to take some more time off, you know, disappear for another couple of weeks, it's okay. We can all cover for you. We'll cover the undergrads, and Professor Muldower will cover us. And you probably got plenty more time on your bereavement leave or whatever they call it."

That did it. Several body blows followed by a knockout punch. I was back. It was all back inside me—my dead wife, the accident that I had survived without a scratch, the way her family blamed me, the fact that it *was* my fault (even if it was an accident), the usual survivor's guilt coupled with the fact that we *hadn't* been getting along coupled with my new feelings for this woman right in front of me coupled with several days of unabated drinking and the pills that I'd been given to keep me calm but that should *not* be taken with alcohol.

I had been, as my students would say, severely fucked up. I couldn't tell you exactly when I stopped being a single individual, when I became a pluralistic observer. Now, it was painful to come back, having watched an older, funhouse version of myself in Dr. Schrödinger for the previous few days. As psychotic breaks go, though, it was less destructive than some. There was at least *that* to cling to as I returned to a sad and guilt-ridden existence. Had I happened upon a genuine, evolutionary explanation for psychosis? I was pretty sure I'd be better off if I didn't pursue the matter, though. It wasn't my table, anyway.

And there was something else, I now remembered, something very, very bad. I got up, headed toward the inside door to the garage.

Dori misinterpreted my abrupt action. "I can go if you need to be alone, you know. It's no problem. I totally understand."

"No!" I said, whirling around, before I even thought about it. Then I thought about it. "What I mean to say is, I'm not sure I'd be in any condition to be inclined to be a, um, lover, as it were. But your presence would be . . ."

"Appreciated?"

"Yes."

"No problem." There would be problems, though. I'd seen to that by rushing things with her, or by letting Dr. Schrödinger rush things, or however one would put it. But I had a more pressing need at the moment. I rushed off to the garage, unlocked the door, and switched on the light, scarcely daring to breathe.

In the garage was the wreckage of what had been my "lab." My chemistry was fairly amateurish, more or less a "hobby" that just so happened to dovetail nicely with the largely theoretical physics that was my profession. A shoddy dodge, really, and no doubt a sadly transparent retreat from what had become an unsatisfying marriage . . . I fought those thoughts off. Understand—it *was* an accident, of this I'm sure. It just didn't *feel* like one.

What was here in the garage, though, *wasn't* an accident, and my stomach heaved with the thought of what I'd done. There would be no forgiving myself for what was here, no way to make up for it if . . .

How long had it been? Forty-eight hours. Maybe less, but definitely more than a day. It was hard to say. It was hard to recall exactly what "Dr. Schrödinger" had done, especially when I "wasn't with him," but I had some memory of this thing: this horrible, unthinkable thing.

I approached what had been a well-organized lab table. Everything had been swept aside, the floor was a mess of bottles and vials, some spilled, some intact. On the desk, though, was what I knew would be there: a box.

I listened, hoping to learn something, and there was no sound. Which meant very little, and, besides, there was no time to waste. Whatever I found out, the longer I waited, the lower the chances of a positive outcome would be, the more likely that I would prove to be, along with everything else, a murderer.

It was a small box, really, cruelly small. It had once housed a seventeen-inch computer monitor. It did not house a monitor anymore. It housed an experiment that was never meant to be real, and that possibly had deprived me of one of my truest companions. Werner. I couldn't bear the thought. I had no choice.

I opened the box.

The funeral was brief, well attended, and slightly less somber than you might think. This was due to all the uncertainty, principally. The service was handled by a Unitarian minister, a colleague of Leonora's. His eulogy was tasteful and appropriate, occasionally pretty, and was of very little pertinence to us here. It spoke of the tragedy of dying young, of the meaning of a life that, however short, touched so many, and of the inscrutable mechanisms of God's largely benevolent universe.

Leonora was flanked by the many people who cared about her. Jack Kennedy stood somewhat nearby.

The three remaining friends kept mostly to themselves. As a group they were still bewildered by what they'd been through. Unlike the throngs who had gathered outside Johnny's house, they couldn't just discount the coroner's report as shoddy work. Something *had* happened, though they were stymied as to what exactly it had been.

From the moment when Arlene had found Grant and Deb entwined in the rain, from the moment they had risen and begun their fruitless search amid the lightning bolts and thunderclaps, from that moment on, Arlene had stuck by what she'd seen. She was the only one watching Johnny just as the truck hit, and she'd seen Johnny, in that instant, simply *disappear.*

After failing to find him and trekking to his house and hearing the news, Grant and Deb were inclined to believe Arlene (though at first they'd been frustrated by her unhelpful attitude toward the search—she saw it, rightly, as pointless). Believing her didn't shed light on anything, of course, but it was a decent enough patch for the yawning hole in their narrative of that night.

For Grant, who was wont to see Mandelbrot sets swirling in the soap scum atop his bathwater, the events of the weekend seemed to have a shape, though he could not yet tell what it was. He knew, however, that by an extremely implausible string of coincidences and events he had somehow been thrust into the situation he'd always wanted but was fundamentally incapable of finding his way into on his own. It was so improbable, in fact, that the always agnostic Grant now found that he believed in something. He didn't know what it was, he was far from putting a name on it, but everything that happened was undeniably a baroque mechanism that had achieved a devoutly desired end. Grant's gut was telling him that there was some sort of Intentionality behind all that, while another part of him quietly whispered that he was *bound* to feel that way, that winners always do.

Either way, he was in a strange place. He'd lost his best friend under bizarre and tragic circumstances. At the same time, he was embarking on a relationship that thrilled him, ennobled him, and scared the living shit out of him. His emotional plate was full. He tuned in briefly to what the minister was saying—the phrase "the power of belief" drifted through his mind. He found it interesting, filed it away for calmer times, when he would set about trying to connect it with something. It would be a long time before he found that it was best connected to *everything*, and to nothing at all.

Deb already missed Johnny horribly. He'd always been, quite

simply, beautiful. She'd never probed or tried to get inside the sweet calm that lay under his exuberance; she'd just loved being with the whole package. To her, in retrospect, he hadn't really been that *different* during the weekend, just larger, brighter, more himself than ever. The sudden lack of him was palpable, especially because she made absolutely no attempts to shield herself from the grief.

And then there was the Grant thing. Deb had never invested herself in a real, serious romantic relationship before, and already she was getting a sense of the deeper joys that might lie in store for her. Glorious and long-burning feelings that she was delighted to be getting an inkling of, focused around the person who had become her absolute favorite in all the world. She'd always thought that her future involved something like this, but it hadn't been time. Now it was time, Deborah Johnstone was taking on a Relationship, and she was determined to enjoy every moment of it, nurture it, and get it *right*. Maddeningly, inevitably, she would.

For Arlene, for now, things sucked. Pure and simple.

She'd be all right, one may suppose. But in the span of a weekend she'd lost a dear friend, a new lover, and a beloved cat, and had found herself on the outside of the new Perfect Couple, who had been her individual friends. If there was any bright side at all, she thought, it was that her usually neurotic and despairing mind now really had something to despair about. Perhaps. At the very least, she had more dark feelings to write about. And though she wouldn't know it until later that day, she had a new kitten, courtesy of Grant and Deb.

The service ended, there were more tears, and there were sandwiches back at Leonora's house. Sometime later, the three friends found themselves in the afternoon sunlight on Leonora's front lawn, waving to Johnny's family, retreating to the curb, and saying some private goodbyes. They hugged and parted, Grant and Deb going one way, Arlene the other.

There's no finality to that, of course. The three of them would be at the Abbey the very next evening, and they'd be seeing a band in Central Square a few nights after that. On their way home from that, the three of them would be flashed by a homeless woman in the most startling of ways, and that would lead to . . .

But endpoints are where you put them, and we'll put one right here. The friends parted, the day ended, and Johnny Felix Decaté was laid to rest.

Oh—one more thing: As she walked away, impossibly enough, deep inside Arlene a zygote was growing at an amazing rate, dividing and dividing and sorting itself out in the ludicrously complex dance that brought us all here in the first place. And at the very same time, *nothing* was growing inside Arlene at all, because its presence was, naturally, impossible. It was simultaneously there and not there.

A conundrum, then. And, as always, there is only one way to find out.

Now that I'm out of the box, I can't believe I was ever in that friggin' thing. Man oh man, that was weird. I was gettin' pretty strange in there, I don't mind saying.

But eventually the light came and there was the guy! My favorite guy.

Everything's pretty much as it was, though someone definitely messed with my scrunchy mouse while I was gone. The guy spends more time with me, which sometimes requires the mighty claw of Enough Already, but I can deal. And I don't sleep in the sock drawer anymore, which is pretty understandable under the circumstances.

Back there, in the box, things got a little weird. I was thinking some pretty crazy stuff, some pretty heavy stuff, some stuff that seemed pretty important while I was inside. I remember I was all like, "If I ever get out of here, I'll be a better cat." "Maybe the box is an illusion, or maybe I am." "Maybe I deserve to be here, or maybe this is just the kind of price you gotta pay for all the good stuff that came before." Jesus fucking Christmas! Man, I was serious.

But that's all way behind me now. I don't think about those things now. Why would you, unless you're in a box?

Appendix

The Real Erwin Schrödinger Stands Up

I'm not the most qualified guy to explain quantum physics or Heisenberg's uncertainty principle to you. But you probably guessed that already. There are scores of places in your local library or on the Web where you can read lucid, well-written layman's explanations of how exactly a particle can't be a wave and a wave can't be a particle and how a cat can or can't be simultaneously alive and dead.

If this book was concerned with anything remotely scientific, it was concerned with explaining the uncertainty principle and Schrödinger's famous thought experiment *badly*. Now, *that's* a task I am eminently qualified to perform. But, seeing as I've devoted so much energy to making a difficult concept even more difficult while simultaneously presenting a not altogether flattering fictionalization of an eminent physicist, perhaps I ought to, in fairness, offer some account of what Schrödinger and his Cat were really all about.

The soup of interconnecting and poorly misunderstood concepts surrounding Heisenberg, Schrödinger, and quantum physics is blurry and hard to define, not unlike the electron probability cloud proposed by Heisenberg himself. Or was that Schrödinger? Or Bohr? It's complicated.

Back in the mid-1920s, both Heisenberg and Schrödinger were hot on the trail of the electron. It was important work: Any physicist worth his salt had realized that the classical model of the atom was incomplete, that a more complete model was going to tell a peculiar story about the nature of our world, and that something very strange was going on with electrons. There *had* to be—if electrons behaved the way larger matter did, there was a big, big problem.

See, the law of conservation of matter tells us that it takes energy to make things move. If electrons have mass and are moving around the nucleus of an atom, they're using up energy. So their orbits ought to be decaying. In other words, if classical physics applied to electrons, then atoms ought to be collapsing all the time, which would put a serious crimp in everyone's vacation plans. This was the problem Einstein, Bohr, Heisenberg, and Schrödinger set out to solve, principally by calculating, theorizing, and yelling at one another a lot.

Heisenberg got there first, by a matter of months. His description of quantum mechanics using "matrix algebra" in 1925 was what eventually won him the Nobel Prize. Schrödinger finished his version in January of '26, producing what's known as the "wave equation."

The odd thing about those two explanations was that Heisenberg's wasn't very popular. It didn't have a beat you could dance to, from a physicist's perspective. Schrödinger's, though it came afterward, was much clearer and easier to understand, and it was an instant hit. Schrödinger was *good* at explaining things, which is probably what led to the whole mess with the Cat.

After the two physicists published, more high-level squabbling set in. A jealous Heisenberg took potshots at Schrödinger's equation. Schrödinger, in a move of colossal intellectual passive-aggressiveness, proved that his and Heisenberg's theories were mathematically identical. By 1927, Heisenberg had synthesized their work (and that of Einstein and Bohr) and unleashed a pop hit of his own: the uncertainty principle. What this boils down to is that when you look at a particle's waveness it loses its particleness. And vice versa. The act of looking shapes the reality, said Heisenberg. At the quantum level, human perception shapes what is and what isn't. And, according to Heisenberg, that was the end of the story. Heisenberg and Bohr were convinced that everything had been explained as fully as was possible, that certain things were just plain inscrutable, and that physicists ought to concentrate on improving their tans and picking up chicks.

Although they acknowledged that much of Heisenberg's work was accurate, Einstein and Schrödinger never embraced the totality of quantum uncertainty. In fact, it drove them nuts. Einstein muttered his oft-misinterpreted "God does not play dice with the universe." Not to be outdone, Schrödinger produced an objection guaranteed to be even more grossly misunderstood, deriving yet another popular smash from Heisenberg's big hit.

In 1935, attempting to prove that there was still something missing from quantum mechanics, Schrödinger created his Cat. To illustrate that the nature of reality really *wasn't* a slave to indeterminacy and human observation, he put together a thought experiment with a device with which quantum uncertainty would have to have real-life consequences. He asked us to imagine a box:

One can even set up quite ridiculous cases where quantum physics rebels against common sense. For example, consider a

cat is penned up in a steel chamber, along with the following dia-
bolical device (which must be secured against direct interfer-
ence by the cat). In the device is a Geiger counter with a tiny bit
of radioactive substance, so small that perhaps in the course of
one hour only one of the atoms decays, but also, with equal
probability, perhaps none. If the decay happens, the counter
tube discharges and through a relay releases a hammer which
shatters a small flask of hydrocyanic acid. If one has left this entire system to itself for an hour, one would say that the cat still
lives if meanwhile no atom has decayed. The first atomic decay
would have poisoned it. The wave function for the entire system
would express this by having in it the living and the dead cat
mixed or smeared out in equal parts.

See? said Schrödinger. Now, *that's* ridiculous. Only a ninny
would think that the cat existed in a state of nonaliveness and
nondeadness *and* aliveness and deadness until the box was
opened. Clearly, we need to knuckle down and—

The world, it turned out, was full of ninnies. And that may
not be a bad thing. At least, not a bad thing for anyone besides
Erwin Schrödinger, who allegedly said in his later years that he
wished he'd "never met that cat." As good as Schrödinger was
at explaining things, as vivid and accurate as his allegory is,
he never quite realized that what survives and propagates is the
story itself, not what the story's about.

A college professor of mine, the polymathic Daniel C. Den-
nett, has often pointed out that what we are, the engine of our
consciousness, is *stories*. To paraphrase one of his neater con-
structs, we are the ape that told the story of the storytelling ape.
Certainly, stories *mean* something, but the meaning can change
in useful and important ways (or in harmful and trivial ways).
We're all wired up to understand, enjoy, and interpret stories. To

most of us there's less of a story involved in rules and equations, and that fact is why most people don't sit around campfires and recite scary formulae at one another. That's also why the Bible is still a hot seller, while "Papa Ishmael's List of Things God Wants Us to Do" is lost somewhere in the remainders bin of history.

Still, the real Dr. Schrödinger probably didn't go to his grave tortured by his Cat and what it had done—to him it was merely a passing annoyance in his fascinating and brilliant career. The weird misconceptions probably didn't really bother him all that much.

However, if he had even suspected what a large number of people all *believing* the same misconception could do . . .

Acknowledgments

GETTING IT WRONG TOOK A LOT OF HELP.

My early readers: Michael Bernard, Peter Sagal, and above all my wife, Jeanne Simpson. Jeanne heard the first few pages on our first date, and this, coupled with the fact that there *was* a second date, speaks volumes about her. My agent, Scott Mendel, served as a reader, critic, editor, fan, and friend.

I realize that when authors lavish praise on the editors who selected and shaped their work, in a way they're really just complimenting themselves. I'd like to thank the stunningly brilliant Stephanie Higgs and her astoundingly ingenious executive editor in chief, Daniel Menaker, at Random House. I'd also like to thank Karen Fink in advance for the fine publicity work that led to all the sales, press, and prestigious awards.

Kent Osbourne drew that wonderful Rube Goldberg cartoon, just when I was at the point where I'd almost given up on the idea. Michael Rizzo at ICM was an early reader and ardent supporter, even though he represents me for Things That Are Not Books. Russell Frost designed the extremely attractive schrodingersball.com.

My eternal gratitude also goes to Mo Rocca, the Felber clan, the Simpsons (neither Jessica- nor O.J.- nor Homer-related), my dear friends at *Wait Wait . . . Don't Tell Me!*, the Bunkdance

Film Festival, and, for their extraordinary support, the Lindsay Milligan Society.

But most of all, I must acknowledge the novelist Edith Layton, aka "Edith Felber," aka "Mom." Watching her craft her first novels at our kitchen table as three school-age children screamed, snacked, spilled, and clamored all around her taught me the invaluable lesson that the real trick to writing a book is *writing*. Until you have a book.

About the Author

ADAM FELBER writes and performs for screens of all sizes and resolutions, performs improv and sketch comedy in venues around the country, and can be heard regularly on NPR's *Wait Wait . . . Don't Tell Me* and occasionally on *This American Life*. His TV credits include *The Apprentice*, Cameron Diaz's MTV travel show *Trippin,* PBS's *Arthur* and *Wishbone,* and *Smoking Gun TV,* and he has taught humor writing at Princeton. He has had screenplays optioned and articles published, and his political-satire blog, "Fanatical Apathy" (www.felbers.net/fa), has been entertaining visitors since 2002. A native New Yorker and graduate of Tufts University, Felber lives in Hollywood with his wife and cat.